A MAN'S LOVE

David's Passion Series
Book 2

Sherrhonda Denice

Lily Bird
PRESS

.

Also by Sherrhonda Denice

David's Passion Series

A Man's Heart (David's Passion Book 1)

A Man's Love (David's Passion Book 2)

Glue

Pathways

A Man's Love: David's Passion Book Two

Copyright ©2020 by Sherrhonda Denice

www.sherrhondadenice.com

Published by Lily Bird Press, LLC

Scriptures taken from the Holy Bible, New International Version®, NIV®. Copyright © 1973, 1978, 1984, 2011 by Biblica, Inc.™ Used by permission of Zondervan. All rights reserved worldwide. www.zondervan.com The "NIV" and "New International Version" are trademarks registered in the United States Patent and Trademark Office by Biblica, Inc.™

Scripture quotations from The Authorized (King James) Version. Rights in the Authorized Version in the United Kingdom are vested in the Crown. Reproduced by permission of the Crown's patentee, Cambridge University Press

Editing: Veronica Hollis for Advanced Tutoring and Editing, LLC

Cover design by Covers in Color

Library of Congress Control Number: 2020906598

ISBN 978-0-9801028-2-6 (Print)

ISBN 978-0-9801028-3-3 (eBook)

Printed in the United States of America

 Formatted with Vellum

Author's Note

Dear Reader,

Thank you for choosing to read *A Man's Love* (*David's Passion Series Book Two*). This story explores deeply challenging yet important topics, such as sexual assault, sex trafficking, and the journey of healing for survivors and their loved ones. While these issues are addressed, there are no graphic scenes; sensitive events are alluded to with care and discretion.

My purpose as a Christian writer is to honor God's holiness while realistically portraying some of life's challenges. I avoid explicit content and would consider my writing to align with a PG-13 rating. At its heart, this is a story of faith—a testament to God's love and grace to heal even the deepest wounds.

If you are a survivor, I pray this story reminds you that healing is possible. For those supporting loved ones, I hope it inspires empathy and understanding. As a licensed therapist, I understand that some topics may be triggering, and I encourage you to prioritize your mental well-being.

Thank you for trusting me with your time and heart.

With love and grace,
Sherrhonda

For Nate and Geraldine Thank you.

Many waters cannot quench love; rivers cannot sweep it away.
If one were to give
all the wealth of one's house for love, it would be utterly scorned.
Song of Solomon 8:7, NIV

Chapter 1

A Beautiful Devil

D ominique Street sashayed across the multi-blue, wave-inspired carpet in Pastor David Kent Cole's church office at Disciples of Christ Ministries, more affectionately known as DOC. She was wearing a pair of five-inch black stilettos that gave her petite height a model-like appearance. She wore a fitted black blouse that was unbuttoned just enough to tease helpless eyes with a barely hidden, black lace, push-up bra that showcased her breasts. Her short, black, wet-look skirt successfully drew attention to her curves. The petite beauty was an astonishing vixen. Her make-up was camera-ready, "beat" with a soft, natural look—not too heavily overdone—just the way David preferred. She hadn't forgotten any of his idiosyncrasies. Her long, naturally curly, dark brown hair had been straightened, and it flowed past her shoulders in gentle spirals, accentuating her smooth, cocoa-brown complexion and innocent-looking eyes. It was an ingeniously beautiful disguise for the devil.

David swallowed the last of his straight black coffee. With jittery hands, he steadied the cup on his desk to keep from dropping it. He wanted to remain calm and professional. He wanted to remain godly. But the audacity of Dominique Street showing up like this after her betrayal quickened an irate blaze in him. David's handsome, honey-brown face, which moments ago had been a divine portrait of masculinity and fineness, was now marred with pure disdain.

David had commanded stages all over the world. He'd been dubbed "The Turn Around Preacher" for his radical way of reaching youth and the work he'd done to usher the city of Detroit into a new era, filled with reduced crime rates and economic stability. His powerful youth and young adult ministries were well-known throughout the country. And having grown up on the northwest side of Detroit, David was no stranger to the hood. Back in his days before Christ, he had earned a reputation as one who was not to be crossed.

Now, the forty-one-year-old, street-bred and Harvard-educated spiritual titan served as a spiritual consultant to top government officials and CEOs of corporations. He had earned both a bachelor's degree in finance and an MBA from Harvard, as well as a master's degree in divinity from Hilltop Theological Seminary, one of the top seminaries in the nation. Known for possessing a calm and reflective disposition, David was a true man of God who held firm to biblical principles. Right now, however, he was on the verge of losing it—feeling like that *old* David. The one he was before he accepted Christ in his late twenties. He still had the kind of swag and commanding presence that could disarm someone with his smile or downright intimidate a person with just a glance, depending on what one's intentions were.

David breathed in deeply and exhaled, determined not to let Dominique undo him. She'd proven in more ways than one that she was never the woman he thought she was. She was nothing like the woman he was going to marry in two short weeks. Dominique Street was something far beneath the woman he had now. For that reason alone, she could take her little too-short skirt, half-buttoned blouse, and five-inch heels, and walk right out of his office. And keep on walking. Period. She didn't matter anymore.

"What are you doing here?" David barked. His face held a cemented scowl. It was unlike him to come unglued. Normally, he was affable and approachable. But Dominique had hit a switch that had turned on volts of angry, indignant energy—enough to power and sustain all the electrical grids in the city.

"Dave," Dominique said, employing the nickname she'd given him during the time they were on more favorable terms with one another. "I really need to talk to you. It's impor—" she started before David's desk phone rang.

David picked it up quickly, successfully ignoring Dominique. He'd been waiting for Ms. Naomi Harlow, one of his church members, to call him. Ms. Naomi had been a foster mother to sixteen-year-old Lorna Jones for a year, and Lorna had run away again. Before her placement with Ms. Naomi, Lorna had been in seven foster homes, mostly due to her uncontrollable behavior.

One could call her placement with Ms. Naomi a success since she'd been with her an entire year—longer than she had been in any foster home. But no one had heard from the sixteen-year-old in two days. Before entering foster care at age fourteen, Lorna had lived on the streets since age twelve. As a habitual runaway, she was used to selling her body to survive. David hoped she hadn't slipped back into the snare of the streets.

Lorna and Ms. Naomi had gotten into a heated argument about Samuel, Lorna's new boyfriend. Ms. Naomi was strict and old-fashioned. She didn't believe in any sort of teenage *courting*. And Lorna claimed to be *in love*. David had met

Samuel, and by his assessment, the kid had his head on pretty straight for a seventeen-year-old. That, however, didn't appease Ms. Naomi in the least. She had her house rules and expected Lorna to abide by them. No boyfriends. No male company.

"Good Afternoon, Ms. Naomi," David said, while his eyes burned through Dominique. "Yes, ma'am . . . thank God! Right . . . I understand. I appreciate it . . . yes . . . yes . . . Cherelle and I will stop by on our way to dinner. You, too. God bless," David said before returning the phone to its cradle.

"Why are you here?" he questioned Dominique for the second time. All the warmth he'd spoken to Ms. Naomi with had dissipated. Dominique stepped closer. David extended his hand in a stop motion and took a step backward. Whatever Dominique had to say, she was going to say at a distance. She looked like she'd come to seduce him.

"Da—"

"Look, I don't have anything to say to you. Please leave," David interrupted in the firmest tone he could use without being flat-out disrespectful. He regretted the very day he met Dominique Street. She had caused nothing but calamity in his life. For a short period in his past, he had allowed himself to be drawn into her web. He still felt ashamed when he thought about it.

Dominique sighed. David wasn't making it easy for her to do what she'd come to do. "I just wanted to say I'm sorry, Dave. That's all . . . I'm sorry." Her soft brown eyes stared deep into David's as if she were some hypnotist attempting to lure him into an alternate state of mind with her charm.

"For what, Dominique? Being a liar? Or are you sorry for *killing* my child? Wait a minute . . . maybe you're sorry for almost costing me my life—three bullets and a year's worth of rehabilitation—learning to walk, talk, and dress myself all over again, huh?! Just what part are you sorry for, lady?" David's voice had elevated at least three decibels. No trance here.

"For everything, Dave. And I need you to forgive me . . ." Dominique whined. She fought hard to bring him into the state of consciousness she needed him to be in.

"Lady, you are forgiven, and you are *dismissed*," David said, nodding toward the door. He unconsciously pinched his bottom lip with his teeth. Dominique knew from experience that David tended to do that on two occasions: one, when he was turned on, and two, when he was about to blow a gasket. The latter was winning for her right now.

Dominique advanced and invaded David's space again. She reached out to touch his face, and he blocked her hand with his forearm. Instead of stimulating him like she'd planned, the sultry look in her eyes only disgusted him.

"We used to be good together, Dave," Dominique said in a tone that used to disarm David in a sensual way.

David was quick to strike back. "No. We never were, but I thank you. Because if you hadn't been the kind of—" he started, catching himself before he said something he would regret. "If you hadn't been the kind of *woman* you are, I wouldn't have the kind of woman I have now. I'm done. You can leave. Thank you. You're welcome."

Chapter 2

Put The Devil in His Place

David's fiancée, Cherelle DuPree, entered his office without knocking on the open door. Because of his position as pastor of one of the largest ministries in the country and his community involvement, Cherelle usually extended David the respect of not entering his office without permission—even if his door was open—to avoid inadvertently walking in on a counseling session or an important meeting. But today, she strolled in without hesitation and walked over to David. "Hi, honey," she said, acknowledging him with a level of reverence and possessiveness that could not go unnoticed. She pressed a chaste kiss against his cheek. The chocolate diva's presence disarmed David like a skilled bomb technician neutralizing a threat. And she looked delectable in the outfit she'd chosen for their special date night.

Cherelle stood five feet six without heels. Today, however, she'd worn a sleek pair of Giuseppe Zanotti heeled sandals. They were nearly five inches tall, placing her at eye level with David, whose stature was six feet. Cherelle owned this particular shoe in three different colors: red, black, and royal blue. She'd mentioned to David that the sandal was called the Cruel Sandal. David couldn't help but agree with whoever had named them because whenever he saw Cherelle in a pair, he had all kinds of thoughts running through his head that he couldn't act on yet. *Two weeks.*

This was David's first time seeing the royal blue pair. The strappy heels had a distinct leather wing design that floated up the middle of Cherelle's beautiful feet and buckled at the ankles. Her lilac-painted toes complemented the color of the sandals and the delicate ankle straps. The design was David's favorite.

Always polished-looking and flawless, even when she wasn't dressed up or wearing any make-up, Cherelle sported a royal blue Roberto Cavalli wrap dress, several gold bangles on her wrists, and intricate sundial earrings to match. She held a gold Louis Vuitton clutch in her left hand. Her outfit was a representation of some of the luxury spoils she had attained from acting in two movies, serving as a producer on three others, and penning several books as a psychologist.

Cherelle turned slightly and set her clutch in one of David's chairs just to her right and stood at his side. She had been in the hallway listening to his conversation with Dominique.

She examined Dominique's revealing outfit—her tight blouse, itty-bitty skirt, high heels, and salon hairdo that had been meant to seduce the man she was going to marry in four-teen short days. A rebuking smirk communicated her disap-proval. Cherelle spoke directly to the devil. "I'm Cherelle," she said, turning her attention to Dominique.

Dominique extended her hand. "I'm Dominique."

Cherelle did not reciprocate. She placed her hands on her solid but soft hips. "I know who you are. You went through the trouble of dressing up," Cherelle said, making air quotes with her fingers, "just to say *sorry*? How contrite."

Dominique stepped forward. "This has nothing to do with you, *Cherelle*."

Cherelle took a step closer. "Anything that concerns *David. Kent. Cole* has *everything* to do with me, Dominique. So, *don't* come back here," she chastised Dominique.

David stepped in front of his fiancée and straight-faced Dominique, "Like I said, we're *done* here. Goodbye." His cool, easy-going persona had returned, partly because when he was in Cherelle's presence, nothing but love oozed from his pores. David's words to Dominique had been spoken with enough quiet power to reiterate that she was neither wanted nor welcome. There was nothing left between them.

Malcolm Porter, a security guard who had been on David's security team for the last four years, entered David's office through the open door. Malcolm was exactly six feet tall, the same as David, with a similar build. He was serious and used few words unless he was forced to do otherwise. His mere presence commanded respect.

"Good evening, Officer Porter. "This lady needs an escort off the premises. Thank you," David said.

Malcolm received his orders like an efficient soldier. "Yes, sir," he said to David before walking toward Dominique. "Ma'am, I'm Officer Porter, and I'm here to escort you off the premises," Malcolm said to Dominique.

"I'm good," Dominique snarled as Malcolm approached her. She hurried in front of him and then turned back to Cherelle. "Insecure?" she goaded.

Cherelle rolled her eyes. "Oh, please! You are dressed for the streets."

Shocked by Cherelle's snide comment, David's eyes bugged wide. In the two years he'd known Cherelle, he'd never heard his normally prim and kindhearted woman of God say anything to or about anyone that wasn't uplifting. He walked over and closed his office door. "Kit, I'm sorry," David said, calling Cherelle by the nickname he'd given her that was short for Kitten. She was two years older than him. So he teased her, saying that she was his kitten instead of his cougar. It was their inside joke. "I didn't know she was coming. I don't even know how she got into this private wing . . ."

"Are you *done*?"

Cherelle's curt tone surprised David. "What do you mean, babe? Am I done *speaking*?"

"No. Are you *done* with *Dominique*?"

David sighed. "Yes . . . Kit . . . you know that."

"I want to make sure that *you* know that, David. She had no business being here . . . in your office dressed like that. She had no business here, period!"

David had enough sense to know that he had to handle this situation delicately. He remembered his pastoral counseling training. A person had to be specific when he or she offended someone. "Sweetheart . . . I apologize that you walked into my private office and found Dominique here. I was blindsided by her presence, and I tried to handle the situation as best as I could. It will *not* happen again." David picked up his desk phone and dialed the security station. "Number One, can you come to my office, please? You can let yourself in."

Juan Gomez, head of security at Disciples of Christ Ministries, was at David's office door in no time. He knocked and waited for permission to enter instead of using his electronic key, despite David having told him to do so.

"Number One, you're clear," David said through the door.

Juan entered and nodded humbly. "Good evening, Pastor Cole and Sister Cherelle," Juan said. He stood at attention and waited for David to address him. He was six feet four with a brown sugar complexion. A regular fitness buff, Juan's solid, muscular frame made him look like a statue of pure muscle.

David got straight to the point. "Good evening, Juan. I just wanted to let you know that we had a breach tonight. Someone let a woman into this private wing without my permission. And I want to make sure that it doesn't happen again. I want to reiterate that the only people who are allowed to access this wing without my prior knowledge are my immediate family members. That would be Sister Cherelle, Gus Merrick, Deacon Lewis, and my parents—no exceptions. Everyone else needs to be cleared with me first. If I'm not available, they need to wait."

Juan nodded understandingly. "Yes, sir. I will take care of it right away, Pastor. I apologize for my team's lack of professionalism. We will rectify the situation and ensure we don't have this sort of problem again." As a retired military police officer, Juan prided himself on ensuring order at DOC, and he settled for nothing less than professionalism and efficiency from his security team. Due to the number of gangs in the area and the high crime rate, it was necessary to have a security team that was up to par.

"Thank you, Juan," David said sincerely, shaking Juan's hand and giving him a few firm pats on his back. He felt safe with Juan's team, and he appreciated Juan's work ethic and his level of excellence. For that, David compensated the team accordingly. He knew there would be a new security protocol in place by morning, and that he would receive the written document from Juan no later than midnight tonight.

"No. Thank you, Pastor. I want to make sure that the team is on top of our job so that you and your family remain safe at all times," Juan said, glancing at Cherelle with a smile.

In Juan's opinion, Cherelle was the epitome of class. She was always gracious whenever she interacted with any of the staff, treating everyone with dignity and esteem. The custodians and groundskeepers received the same level of respect she gave to visiting dignitaries, senators, and various celebrities she'd hosted at DOC with David. Cherelle smiled back at Juan, thanking him silently with her eyes for acknowledging her. Although some of the teens already referred to Cherelle as FLODOC, an acronym for First Lady of DOC, the security team only did it secretly to maintain professional decorum.

"That's it, Juan. We'll be leaving in a few minutes," David said.

"Yes, sir," Juan said. He shook David's hand again and exited.

When Cherelle turned to David, her smile was gone. "She came here to seduce you, David! In the church . . . in your office! I'm not okay with that!" Cherelle continued. "You have to be on guard!"

"Babe, I *am* on guard," David said calmly, empathizing with Cherelle. "I wouldn't do anything to disgrace the Lord's house or put my relationship with you in jeopardy. I'm fully aware that Dominique's being here was a trick of the enemy. I sensed it as soon as she walked in. It's done."

"She's obviously not finished."

"But *I'm finished*, babe," David pleaded. "You *know* that, Kit. So please, let's not spoil our evening over *her*. I accept full responsibility for her entering this office. I should have had something in place with my security team beforehand. Moving forward, though, it *won't* happen anymore. I promise, babe." David stepped closer, compromising the space between them. "Please know that I try my best to make you feel safe and secure with me as your man—as your soon-to-be husband. I don't purposely do things to hurt you or make you feel uncomfortable, Kit. You know that, babe," David said, taking Cherelle's hands in his. The sincere, sensuous timbre of his voice, coupled with his handsomeness, was enough to make any woman forget her anger and be under his spell, agreeing to or accepting anything he might say. He hadn't intended to be sexy or sensuous, but his low, tenor rumble infused with frankness and his genuine will to protect her almost had Cherelle forgetting what she needed to say to him.

Cherelle stood in front of David and stared at her handsome beau for a long moment. She studied his caramel face and his strong jawline that held just a hint of softness. There was a polished ruggedness to him. Any other time, she would have been captivated by his six-foot athletic build, his low-cut fade, and his dark, hypnotic eyes. But right now, she was arrested by a Molotov cocktail of emotions. Anger. Hurt. Jealousy. The thought of another woman seducing David induced a vomitous feeling in her gut. And the mere consideration that he might desire another woman—especially Dominique—*that* way made Cherelle's stomach churn.

She looked away and then held her head down. Her right leg wiggled nervously as she finally looked up at David and spoke softly. "I need to know that you are *completely* done with anyone or anything that happened in your past, David. I have saved myself for you emotionally *and* physically, and I have given you everything the Lord has allowed me to give you . . ." Cherelle's voice trailed off.

When the first tear trickled from Cherelle's dreamy, slanted eyes and slid down her soft chocolate face, David knew that his supposed-to-be romantic evening was on skates and a rollercoaster quickly heading south. Cherelle was rarely overly sensitive, so David knew he had to douse the growing wildfire in the room.

He blew out a breath and soaked up her tears with the pads of his thumbs, "Kit, I'm really sorry. I mean it. I—"

"I need to have a quick word with you, it's important!"

Deacon Lewis, David's long-time armor bearer and surrogate grandfather, said through the door while knocking simultaneously.

"Give me a minute," David returned loud enough so that Deacon Lewis could hear him.

Deacon Lewis entered the office dressed in a casual pair of navy slacks and a baby blue button-up. It was an updated departure from his signature deacon's *uniform,* which always consisted of a suit and tie. He claimed he was trying to relax a little and blend in more with the young people, but David had a feeling that it had more to do with Sister Nadine Harper, a seventy-five-year-old widow who had recently joined the church's gardening ministry, of which Deacon Lewis was the chairperson.

"I said—" David started, but he remembered that at eighty-two, Deacon Lewis's hearing was not what it used to be. He probably thought that David had said, '*Come in.*'

"Daughter," Deacon Lewis greeted Cherelle, hugging her and kissing her on the cheek. His soft and silky salt and pepper waves and café au lait skin reminded Cherelle of Cab Calloway. Deacon Lewis was the spriest eighty-two-year-old Cherelle had ever known.

"Hi, Deacon Lewis," Cherelle said. She hugged him and quickly rubbed her eyes to get rid of the evidence her tears had left behind. "My allergies are acting up," she lied.

Deacon Lewis nodded, but an unbelieving look danced in his eyes.

"Excuse me, I need to use the restroom," Cherelle said. She grabbed her tote and sprinted into David's private restroom.

With his jaw firmly set, Deacon Lewis closed the space between David and himself. He whispered his reprimand. "Look what you've done! You made her cry, didn't you? You know better, son."

David knew from Deacon Lewis's tone that Deacon Lewis was no longer addressing him as his armor bearer, driver, and church deacon, but instead, he was operating in his role as David's surrogate grandfather. David threw his hands up and whisper-argued back. "I didn't mean to . . . Dominique just showed up!"

"Dominique had no business in this office with you!"

"I don't even know how she got back here! It wasn't my fault!"

"Louis, that new security guard, got his eyes and mind stuck in places they shouldn't be; that's how. He let her in. He stays on his cell phone more than he does securing anything around the Lord's house. I'm sure Juan is gonna fire him, but that ain't no excuse for you! Ms. Dominique is full of the devil and bent on corrupting you *again*! She has no place here!" Deacon Lewis fumed.

David had shared most of the details of his and Dominique's past relationship with Deacon Lewis. He had to fight to keep their argument at a whisper level. "If you saw so much, why didn't you do something!?"

"I did! I sent Malcolm in. Besides, I saw Ms. Cherelle coming, and I knew she would put the devil in his place." Deacon Lewis wagged his finger in David's face. "But *you* better be on guard! Don't you dare hurt Ms. Cherelle over something that was meant to tear you and your ministry apart! Ms. Cherelle's been through too much with you—for you!" Deacon Lewis continued. Then, in a sudden mood shift, he paused for a few moments and eyed David pensively. In a loving gesture, he placed his hand on David's shoulder. "Son, giving the devil even one second is too long. And I know you know this very well. See to it that you stay *away* from Ms. Dominique, even if she don't stay away from you. I love you, son. Good night."

Deacon Lewis left just as unassumingly as he'd entered. David rubbed the sides of his temples. Then he walked over and tapped lightly on his restroom door.

"Kit . . . open up."

The door creaked open slowly, and Cherelle stood in the archway. It appeared as if she'd washed her face and reapplied her makeup. She spoke first. "I'm sorry, honey. I didn't mean to be so emotional. I have a lot on my mind with the wedding and stuff. I guess I'm a little stressed."

"No, I'm the one who needs to apologize, babe. I regret that our date night has started this way. And I want to make things right with you. Can we please start over right now, babe?" David asked. "I never want the enemy to win when it comes to me and you."

Cherelle knew David was right. It was the enemy's plan to upset and rattle what God was doing in their relationship—bringing them together in a holy union. "Okay, I would love to do that, my king," Cherelle said.

David warmed all over, and a simple joy spread across his face, exposing his straight white teeth. Cherelle had been addressing him as her king since their engagement. It was another one of their inside jokes. She had previously referred to him as King David because of the way he managed others. But now, he was her king in a way that claimed her whole heart and his.

David leaned against the doorframe. "Kit, babe, you are absolutely gorgeous. Your hair is lovely . . ." David said honestly, touching Cherelle's natural mane that she wore in a twist-out. "And you got this dress speaking to me," he chuckled. "And for the record, since we're in the Lord's house, and He already knows what I'm about to say . . . The *only* woman I've been thinking about, dreaming about, and wanting is *you*. In fact, I've had to do quite a bit of repenting for thinking too hard about our wedding night and honeymoon. I love you more than anything in this world, and I *know* that you are my blessing from God. I honor that, and I can't wait to show you just how much—how deeply in love with you I am . . ." David said. He pressed his forehead against Cherelle's and gently rubbed his nose against hers. He hugged her close for a moment and kissed her on the cheek.

Months ago, before they'd become officially engaged, David had been led by the Lord to place a moratorium on kissing until their wedding day to keep their courtship holy. He knew it wasn't a sin for Christian couples who were courting to kiss, but for him and his fiancée, he knew they couldn't; his attraction to Cherelle was too strong.

He'd learned from his past mistakes with Dominique that not sticking to boundaries was a prelude to disaster. His sexual indiscretion with her had cost him more than he'd been prepared to pay. Beyond placing a strain on his relationship with God and costing him his spiritual peace, it had almost cost him his life. Over a year ago, Dominique's romantic involvement with Brent King, a dirty narcotics officer, led to him ordering a hit on her for her lack of loyalty. David had subsequently been caught in the crossfire, sustaining three gunshot wounds, one of them to the left side of his brain, which left him in rehab for almost a year, learning simple tasks again. He was a walking miracle.

He was determined to protect himself and Cherelle from falling. He wanted their union to be blessed, so he took extra care in keeping it pleasing to the Lord—except for the occasional thoughts he'd been having for the last few weeks. But that was another problem altogether. One that would be resolved soon enough.

Chapter 3

Walk and Talk

After they'd checked on Ms. Naomi and given Lorna Jones a good talking to, Cherelle begged David to see one of the new homes the church had helped to renovate in the surrounding neighborhood. Disciples of Christ Ministries was involved in a joint initiative with the city to provide homeownership through a strategic housing program. Being a regular HGTV junkie, Cherelle loved looking at new and renovated homes. Standing in the kitchen of one of the new homes, she trailed her fingers over the white quartz counter in the kitchen. "They did such a wonderful job," Cherelle beamed, as she studied the espresso-stained cabinets and opened each one, admiring the workmanship.

"Yeah. Dad's construction company handled most of the work, but he employed a lot of workers from the church. It does look very nice. I'm proud of it."

Cherelle winked at David. "You should be, my king," she said. "You are really helping to turn this neighborhood around. People are moving back into this neighborhood because of all the new housing and businesses. And neighbors on the block are taking pride in their homes and this community. It looks beautiful."

Cherelle's half-brother, Corey Perry, pastor of Greater Christian Center Church, focused on economic empowerment for his congregation so that they could be good stewards of the resources God had given them. He'd shared some of his ideas with David, which prompted David to take up a new charge in the community surrounding his church.

"Well, Corey gave me the idea to help the young adults focus on financial literacy and economic stability through homeownership. As a church, if we can teach them how to properly steward their finances so that they can use their resources to further God's mission, I see it as a win-win. But let's get moving so we can start our date night. I've been looking forward to it," David said.

Cherelle sauntered over to David and reached for his hand. "Me too, my king," she said. David took her left hand in his, brought it to his lips, and placed soft, wet, lingering kisses all over it. He pulled her closer. "I love you so much, babe," he whispered into her ear.

"I love you, too, my king."

"I need you to do me a favor, babe . . ."

Cherelle pulled back and eyed David seriously. "Yes, honey, what is it?"

"Don't wear this dress or these shoes again until we are *married!*" David said. He nudged her playfully. "As a matter of fact, I think I need you to stay away from me."

"You know you are incorrigible, right?"

"Yes, I do. Come on, let's go."

They walked hand in hand to the front door. David turned on the alarm system, and they exited. It was now dusk, and an orange-blue sky greeted them as they stepped out onto the porch. Three young men walked toward the house with purpose. David surveyed their surroundings cautiously. There were no other people visible aside from an elderly man across the street who was walking his dog. In a protective stance, David stepped in front of Cherelle as they walked down the porch stairs and onto the home's walkway that led to the sidewalk.

How are you brothers doing tonight?" David greeted them when he and Cherelle neared the sidewalk. He'd learned that it was better to address people on the streets in rough neighborhoods, rather than automatically assume they were up to no good. But the neighborhood surrounding his church had one of the highest crime rates in the country.

"Oh, we doin' real good, Pastor Cole," one of the young men said. David could tell by the young man's persona that he was the one in charge. David supposed it was the job of the other two to stand around and look intimidating while the leader spoke.

"That's good. Be blessed," David returned, relieved that the young man had addressed him respectfully by name. That at least meant the trio was friendly.

The young men stopped just as David and Cherelle stepped onto the sidewalk. The couple was just a few feet away from David's truck. Cherelle squeezed David's hand, and he felt her tension. Maybe these *weren't* friendly young people. Ordinarily, Cherelle felt protected with David, but these days, and in this neighborhood, people carried guns. She feared him getting into any kind of scuffle. Despite his miraculous recovery from the shooting incident that happened a little over a year ago, Cherelle knew that any sort of re-injury could cause David a devastating setback.

"How can I bless you?" David asked the young men.

"We just want to talk to you for a little bit, Pastor Cole," the leader said. There was something deviant in the young man's eyes.

"Okay, but can we keep it brief, fellas? My fiancée and I have an important event to attend tonight."

The three young men formed a circle wall around Cherelle and David.

"Oh. Pardon my manners," the leader said. He used hand gestures as he introduced himself and his partners. "I'm Rico," he said, spreading his fingers over his chest as if he were reciting some oath. He was tall and slim, with hard features and dark eyes, set against skin the color of honey. "This is Dre, and this is Skip," he continued, gesturing to the other two like a used car salesman. The other two grim-looking young men nodded. They resembled one another and could have been brothers. They had the same dark complexions and stocky builds. Then David noticed the tattoo in the center of Rico's right hand. It was a horizontal marking with the letters T and S in an elaborate Victorian font, the symbol for the gang who called themselves The Sect.

"Okay, Rico. Dre. Skip. What can I do for you?" David asked, keeping his eyes on Skip and Dre.

"Are you familiar with a young lady named Sharia Tate, Pastor Cole?" Rico asked.

"Sharia . . . yes . . ." David recalled. He knew her well, and she was a handful. She'd gotten saved and was new to the church. She was learning how to walk as a Christian, and it was taking a little more effort than she thought, but David had employed some of the mature young women in the church to mentor her.

"Is she your girlfriend?" David asked. Perhaps this young man was angry because his girlfriend was in church now. It wouldn't be the first time David had been confronted about an issue like this, especially from gang members.

"Nah, she's my little sister ..."

"Okay . . . is there something you're concerned about, Rico?"

Rico smiled slyly. "I think we should take a walk and talk about it," he said.

David knew that was altogether a bad idea. "I really don't have the time right now, fellas. But you can schedule an appointment, and I can meet with you at the church." David said, attempting to bypass them. Rico blocked David's path.

"Nah, I think right now works better for me."

Dre opened his jacket just enough so that David could catch a glimpse of the weapon he was carrying. Skip did the same. David was certain this *wasn't* a friendly greeting after all, and his first concern was Cherelle. He wasted no time acting. "O-o-kay, but she needs to go. This doesn't involve her."

Rico shrugged. "That's up to you."

"Kit, go back to the church and wait for me," David said. He pressed his car key into Cherelle's palm. "Let Deacon Lewis and Pastor Clint know that I took a walk with some of the neighbors."

Cherelle spoke in a quivering voice. "No . . . I—I'm gonna stay with you." Her heart pumped so furiously; it echoed in her ears. A welt whipped across her face in an instant. Whenever she was nervous or upset, it happened. Her eyes held the terror she felt in pools of water.

"*Cherelle*," David said firmly, "I love you. Do as I *say*, babe." With a nod of his head, David gestured toward the truck. Cherelle hesitated. David kissed her quickly on her forehead. "*Go*," he said, reiterating his command.

Shaking, Cherelle sulked to the truck on unsteady legs. She climbed in slowly and started the engine with her eyes still glued on David. And David didn't move until she had pulled off.

Rico let out an expletive. "Fine and obedient! I likes that! That's the kind of chick I need in *my* life!"

"Don't ever disrespect her," David warned.

Rico erupted in a sinister laugh. "This dude right here, he got heart!" he said to Dre and Skip. He turned to David. "Now let's walk."

CHERELLE BURST into DOC's Friday night youth event held in the church's grand meeting hall; she searched the room for Pastor Clint Hobbs, David's twenty-eight-year-old assistant pastor. The grand meeting hall was filled with over a hundred teens. Cherelle couldn't find Deacon Lewis either. Pastor Clint was talking with his wife, Stormie, when he noticed Cherelle's frazzled state. He and Stormie hurried over to Cherelle and escorted her out of the room. Hyperventilating, Cherelle blurted out without taking a breath. "We went to look at the renovated houses around the corner, and a group of guys came and made David go with them. He made me come back to the church. He said to tell you he took a walk with some of the neighbors."

"*The neighbors*—that's The Sect," Clint said calmly. David had developed code names for each of the gangs in the area since he and Clint encountered them regularly. "Did you hear any of their names?"

Cherelle breathed rapidly as her chest tightened. "Rico. Dre. Skip. I called 911 already. They said they would send a patrol car to the area and one to the church."

Clint seemed to be unfazed. "Hmm. Maybe we should have done something last week."

"What do you mean?" Cherelle asked.

"Let's go back to my office and wait for Pastor," Clint said. "Stormie, please find Deacon Lewis," he instructed his wife.

"Okay," Stormie said before hurrying back into the grand dining hall.

"Last week, The Sect sent Pastor a love note, as he calls them," Clint informed Cherelle.

"W—w-hat d—did it say?"

"It was a verbal note—not an actual note. A guy came up to us in the parking lot as we were leaving last week, and said: 'You're tangling with The Sect. You're on the list.'"

"What does that mean, Clint?"

"*Tangling* means that Pastor's sparring with them—in their way, because he's been getting to some of these kids, and they haven't been joining their gang. As you know, most of the other gangs haven't been recruiting kids who are involved in the city's youth project. But The Sect has been recruiting and harassing the kids anyway. They've got some infighting. There's supposed to be a new guy in charge now. They call him Jag. When they say Pastor's on the list, it means on their hit list—as in to be killed."

"Oh, my God!" Cherelle heaved. She buried her face in her hands.

"Sister Cherelle, calm down. The gangs have been doing stuff like this for years. Pastor gets love notes all the time. He didn't think anything of it. He'll be back. He's okay. I can feel it. I'm positive."

Pastor Clint Hobbs was a younger version of David. He'd been educated at the University of Michigan in engineering, but knew he was called to preach. He'd already begun working on his doctorate in divinity. Like David, he had a brilliant mind, and he'd grown up in the hood, so he had a knack for communicating with all types of people. And he had David's same calm disposition, no matter what was happening.

Cherelle didn't *feel it,* and she didn't know anything except that her head was swirling. She prayed as she rocked back and forth in the chair. Deacon Lewis entered with Stormie, and Pastor Clint relayed all that had taken place. They sat in Clint's office and waited. The police unit arrived and asked Cherelle routine questions. They'd already sent a patrol car around the neighborhood, but there'd been no sign of David or any of the young men Cherelle had described.

Cherelle couldn't track David's phone because he'd left it in the truck while they visited the renovated home. She was attacked by a headache. She wanted to call Leah and Joseph, David's mother and stepfather. But Deacon Lewis forbade her.

"I feel like I'm losing my mind. I shouldn't have left him. I should have stayed with him!" Cherelle cried.

"No . . . no. If Pastor told you to come back to this church, that's what he *meant.* That's what he wanted," Clint said. He propped himself on the corner of his desk.

"Yes, indeed," Deacon Lewis agreed.

"He knew what he was doing. He was protecting you in case anything *did* happen," Clint offered. "Pastor's been at this for a long time, and he knows—"

The door opened, and David walked in. Cherelle sprang from her chair and ran into his arms. She let go of her tears. "I was so . . . scared. What did they do to you?" Cherelle cried. She squeezed David around his neck.

"Nothing, Kit. I'm good. Don't cry. I'm good," David said into her ear. He hugged Cherelle close. She was still shaking. "Shh . . . I'm okay, babe," he reassured her.

The group was drawn to every word David spoke as he explained. "It wasn't what it looked like. He was *thanking me.* You all know Sharia Tate? Well, it turns out that Rico is her older brother, and before she became a member of this church, he was at his wits' end with her. He said Sharia had gotten wild and was running the streets, getting into all kinds of trouble and making out with a bunch of different guys. He said he'd done everything except put his hands on her because he doesn't believe in that. Their mother has been in prison for armed robbery for over seven years, and he's been raising Sharia on his own all this time—since he was seventeen. He's only twenty-four years old, but he's like her father and brother all rolled into one.

"Why did they have the guns? I thought they were going to hurt you," Cherelle said.

"No, it was just appearances, Kit. We walked a safe distance away from the other two. They didn't even hear what we were talking about. Rico told me that he doesn't trust too many people on the street. He mentioned some 'technical difficulties' with the gang and said he was being careful with information. I interpreted technical difficulties as in-fighting."

"So, then, the rumors are true? The Sect really has a new leader?" Clint asked.

"That's what he said. He called it a *transition*. Made it sound like he was running a business that was being taken over by another company."

"Well, they are running a business, albeit a dirty business of drugs and other illegal stuff," Clint added.

"That's what was funny. This kid has a good head on his shoulders. He told me that his vision for The Sect isn't the same as the new leadership—said he had a *moral* disagreement about the things The Sect was getting involved in."

"Hump. That is strange—ironic at best," Clint said.

"Yes, but I have a feeling that there is room for Jesus in this young man's life. There was something there. I even asked about the shooting last year. He point-blank told me that he didn't have anything to do with that part of The Sect."

"You believe him?" Pastor Clint asked.

"Yes, I do. When talking about his little sister, he was almost moved to tears. He said the change in her is real. I know this young man is running drugs on the streets, but I also know that God can change a man's heart. Rico sees the Holy Spirit working in his sister's life. That has turned a light bulb on for him. I hope he gets out before it's too late for him."

"Well, I'm glad you're safe, son. I'm gonna get on back to the kids. Can't leave 'em alone too long. They'll miss me," Deacon Lewis said, even though several adult volunteers were managing the teens..

"We're gonna head back in too. You two enjoy your date night," Clint said, leading his wife out of his office to give David and Cherelle some alone time.

When they were alone, David turned to Cherelle. "Kit, listen, this neighborhood is changing, but it is *still* dangerous. The violence—the gangs—this stuff is *real*. I want you to always be on the lookout for people who may be up to no good, sweetheart. Always be on guard. Pay attention to what's going on around you—watch people's moves," David said. "Make sure you know the number of people around you. Watch what everyone is doing. Don't allow anyone to get too close to you and scope out someplace you can run if you have to run. And if we are ever in a situation like that again, I need you to comply right away. Don't think. Don't hesitate. Just do as I say. Please. Do you understand, babe? It's for your safety, sweetheart. I need to know that you will love and trust me enough to do exactly as I tell you, Kit."

Feeling as if David had scolded her, Cherelle's tears returned. It was the second time this evening that David had made her cry. "Yes, honey. I was just so scared and worried. I didn't want anyone to hurt you. I'm sorry. I just didn't want to leave you . . ." Cherelle said, swiping at her tears.

Instead of apologizing for his tone or the necessary admonishment, David cupped Cherelle's face in his hands and broke his own rule. He kissed her full on the lips and allowed his lips to linger and caress hers with kisses; there was no other way to convey what he felt in his heart. After a few moments of pure bliss, he said, "Kit, I love you with everything in me. I *love* you. If something were to happen to you because of me—because of someone's attempt to get to me—I wouldn't be able to live with myself."

Chapter 4

No Permission. No Blessing.

D avid sat confidently in front of Cherelle's mother, Eleanor Dupree. Whatever problem he and Eleanor were having—and they were having one—David wanted to know what it was so it could be handled and put aside before he and Cherelle married. Their wedding was one week away now, and David could tell that trouble was already brewing in paradise.

Cherelle had successfully avoided telling David the whole truth about why her mother had turned so cold toward him. She'd claimed that her mother was just reacting to her only child getting married. David, however, was astute enough to know there was something deeper than that going on. He was sure of it. He guessed that he'd inadvertently offended Cherelle's mother somehow, and he wanted to right whatever wrong he'd committed so that he and Cherelle could start their lives together without any in-law drama. He'd been a pastor long enough to know that the little foxes in a relationship could tear a marriage completely apart.

"What brings you here, David?" Eleanor Dupree said coolly. Even though her voice sounded slurred as a result of having a stroke some years ago, David heard the ire in her tone.

Cherelle shared the same chocolate complexion as her mother and the same long, beautiful, natural hair, but there were no other resemblances. Cherelle favored her deceased father, Pastor Charles Perry. Eleanor looked much older than her sixty-something age. She didn't have the spunk or sexiness of David's mother, Leah, or Corey's mother, Cynthia, and they were all around the same age. Something had zapped Eleanor Dupree's vibrance and youth, and the stroke she'd suffered some years ago due to a ruptured aneurysm was not to blame. David discerned that something emotional had robbed her of living life to the fullest.

David scooted to the edge of his seat and looked Eleanor right in her eyes. "Well, for starters, Ma Dupree, I sense that there is some tension—some kind of problem between us, and I want to know what I've said or done to offend you."

Eleanor maintained a stern disposition. "Have I ever said you've offended me, David?"

"Well, no. But I know there is *something* wrong, Ma Dupree. I don't expect you to be the president of my fan club, but you treat me as if I've done something wrong to you—or Cherelle. And I'm not aware of anything," David said humbly. "But if I have done something, I'd like to apologize, and I'd at least like to know what it is so that it doesn't happen in the future."

Eleanor wrapped the thin throw around her shoulders and reached for her teacup. David leaned over to the end table next to her and handed her the cup and saucer. She nodded.

"Thank you."

"Ma Dupree, I love Cherelle. I try my best to do for her and give her whatever she needs, so that she can see an outward manifestation of what I feel on the inside. I'm good to her. I'm always asking her if there is anything that I need to do to be the kind of man she wants."

"I understand that, David. I've never denied that."

"Then, I don't understand the coldness. I'm not trying to compare, but the way you treat Corey, as opposed to the way you treat me, is like day and night. If I've offended you, I want to ask you for forgiveness because—"

"Stop right there, David," Eleanor said, interrupting him. "Let me be honest . . ."

"Please do . . . I welcome that."

"I find your relationship with Cherelle disturbing . . . that's the truth of the matter."

David was initially confused and taken aback. Then offense settled in. He smirked indignantly, and his jawline tightened. "There is *nothing* disturbing about my relationship with Cherelle. Our relationship is beautiful. I don't mean to be disrespectful, but you're on the outside looking in, so I have no idea what you're basing your assumption on."

"You wouldn't. But it's very simple, David. This—the way Cherelle feels for you—can destroy her. It's 'David this . . . David, that . . .' It's like you're the center of her world."

David shook his head from side to side. His aggravation was noticeable. "That's not true, Ma Dupree. *God* is the center of Cherelle's world, as He is mine. I'd like to think I come second, but I'm definitely not the center."

"You wanted honesty. I'm giving you honesty, David. It's too much. Love like that is destroying."

"No, it's not. It's good and it's pure. What Cherelle and I have isn't destroying."

"It may not be destroying to *you*, David, but I see Cherelle. I *know* Cherelle."

"You don't know Cherelle like I do—in the ways I do. You can't. And you'll never be able to," David retorted.

Eleanor sat straight up in her chair and glared at David. "Are you trying to tell me that you know Cherelle *intimately,* Pastor David Cole?" Eleanor insinuated.

David sensed her indignation. "Yes, but not *physically.* I haven't touched her that way. We made a commitment to save one another for Christ. The most we've done is kiss, Ma Dupree. That's it. So, if you're angry with me because you think I've taken advantage of her, that's not the case. Cherelle and I have honored God in our relationship. She's worth waiting for."

Eleanor breathed a sigh of relief. "I know that topic is of a personal nature, so I do thank you for clearing that up. I suspected otherwise because of the way Cherelle fawns all over you," Eleanor said with an eye roll. "There is a pull between you that reminds me of—well, it doesn't matter. I know the two of you are far beyond grown. But your relationship just doesn't seem healthy to me. And no matter how old she is, I feel compelled to speak my mind on that."

"Ma Dupree, God is right in the middle of our relationship. I love Cherelle with all of me, and I know she loves me. What we have is ordained and blessed by God. There can be nothing disturbing about that."

"You hold Cherelle's heart in your hands, David. I think you know that. You're a well-educated *and* street-savvy man. You have too much power over Cherelle, David. That's my opinion, and that disturbs me greatly."

"Ma Dupree, Cherelle has my heart right in her hands, too. I have willingly given it to her with no reservation. I've held nothing back from her," David explained. *Except for one little incidental thing,* he thought to himself. "And I can tell you with all honesty that I have *never* loved another woman the way I love Cherelle. And I *welcome* the feeling. I know my heart is safe with Cherelle, and her heart is definitely safe with me. I would never hurt her intentionally. I'm preparing to build my life *around* her and *with* her. A week from now, she will be my wife, but even right now, she is the best part of me."

Eleanor was not at all moved by any of David's explanations or confessions. "David, Cherelle refers to you as *king*—her king. You don't see how that's disturbing?"

David smiled slyly, then checked himself so that he wouldn't come off as being too cocky. "No, I don't," he said. He stroked his goatee, accessing a private memory. Even Eleanor couldn't deny David's handsomeness. She could plainly see why Cherelle was so mesmerized by him. "Actually, I see it as *sexy* and *passionate*. Cherelle calling me that started as a joke about the way I manage people—how I handle business, Ma Dupree. It morphed into something personal as Cherelle and I started courting. It's passionate. She calls me her king because I treat her like my *queen*. It's her natural response to me and the way I treat her. Again, ain't nothin' disturbing about that," David said, eschewing his Harvard education to make his point.

"My feelings about the matter won't change. I cannot say you have my permission or blessing to marry her. I know that no matter what I say, Cherelle loves you and is going to marry you anyway, but I cannot and will not give you my blessing."

David rose from his chair. "I didn't come here for your permission or blessing. I'm more than positive that Cherelle and I have God's permission and God's blessing to proceed with becoming one in marriage," David said as respectfully as he could. "How you feel about me and my relationship with Cherelle is not going to change what I feel for Cherelle. It's not going to delay or negate my plans to marry her. As a matter of fact, it won't interfere with our relationship at *all*, because I won't allow it to. I love Cherelle. She is *mine*. And she will *always* be mine. And I don't care who has a problem with that. Thank you for your time, Ma Dupree. I will let myself out," David said. He turned and walked toward the door.

Eleanor Dupree's stern, pouted lips curled into a defeated smile.

Chapter 5

Hot Market

Greg Kingston greeted David and Cherelle at his front door. He'd been providing pre-marital counseling to the pair since they announced their engagement earlier that year. Being a pastor of a relatively small church, Greg and his wife, Norma, a psychiatrist, provided pastoral counseling to a select few from their home office. David was one of the few clients who used the couple's front door since Greg had been his spiritual and financial mentor for many years.

"Hey, Greg, I see you've gotten wiser since the last time we saw you," David said, referring to Greg's curly salt and pepper shade hair.

"I'm getting wiser every day, sir," Greg chuckled, rubbing his hands over his head.

"You look wonderfully handsome *and* distinguished," Cherelle said.

Greg hugged her warmly and kissed her on the cheek. "Now, I see why you're making this woman your wife," he said to David. "Not only is she incredibly beautiful, she's also incredibly smart."

"I can't do anything but agree," David returned.

Greg opened the door wider and allowed the two to enter. "Greg, I need to run to the restroom before we start. I just had a big cup of Mama Leah's lemonade," Cherelle said.

"Go ahead and use the one on the main level. You can meet David and me downstairs in the office when you're done."

"Thanks."

* * *

WHEN DAVID and Greg were alone, Greg took the opportunity to probe David about the couple's progress since their last counseling session.

"Did you guys come to an agreement about which one of you is going to move into the other's home?"

"Nope," David said, shaking his head.

"You know you're a week away from being tied together for the rest of your lives, right?"

David chuckled. "Yes. But I've been praying, and I still don't feel comfortable moving into Cherelle's home. I know these are modern times and all, but that's not me. I'm not saying it's wrong or unmanly for any other man. I know marriage is about being a team. But for me, it doesn't sit right in my spirit."

"I understand. But Cherelle says your house is much smaller and she's going to lose a lot of space—the lake view and the woods—her muse for writing. That's important to her."

"Hopefully, today we can work this out. I'm hoping my fiancée will agree to move into my house until we can find a home both of us can agree on."

"But you two haven't even been looking for a home."

"I know. I was hoping Cherelle would see things my way.

It's a hot market right now. She won't have any problem selling her home."

Greg's eyes grew wide, and they both laughed. David especially was tickled by his own silliness.

"Did you tell Cherelle about your little *girlfriend* in Tennessee?"

"Uh . . . I want to wait until after we're married."

David's *girlfriend* was a lavish, four-acre lakeview estate near Knoxville. David called it the Escape. He had managed to keep the property a secret, even from his parents. The only people who knew about the escape were Greg, his wife, Norma, and his soul brother and best friend, Gus. David purchased it at a good time when home values were low, and now it was worth quadruple the price he'd bought it for. He stayed at the Escape when he needed rest and rejuvenation. His day-to-day schedule was demanding, and the property was his hideaway spot, his getaway from the world. It was a serene space that provided him with just the privacy he needed. One day, he would retire there.

Greg shook his head. "You can't be serious, David. You must have forgotten that you're only *days* away from being married. We're on what Norma and I call full disclosure status. Nothing hidden. Everything in the open. Today, we've got to get the finances out in the open, too. *All* of the finances."

David shifted uncomfortably, and stress lines took over his brow. He let out a sigh and relented. "Okay, but can we just wait on the Tennessee thing? I want to hold off on that. I have something special planned for Cherelle."

Greg began to protest with his forefinger raised.

"Everything else is on the table—I promise. I even brought a copy of the investment portfolio, the property deeds, and bank statements—everything."

"You know Norma and I usually tackle finances and have

this topic out of the way by this time in the game, David. I've given you more than enough time to come *clean*."

"I know. And thank you for giving me some more time."

"Are you sure you trust Cherelle *fully*, David?"

"Yes. Certainly."

"Well, Norma and I were curious as to why you wanted to wait until the week before you get married to have a *full* financial disclosure session. We usually do it at least six weeks *before* the wedding. We like to reserve this last session to discuss intimacy—we need to discuss a few points regarding that today."

"Greg, I trust Cherelle. I've given Cherelle my whole heart. I've never been out on a limb like this in my life. I just wanted to wait. To be honest, I don't know why I've been stalling. Once I put everything on the table, that's it. She'll know everything about me."

Greg sat pensively for a moment, then said, "I want to respond to that, but I'll wait until Cherelle's here." At that moment, the two heard Cherelle's heeled footsteps. She cracked the door open.

"I'm ready. Hope I didn't take too long, Greg. I know I've been here a million times, but every time I come here, I can't help but feel like I should own this house! It is so beautiful. I love it." The two-and-a-half-acre modern residence had seven thousand square feet of living space, which included six bedrooms, a movie room, an outdoor kitchen and pool, and a dance studio in the basement.

"Thank you. I have no plans to move," Greg said, winking. Cherelle scooted next to David on the loveseat.

Greg led the two in prayer before beginning the session. "Cherelle and David, Norma wanted me to tell you that she's sorry she couldn't be here," Greg said as soon as they were finished praying. "Our youngest daughter, Joy, is having her first baby by C-section in the morning in Arizona. Norma wanted to go down early and be with her. I plan to fly out later tonight. And as you both know, the Lord led me to step down from pastoring Spring Hill Church. Another church in the area has inquired about me coming there. Norma and I are on standby, just waiting for further instructions from the Lord. As a result, things are a little hectic right now. You two will be our last counseling clients so that Norma and I can fully devote ourselves to the next mission the Lord sends us on."

"It's no problem, we totally understand," Cherelle said.

"Thank you. Did you both get a chance to go over each other's credit reports thoroughly?" Greg asked.

"Yes," David and Cherelle answered in unison.

"Did you two have any questions or concerns?"

"No," they answered in unison again.

"Okay. I gave you a task to decide how the household finances will be handled. Did you do that?" Greg asked.

Cherelle spoke first. "Yes, but we didn't really come to a *consensus* on it." Greg noticed that Cherelle used the word *consensus* instead of *agreement*.

David's face held no expression. "Explain, Cherelle," Greg said.

"Well, David would like to put everything together in one pot—and there's nothing wrong with it—but I've been on my own for a while, and I'm independent. I would rather he assign me the bills he would like me to take care of. I agree that he should be the person to handle the finances because of his skill, but I'm not comfortable handing my money over to anyone."

Greg knew then that David was frustrated. All the other sessions had gone well. They'd left all luvvy-duvvy. This evening would be a different story.

"Kit, you're not handing over your money to me like you're putting it. Let's be clear: I don't need your money to take care of you. It just doesn't make sense for two people to bring money into the same home, and it's not coming together. It can be better planned and invested when it's put together. Besides, your income isn't steady. There may be times when you don't have anything to put in anyway."

"Why can't you just tell me what you want me to pay, honey?"

"Because there is no such thing as my bill or your bill. They will be *our* bills. And I'm not 'anyone,' I'm about to become your *husband*."

"Sorry, I didn't mean it like that, honey."

"Cherelle, why are you uncomfortable giving—rather, sharing your money with David? Is it because that would make you feel vulnerable?" Greg asked, eyeing David. David received the message that the question applied to him, too.

"I don't know. I just need to be independent."

"Kit, I don't understand how that will keep you from being independent."

"Honey, I don't know. Are you going to decide how much of *my* money I get to keep for myself? I don't like that."

David sighed. As much level-headedness as he possessed, Cherelle knew she was pushing it. And she hated that she was disappointing him or aggravating him, whichever she was doing right now. But as a therapist, she was being completely honest with herself and him.

Greg sat back in his chair and let the two hash it out. He knew it would be better this way.

"No, Kit," David said patiently. "You can do or buy whatever you want—whenever you want, babe. I'm not trying to put you on a leash. I'm trying to exercise good stewardship over the Lord's resources."

"If I just keep my money, you can still do that. I can give a certain amount to you if you want to invest some of it. Why do I have to pool it with yours?"

"First of all, babe," David said in his minister's voice. It was laced with compassion, but at the same time, it was chastening. "Everything we have or earn belongs to God—not to me or you. It just makes good financial sense. Greg, as a financial planner, don't you agree?" David asked Greg, pleading for an ally.

Instead of answering, Greg said, "You two don't trust one another."

"I trust him."

"And I trust her."

"No, you don't. You two *love* each other—you're *in love* with each other. But you haven't learned to *trust* each other yet. Money is the main thing that keeps people in divorce court, more than cheating or anything else. You're going to have to resolve the trust issues as far as money is concerned. Please take out your bank statements and financial portfolios and exchange them."

David reached down and lifted his briefcase off the floor. He placed it on his lap and opened it. He took out two slender binders and handed them to Cherelle.

"The first one contains a copy of my investment portfolio. The other contains my bank statements for the last year, along with a list of all the real estate and land that I own. And the information about the private jet charter company I'm heavily invested in, called Maverick Charter Jets. As you know, I'm a private man, Kit. The majority of my assets are held through LLCs and a trust. That's why we're meeting with the attorney tomorrow so that I can revise the terms of the trust to include you. I created an easily readable pie chart for you, so you can see the financial percentages in terms of how much each sector is worth. And I also created an easy-to-read spread chart with just my assets, liabilities, and total net worth."

Cherelle handed David a one-inch, purple binder with her information in it. He didn't look at it. He focused his attention on Cherelle as she read through his financial statements. No part of him was hidden from her now. He'd exposed all—except for the little matter in Tennessee. Cherelle sank back into the cushion of the loveseat and thumbed through David's portfolio and statements. After several minutes, she was thoroughly embarrassed. She pursed her lips together. She'd been afraid to let go of her independence, but it was obvious that David was much better off financially than she was. Why was she holding back?

David read through Cherelle's financial statements and handed her back the thin binder she'd given him. They sat without saying anything, each pondering Greg's statement. They didn't trust one another. Both were afraid of being vulnerable.

"How did you acquire this much money at your age?" Cherelle asked quietly.

"Kit, I've always been a good saver and investor—as soon as I learned about stocks in the seventh grade," David said. The memory caused him to chuckle. "I had the first hundred thousand dollars by the time I was eighteen years old," David continued. Cherelle's mouth flew open. "Listen," he said. "I've worked since the time I was fourteen—twelve if you count the times that I worked for Joe at his construction company unofficially. I literally invested almost every dime. My mom established a custodial account for me in seventh grade. She turned it over to me when I turned eighteen. At that time, I had fifty thousand dollars in my portfolio. My grandfather had been keeping up with me and what I did with stocks, so he surprised me when I graduated from high school and gave me fifty thousand dollars to match what I already had.

"I was blown away because my grandfather had an old, raggedy pick-up truck and a small home on a nice plot of land in Knoxville, Tennessee. He pastored a tiny church, and the salary was meager. He worked a full-time job as a carpenter. He didn't own anything that would have led me to believe that he had enough money to give me fifty thousand dollars. He made me promise that I wouldn't tell a soul—no one. I thought he'd given me his life savings to invest, so I worked extra-hard to grow that money, Kit."

"To fifteen *million* dollars?"

"No, not quite, Kit. When I graduated from Harvard with my bachelor's degree, my grandfather gave me *one hundred thousand* dollars to play with. He also gave me the name of someone he said he'd researched who was good at handling money to help guide me. Two years later, the money had grown significantly. My grandfather's guy, Kirk Blum, helped me diversify a little better. My grandfather gave me *another* hundred thousand just two years later, when I got my MBA and started working on Wall Street. He was always keeping track of my portfolio with me. And I made a lot of money when I worked on Wall Street—good money."

"Between what you saved and what your grandfather gave you, that only adds up to three hundred thousand dollars, not counting any money you may have made investing it. How did you grow that to fifteen million, David?"

David smiled. "While I worked on Wall Street, I invested most of my salary along with the seed money my grandad had given me. And I had some good hits—amazingly good hits. But when my grandfather died, the shocker came. I thought Kent Cole had given me his life savings of two hundred fifty thousand dollars. I was sure of it. It made sense. But my grandfather's investment portfolio was worth a little over *three million* dollars.

Cherelle's eyes grew wide. "What?" she asked, hooked on David's story.

"Yep. And in addition to that, the land that he owned was

worth a million and a half, Kit. He was seventy-eight when he passed; he amassed all of that on a carpenter's salary. And he left everything to me. Between selling some of the land a few years later for double what it had been worth initially, the buying and selling of properties, income from my rental properties, profits from Maverick Charter Jets, plus two million from my book sales, that's how," David said, reflecting. "What I didn't know was that the Blums had been managing my granddad's money for a long time—over fifty years—since he came home from the army.

"It was humorous. My grandfather had been testing me. At the same time, however, he'd been showing confidence in me. God has given me a gift when it comes to finance and money. This thing about money has been my little secret—something that has always been just between me and my granddad. And when he passed, I just kept it to myself. My grandfather had taught me so much. That's why I live the way I do—simply, modestly. I take a small salary from the church. It's been the same since the church started. I don't charge any expenses to the church. I pay for travel and hotels out of my own pocket. It's the same way my granddad lived. The money is like a game to me. I love to see how much I can make it grow. It's not to show off or flaunt. It allows me to do good things for others—to serve Christ in tangible ways." David looked at Cherelle seriously and said, "I'm no Bill Gates, but I don't *need* your money to take care of you. You know all my business now. I just put everything out there. And for me, it's a little uncomfortable. I *love* you, and I know you love me. But being fully exposed is a bit uncomfortable. It's like I have let you into every part of my life. It's a good thing, but at the same time, I feel emotionally naked—vulnerable," David admitted.

"I know. I feel the same way. I understand completely. I'm so sorry. I'm feeling a little bit vulnerable, too, just like Greg said. I know that you want us to be a true team in every sense, and I do too. I just need to take baby steps when it comes to money. I know I have a lot to let go of. Let's be patient with one another, honey." Cherelle said.

"We will," David said. He lifted Cherelle's hand and planted a kiss on it. He let his moist, full lips linger, communicating to Cherelle with his heart. She felt the sensuous vibe, and she savored it.

Chapter 6

Garden of Eden Collection

Cherelle stood in front of David, stammering over her words. "Um . . . ah . . . uh . . . there's something I need to talk to you about, honey. It's important . . . but . . . I . . ."

Concerned, David stepped from behind his desk. His stomach sank. Did Cherelle want to postpone the wedding? It was less than forty-eight hours away. David watched sweat bead on Cherelle's forehead. He knew whatever she wanted to talk about was serious. Had her mother told her about his visit?

"Babe, what is it? What's the matter?" David asked. Now that Cherelle had his heart, was she backing out?

"It's just that . . . I—I want to um . . . I need to . . ."

David's gaze was intense. He massaged the back of his neck with his hand, kneading the spot that had knotted up in the last few moments. "You want to what, babe? Are you having second thoughts? You want to postpone the wedding? *What?*"

"No, honey," Cherelle said. She took David's hands in hers. She looked up at him lovingly. "I just want to . . . uh . . . please you—I—I mean I want our wedding night to be special. I

45

bought some things, and I want to know what you'd prefer—I mean . . . I don't know what you'd like me to wear. If you'd like something short or long or—what color?" A welt appeared on Cherelle's cheek. David touched Cherelle's face lightly and breathed a sigh of relief.

"Kit, calm down. Your skin is welting."

Cherelle touched her face. She could feel the hives. "Oh my goodness. I've got to put cortisone on it," she said. She covered her face with her palm. "But can you tell me what you'd like?"

"So . . . you want to know what I'd like you to wear on our wedding night? Is that what you're asking me, Kit?" David asked straight-faced. His blankness caused another welt on Cherelle's arm. She scratched at it.

"Yes . . . I just want you to be pleased with my selection . . ."

David looked up at the ceiling as if he were praying. He looked back at Cherelle. He stared at her directly without flinching. Cherelle was undone. She scratched at the welt on her arm again.

"David, honey . . . did I say something wrong?"

David stepped back to ensure physical separation between Cherelle and himself. His eyes roamed over her. He took note of her gold asymmetric top, distressed skinny jeans, and high-heeled ankle boots. Then he spoke seriously with no expression. "Kit, I can't answer that question right now."

"Are you going to call me *later* and let me know?"

David continued to stare at Cherelle with a blank look that made her feel like she was three years old. He shook his head. "No. Listen, I've got some things to take care of, sweetheart. And I need you to leave. See you tomorrow night at the rehearsal dinner, okay?"

"David . . . honey?"

David bent down and kissed Cherelle's forehead. "Tomorrow, babe."

"But David, honey . . ."

"*Cherelle*, I need you to leave," David said gently. "I'm sorry. I've got some things I need to do. I love you," he said, turning her gently toward the door, while he took the opportunity to check her out fully. He closed the door behind her as she stepped into the main hallway of his office wing. His best friend and soul brother, Gus, exited from the restroom with a grin that made David throw a stress ball at him. The ball bounced off Gus's head.

"Ouch, bro!" Gus snickered. He walked over to the mirror that hung above a credenza near David's desk. Gus raked his hands over his blonde hair and eyed his low-cut fade and goatee. Gus and David had been friends since seventh grade, when Gus came to David's assistance as he fought off three boys by himself. Gus had been the lone white boy in a neighborhood full of black kids, and they'd affectionately nicknamed him Ghost because of his pale skin. These days, CIA agent Gus Merrick had built a life for himself that was vastly different from the scrawny kid who'd lived most of his life in a foster care home just a couple of doors down from David.

"Were you in there eavesdropping?" David asked.

Gus turned from the mirror, picked up the stress ball, and tossed it back at David. "I couldn't help it. I didn't want to come out and embarrass Cherelle. She was already nervous.

David shook his head. "Did you hear that? That woman just asked me what I would like her to *wear* Friday night. Is she kidding me? Oh, my Lord, she is driving me crazy! She has no clue. Jesus help me!" he kidded.

Gus's blue-grey eyes danced with amusement. "She sounded so serious, bro," he chuckled.

David burst into laughter, and a bright smile danced across

his lips. "She *was* serious, bro! My goodness! My baby has a type-A personality. Everything in order. Everything perfect," David said. "It was taking all of me to keep a straight face. She has no idea what I'm dealing with right now. I wanted so badly to say, 'Cherelle, I don't want you to wear *anything* Friday night.' Right now, I feel like skipping this rehearsal dinner and wedding ceremony and jumping right into my honeymoon! I'm coming out of my skin! That woman was hilarious. And she was looking so good with her little skinny jeans and heels on. Whoever invented that needs a raise!"

Gus laughed. "You should have said, 'Honey, I'm really into the Garden of Eden collection these days!'"

"Right! Aw, man . . ." David chuckled. "Ooh, she was lookin' good too! And she gon' come up in here all cute asking me what I want her to wear on our wedding night? That's a no-brainer for me. David shook his head back and forth and continued his rant. "Asking me something like that. I was thinking, *'Woman, I'm trying to keep my mind right in the Lord's house!'"*

"Well, you know how women are, bro. They think we want all the lingerie and stuff all the time."

"Man, God knew what He was doing the first time! Adam and Eve didn't get clothes until they messed up and got kicked out of the garden. I want my fashion to be how God intended it to be!"

Gus turned serious. "So, are you good, bro? Are you ready? I mean, *really* ready?"

David was ready. He felt peace in his spirit, even if he and Cherelle couldn't have children. Cherelle had been diagnosed with Polycystic Ovarian Syndrome a few years before she met David. They both understood that the diagnosis could present a real barrier to having a family. Besides that, Cherelle was concerned about her age. At forty-three, she wasn't exactly young anymore. Even after their engagement, she'd cautioned David to be absolutely sure he wanted to marry her, because there could be a possibility with PCOS and her age, she wouldn't be able to give him the children she knew he wanted. David knew Cherelle had secretly given up on being a mother, but he hadn't given up on being a father.

After praying about it, David gave his last want to God. He'd wanted to be a father for so long. That was the reason why Dominique's betrayal had been so cutting. But God had let David know that He would provide. He didn't know how God was going to give him a child, but he trusted that somehow, He would, even if he and Cherelle had to adopt.

"Yes. I'm ready. No fear. Complete peace," David said.

Chapter 7

I Do. I Will. I Am.

T he sanctuary of Disciples of Christ Ministries was splendidly adorned with hundreds of freshly cut Calla lilies and greenery. The peaceful sanctuary was a secret romantic garden with soft, glowing tree light floor lamps at the ends of every pew in the center aisle. A gentle calm hung over the sanctuary's tall arches. Baria Jennings, Hollywood's most sought-after celebrity wedding coordinator, directed several assistants masterfully via headsets and discreet signals that could rival those of DOC's Sunday morning ushers. Wearing pale pink suits, Baria's assistants moved inconspicuously around the sanctuary under Baria's command. The last guests were seated, and Baria was vigilant about adhering to David and Cherelle's instructions to begin the wedding on time.

In his church office, David stood in the center of a prayer circle created by Deacon Lewis, Gus, and Joseph, his stepfather. David was unable to concentrate on Deacon Lewis' words because he was immersed in a private, glorious conversation with his Father. It was a spiritual vocalization of praise and thanks. He could no longer feel the touch of the trio's hands on him. In his spirit, he was kneeling at the Lord's feet. He could feel the Lord's touch, and it felt wondrous. The firm pat on David's back from Joe after Deacon Lewis' prayer had ended did not disturb David as he communed with God. The trio left him alone at Deacon Lewis' prompting. When the door closed behind them, Gus whispered, "You think he'll be okay? He only has ten minutes left before the wedding starts. It's like he's in some kind of trance."

"He'll be fine, Young Gus. The Holy Ghost will release him when it's time. He's talking with the Lord. He's right where he needs to be," Deacon Lewis said.

"That's right," Joe agreed.

Gus joked, "This is his last few minutes of singlehood before he gets that ball and chain. I guess praying is the best thing to do."

"Marriage will be good for him," Joe nodded.

"Humph. And watch what you say. Your ball and chain is just around the corner," Deacon Lewis warned Gus with confidence.

Gus shook his head. "Unh-uh. Not ready for that, Deac. I'm okay with being saved and all, but settling down with *one* woman for the rest of my life? I fa sho ain't ready for that. No . . . no . . . no . . ." Gus sang, mimicking Amy Winehouse.

Deacon Lewis's eyes hinted at something he was certain of. "Mark my words, Young Gus," Deacon Lewis said.

Joseph shook his head in amusement. He wanted to tell Gus that when Deacon Lewis spoke like that, he knew what he was talking about. *Better get ready, Gus.*

"Yes, Father," David said when the Lord released him. It was time. There were no words David could adequately use to describe the peace that enveloped him. He glanced at his watch; he had one minute. He walked to his mirror in his closet and evaluated himself. He blotted his tears with a handkerchief and smiled. He looked good. The young brothers in the hood would have told him that he was "crispy." The older gentlemen would have said he was "clean." Cherelle had picked out his white tuxedo and baby blue boutonnière. It was fall, David's favorite season, and today was the second "best day" of his life —the day he would receive God's second, most precious gift to him—his wife.

Baria let out a breath when she spied David entering the sanctuary from the left wing. Whispers filled the sanctuary. David took his place in front of Gus casually and nodded to Greg Kingston, who was officiating the ceremony. Gus covered his mouth and spoke. "I thought I was gonna have to come and get you, bro," he said.

"Nope. I'm real good. Tonight's *my* night," David teased, barely moving his lips.

Gus patted his shoulder, "For sure. I—I bet," Gus said, stammering over the last of his words. His attention had been hijacked. *Dominique.* If it wouldn't cause a scene, he would march right over to her and throw her out personally. He'd warned her right after David's shooting to steer clear of David. Now, she was swimming in dangerous waters, ignoring what was in store for her if she kept this up. Positive that David hadn't seen her, Gus tamped down the ire boiling over inside him.

To David, the few minutes it took for the wedding party to enter seemed to drag by. When Greg Kingston said the blessed words, "Please rise for the entrance of the bride," the huge wood-carved double doors of the main sanctuary entrance flung open, and David felt his stomach tighten with anticipation. Cherelle appeared seconds later with her arm locked inside of her brother, Corey's. Her natural hair was styled in an updo, and her dark chocolate skin glistened against the celestial-white lace V-neck, mermaid dress with cap sleeves. Cherelle looked stunning. She floated down the aisle toward David, and he couldn't do what he thought he could—contain his tears. His eyes glossed over from the sheer joy of his blessing.

"She. Is. *Everything*," David said.

Gus agreed, "Yeah. She sure is, bro."

"God is so good," David said. Despite his will to contain them, teardrops fell, and David resigned to the fact that there was no sense in trying to be macho at a time like this.

As Cherelle neared the altar, it was apparent that he and Cherelle shared the same emotional state. Corey exchanged a quiet conversation with David before he finally unlocked his arm from Cherelle's and released her to David. This *last warning* conversation caused chuckles from their family and friends. Cherelle's best friend, Lynn, exited her spot around the altar and dabbed Cherelle's face lightly with a handkerchief. But when Cherelle looked back at David, the tears came again. David leaned over and kissed her cheek. Greg Kingston smiled and cleared his throat. Kissing of any kind would have to wait until they made it to that part of the ceremony. Greg read a scripture, and before David knew it, it was time for him to say the words he'd asked many other grooms to say during wedding ceremonies he had officiated.

David steadied himself and peered deeply into Cherelle's eyes as Greg Kingston posed the question. "David Kent Cole, do you take Cherelle Eleanor Dupree to be your lawfully wedded wife, to live together in marriage? Do you promise to love her, comfort her, honor and keep her for better or worse, for richer or poorer, in sickness and health, and forsaking all others, be faithful only to her, for as long as you both shall live?" Greg asked.

David squeezed Cherelle's hand with tender reverence without taking his passionate gaze off her. He spoke with surety, emphasizing every word. "*I do. I will. I am.*"

Some of the teen girls from David's youth ministry swooned and whisper-giggled in awe, living vicariously through Cherelle, their first lady. Even Baria, the wedding coordinator, was bedazzled by David. "Not only is he one of the finest men on the planet, he is ever so romantic," Baria said to herself, forgetting that her mic was still on and her assistants could hear everything she said. One of them responded, whispering into the mic on her headset.

"He sure is. I pray to God my man says that to me when we get married. He's so romantic."

Cherelle felt David's love for her coursing through her veins as he held her hands. When Greg Kingston posed the same question to her, she followed suit, answering just as David had answered. "I do. I will. I am."

David had never been more certain of what he'd known all along. Cherelle had been created to worship God, and yet, He had designed her with David in mind. She was his perfect fit. When the grand moment finally arrived and Greg Kingston pronounced them husband and wife, David cupped Cherelle's face in his hands and saluted her with a slow kiss that was deliciously mesmerizing. This act of possession caused everyone in the church to "ooh" and clap loudly, especially the young people. David pulled apart from his new bride momentarily to allow her to take in air.

Then Cherelle said something that only David and Greg were privy to due to the happy noise in the sanctuary. Instantly, David swept Cherelle in his arms and dipped her as if it were the final act in a well-choreographed dance routine, and laid another slow-cooking kiss on her. When he lifted her and planted her steadily on her feet again, the whole congregation celebrated with whistles and applause.

"Well, I guess that settles that," Greg Kingston said. He lifted his hand and quieted the church and said, "I present to you, Pastor and Mrs. *David. Kent. Cole.*" More applause followed as the couple filed out of the church joyously, ahead of the bridal party. Cherelle smiled from ear to ear, still floating from the kiss David had laid on her.

"What did she say? What did she say to make him kiss her like that?" one of David's cousins asked from the pew behind Leah and Joseph.

"I don't know, but whatever it was made Punch stake his claim!" Leah answered.

"That was so romantic!" David's cousin Geena beamed.

Chapter 8

Welcome Home

David and Cherelle sneaked out of the reception hall through a kitchen exit. They were secured in a large refrigerated container that allowed them to stand up. Pressed against one another in the darkness, David took full advantage by stealing kisses from his wife. The container was carefully wheeled down a ramp that was used for shipping and receiving, then loaded inside a truck that had a pink, purple, and red florist logo on it. Gus had come up with the idea when David mentioned that he was concerned about his and Cherelle's wedding night location being spoiled by all the paparazzi that would be in town because of the number of celebrities and dignitaries attending the wedding.

Three miles away from the banquet center at a nearby church, David and Cherelle exited their escape cover and transferred to a Moroccan Blue Bentley Mulsanne Grand Limousine loaned to David by construction and real estate billionaire, Lance Kimbrough, who also owned two sports teams and was a fan of the work David did with youth.

"Oh, my goodness! This is so nice . . ." Cherelle said,

sinking into the supple leather seat of the luxury vehicle. "Is this in our budget?" she teased David, knowing how financially conscious he was.

"This is a *loan* so that my wife and I can ride to our first destination in style," David said. He removed a blue silk scarf from his pocket. "And unfortunately for you, you'll have to check it out later. I'm gonna need to blindfold you, wifey."

Cherelle eyed David skeptically. "Where are you taking me, King David?"

"I'm taking you someplace where no one is going to hear you but me," David teased as he tied the scarf around her eyes.

Cherelle gasped. "David Kent Cole, I should start calling you Mr. Incorrigible."

"Oh, you ain't seen nothin' yet, woman," he said, adjusting the knot so that it wasn't too tight or too loose. "How's that?" he asked.

"Well, if your goal was to prevent me from seeing anything, I guess you get an A, King David."

David chuckled. "Oh, I plan to get *straight* A's on my report card tonight, Mrs. Cole."

Cherelle lay her head on David's shoulder. She marveled at how tender and patient he'd been. But his inner man was inching to the edges of a sensuous plunge. David traced the outline of Cherelle's face with his fingertips, and her breathing pattern changed. "Mrs. Cole, you're not afraid of your husband, are you?" David asked in a tone that was sprinkled with mischief.

"No . . ." Cherelle lied.

"Well, you're trembling. I know you're the psychologist in the family, but I think that's a sign of nervousness. Relax, babe," David said as he removed the decorative bobby pins that held Cherelle's up-do in place and slid them into his pocket so that his hands could roam free in the hair he loved to play in. He combed his fingers through her hair until it fell softly on her shoulders. "*Mrs.* Cole, you can breathe . . ." he said.

"I feel like a nervous wreck," Cherelle replied honestly.

"Not for long. I've got the perfect remedy for nervousness. Besides, you weren't nervous when you wrote that steamy little love note yesterday, were you?"

Cherelle giggled. "No. Is that why you're torturing me?"

"The sweetest torture, babe. So . . . you thought it would be a good idea to tease me with that letter, huh?"

"I just wanted you to *think* about me."

David smiled. "Oh . . . I see. Did it ever occur to you that I was already *thinking* about you, Mrs. Cole? That little note of yours pushed me right over the edge. That was very naughty of you, Mrs. Cole . . ."

Cherelle relaxed and engaged in the sensual banter her husband started. "Well, then my plan worked."

"Oh, it worked alright. Had me taking a cold shower at two o'clock in the morning. And you tricked me. You've had me believing all this time that you're all nice and sweet, but you're just a bad girl in disguise," David teased.

"Maybe . . ."

"There's no 'maybe' to it. *You* are the incorrigible one, ma'am," David said.

Cherelle laughed heartily, and David became lost in her essence. She was all his, just like she'd told him at the altar. The limo pulled to a stop, and the driver got out and opened their door. David stepped out first and helped Cherelle out. He adjusted her blindfold to ensure she still couldn't see anything until he was ready.

"Where are we? I hope nowhere public because I probably look a mess with my hair all in disarray," Cherelle said.

"You are the most beautiful woman in the universe, babe."

Cherelle heard the quiet hum of the Mulsanne pulling away.

David walked her up cobblestone steps, then Cherelle heard a door creak open. David took her by her hand. "This way, Mrs. Cole . . ."

The smell of jasmine permeated throughout the vicinity, and Cherelle heard soft rushing water—some type of fountain. Where on earth had he brought her? The space was absent of the sounds of voices or movement. It wasn't a public place. David swept Cherelle off her feet and carried her up a flight of stairs. Another door creaked open. David placed Cherelle on a high-back settee. "Sit here," he said as he guided Cherelle onto the plush seat. He bent down in front of her and removed her shoes. He removed his tuxedo jacket and laid it over the back of the settee next to Cherelle.

"Stand up, babe," David coaxed, pulling Cherelle to the center of the room. He circled her like a trained art connoisseur. "My, my, my . . . Mercy! Look at God! Mm. Mm. Mm. Lord, your workmanship is incredible. Absolutely phenomenal," he said.

Cherelle blushed as David moved around her; she felt his admiring eyes on every part of her body. Finally, David stopped behind her. "Now, for your blindfold. I'm gonna take it off, but I want you to keep your eyes closed until I say open them. Can you do that for me, Mrs. Cole?"

"Yes . . ."

David untied the scarf and tossed it. Then he stood at Cherelle's side.

"Open your eyes, Mrs. Cole."

Cherelle was saluted by two thousand red rose petals that were strewn about, creating a red carpet effect in all directions, before diverging into two distinct trails. One led to a massive cream-colored, velour, upholstered bed with a six-foot-tall tufted headboard, and the other led to the master bath spa retreat. The turned-down bed was dressed in all white with luxurious bamboo sheets, an assortment of white throw pillows, and a plush duvet. A sea of rose petals floated on top of the linen.

A corner fireplace burned brightly but could not compete with the one hundred LED candles that illuminated the room and cast a beautiful glow on the hand-crafted California King bed. "Oooh . . . this is so beautiful! Where are we?" Cherelle asked. David's smile was filled with accomplishment.

"Welcome home, babe," David responded.

Cherelle looked back at David. "What?"

"Take a look," David said. He opened a drawer of the antique dresser to reveal Cherelle's personal belongings.

Cherelle walked over and peeked in the drawer, and then another. She turned and walked into a fabulous closet that was the size of a bedroom. Complete with two white-crystal chandeliers and a gold dressing table. The celebrity-worthy closet housed all Cherelle's clothes. Her shoes lined the shelves in perfect order of color, divided further by type. Her handbags were on a glamorous display behind glass cabinets with recessed lighting. Cherelle touched her clothes as if she'd never seen them before. Perplexed, she exited the walk-in closet, walked deeper into the room, following the rose petal trail which led to her spa-style en suite. Artwork that had graced the walls of her condo now hung here.

David followed his wife into their sumptuous master bath and watched as Cherelle walked in and stared at the tub in the middle of the room. It was filled with roses that floated about with the gentle rush of the jet streams and reflected in the fireplace glass. The fireplace's glass rocks changed colors with LED lighting. Cherelle looked up at the skylights overhead that let in brilliant moonlight. She walked over to the shower with its iridescent glass tile and marble bench. It was big enough for a family. Where had she seen this shower and this bath before?

She hurried over to the double-sink vanity and opened several cabinets and drawers; they were filled with her oils and delicate hairpins. Then, the realization settled in her mind.

"David?"

"Yes, babe . . . what is it?" David appeased her proudly.

"All my things are here. B-b-but this is *Greg and Norma's* house. The master retreat. The fabulous closet. The fireplaces in the bedroom and bathroom. The skylights. The spa shower. This is their house . . ."

David strode over to his wife with a sexy, confident swag that was incontestably appealing.

"Babe, this is *our* new home."

"But, honey—" Cherelle started before walking out of the succulent spa bath. She made her way through the bedroom and into the hallway to the bedroom next door and found items from David's home. David watched her hips sway as she moved through the rooms and decided that the view was lovely. Only God could create such a masterpiece. He followed his wife down the stairs and into the kitchen. White Shaker cabinets were paired with white and gray Carrera marble countertops and backsplashes. Cherelle opened a glass-door cabinet and removed one of the antique goblets she'd purchased while on vacation in Rome. Confused, she looked back at David again, questioning him with her eyes.

"David, this is Greg and Norma's house. But all our things are here. Why are our things here?" She couldn't imagine that the couple would have ever sold their home. Greg had said so a million times. He vowed to die in the home he'd built for his wife, Norma. David stood peering down at Cherelle in all her girl-like wonder and cupped her face in his hands again, as he always did when he wanted her complete attention.

"Mrs. *Cole*, this is *not* Greg and Norma's home anymore. *This* home belongs to David and Cherelle Cole," David said with a sensual, penetrating stare that left Cherelle undone. "Quick story," David said, backing up to the island in the middle of the kitchen, pulling Cherelle with him. He rested his backside against it and circled Cherelle's waist with his hands. He pulled her flush against him, claiming the right to infringe on her space. "When Greg got to Arizona a week ago, his oldest granddaughter clung to his son-in-law's father and refused to come to him because she hadn't seen him in a while. To her, he was a stranger. Then, while at the hospital, he ran into a local pastor who told him about a church in the area that was looking for a pastor. Greg said that as he was standing there talking to the man, he could hear the Lord telling him that now was the time to start his new life. That's the phrase Norma always used. She said they needed to move to Arizona and start a new life with their kids, grandkids, and other family members who live there. Greg submitted his resume and credentials to the church in Arizona, and he's waiting to hear from them. In the meantime, he stepped out on faith and followed the Lord's leading, and immediately prepared to move to Arizona.

"He called me that night and told me the home was going on the market, because he knew of a certain beautiful woman named Cherelle, who has been in love with this home ever since she stepped foot in it one wintery night when a certain suave, debonair king named David Kent Cole drove in one of the worst blizzards of Michigan's history to rescue her. And to please this beautiful woman and give her the home of her dreams, I made Greg an offer he couldn't refuse. Within twenty-four hours, I had a moving company come in and pack and move all of Greg and Norma's belongings to a storage space in Arizona near the condo they own there. Norma spied on your Pinterest account and had her interior decorator crew come in and paint and decorate. The same moving company packed and moved our stuff here the next day. And Norma had her little designers working around the clock to have this house ready for tonight . . .

"So, all the time you thought your furniture was being moved to *my* home, it was—not to the house you thought it was going to, but to the house you've always wanted . . ." David said, stroking a finger down Cherelle's soft brown cheek. "And in case you're wondering, I do have a fabulous two-week honeymoon planned for you in some private, exotic locations. But I wanted the first time we came together as husband and wife to be in our new home—in our bed, so that as the years go by, we could always recreate our wedding night at home.

"Now, I would love to give you a tour of all the updates and new designs that have been done in this home to accommodate your taste and style, but um . . ." David started as he moved his hands from Cherelle's face to her hips. He kissed and suckled her neck hungrily before allowing himself enough air to say, "The only tour I'm interested in right now is the Cherelle Cole tour." He lifted her off her feet and into his arms, drowning her in kisses before carrying her up the stairs to their new master retreat.

* * *

DAVID AWOKE with the comfort of his wife sleeping peacefully and soundly on his chest. He could feel her warm, steady breath caressing his skin. The contrast of her softness against his stone-chiseled chest reawakened his desire for her. He glanced at the clock. It was already past eight a.m. Like David, Cherelle rarely slept past five a.m. But that was before she married David Kent Cole. "Lord, you are so good," David whispered. "I don't deserve anything, but I am thankful for Your many blessings and Your mercy toward me, Father. I asked, and You delivered in a way that only You can. And if You come back right now, I'm good. I'm ready. I'm *so* good. I had my blessing. Amen," David said with a chuckle. Then he erupted in laughter. He hadn't intended to wake Cherelle, but he couldn't hold it in.

Cherelle awakened in a state of love drunkenness. She mumbled into David's chest. "What's so funny?" she asked drowsily.

"I'm so blessed it's ridiculous," David said, working his fingers through Cherelle's hair.

Only half-awake, Cherelle's head popped up. Startled and disoriented, she shot David a suspicious glance. She didn't know where she was, what day it was, or why she was in *bed* with *David!*

"David! What are you do—"

David peered down at his wife and smiled. "Babe, we're married now, remember?"

Cherelle rubbed her eyes. She looked around the splendid suite where two thousand red rose petals still graced the bed and floor, and one hundred LED candles still flickered, only upstaged by the sunlight that dominated the room. A smile swept across Cherelle's half-awakened face.

"Oh . . . that's right. I'm *Mrs.* David Kent Cole now, aren't I?"

"Oh yes, indeed . . . you definitely are. Fa sho . . ."

Chapter 9

Beautiful

In the four-seasons sunroom of his opulent new home, surrounded by his three aunts on Joseph's side of the family, David sat sipping his Aunt May's sweet tea. He stole furtive glances at Cherelle in between the fawning women's eager queries and awestruck praise over his wedding and reception, and his new home. David had achieved the perfect coup. He'd successfully secured the home he knew his wife was in love with, and she had thanked him continuously since their wedding night two days ago. Movers and designers had worked down to the wire, but the look of appreciation on Cherelle's face and her display of girl-like joyfulness, when she realized David had purchased the home for her, made that whole frazzled week before the wedding worth every second. It pleased David immensely to be able to give her this gift.

It was the Montgomery family tradition to have a gift-opening brunch to celebrate a new marriage in the family. David and Cherelle had only been married for two days, and impossible as it seemed, he felt more in love with her. In the gathering space in the kitchen nook, Cherelle stood against the doorwall, laughing at the story Joseph was telling her about the hard time Leah had given him when he first tried to court her.

"Punch, you made us so proud. Everything was just so lovely," David's Aunt Bertha said. His entire family still called him the nickname his biological father, Jeff Ford, had given him when he was just a few weeks old. The nickname stuck with him, unlike his father, whom David hadn't seen since he was five.

"Thank you, Aunt Bertha," David returned humbly. He took the last gulp of his tea and smiled.

David's Aunt May rose and reached for David's Mason jar glass that was scripted with the words: *King of the Castle*. The words were in a fancy script painted in red and outlined in bright yellow. She had hand-painted it herself, as well as the others in the set. "Let me get you some more tea, Punch."

David felt guilty that his aunts doted on him so relentlessly. He felt undeserving. "It's okay, Aunt May . . . I'll get up."

May refused. "Oh no, honey. You save all your energy for your honeymoon. When you do right by God, you get to enjoy *all* His blessings!" she said slyly.

"May, you know you somethin' else," Bertha retorted, winking at David knowingly.

David handed Aunt May the glass. Again, he looked over his shoulder at Cherelle, who was laughing so hysterically she had started crying. She did that when she allowed herself to let go and live in the moment. Being a natural-born priss, who'd been raised to remain refined and adhere to all social graces, she rarely allowed herself these moments. David loved to see her this free.

Sue Ann nudged Bertha. "Chile, look how he lookin' at her. That boy's in love for sure. He can barely take his eyes off her."

"Well, just keep on admiring her just like that—even when y'all get our age. Love don't get old. It just matures into something more beautiful," Bertha said to David, pulling him out of his gaze.

David nodded."Yes, ma'am," he said.

"Ain't nothing wrong with that. My Wilbur still looks at me like that. And I love him like I did fifty-seven years ago. We are still good," Sue Ann teased her sister, Bertha.

Bertha playfully swatted her sister. "Girl, you just as fast as you were at fifteen!"

"Sho nuff," Sue Ann returned. David laughed at their naughtiness. He couldn't believe Aunt Sue Ann was eighty-three. She looked like she was still in her sixties. Bertha and May were eighty and seventy-nine, respectively. They looked stellar for their ages. David called them The Golden Girls, the name of an old TV show Leah used to love that featured the antics of some spunky older women. And Joseph's mother, who David called Grandma Hannah, was ninety-eight. She was a lively one as well. She moved more slowly, but she still had her 'right mind,' as the sisters often attested.

"We finally got us a daughter-in-law!" Bertha said to her sisters, because each of them had all girls.

"Yes. The Lord sho is good," Sue Ann confirmed.

Joseph married David's mother, Leah, when David was just seven years old, making David the second family prize in a *world* full of women. Joseph was the youngest sibling, and he had been the sisters' baby until Joseph married Leah. Then David became their baby.

* * *

GUS SIDLED UP TO CHERELLE. "I must say, Cherelle, I am completely outdone."

"Why do you say that, Gus?" Cherelle asked.

"Because of DC," Gus said, calling David by his hood nickname.

The kids in the neighborhood had taken to calling David DC when he was in middle school because he always introduced himself by stating his whole name. "I have *never* in my entire life seen him look at a woman the way he looks at you," Gus continued. "I don't even know who that man is sitting over there on that sofa, and I've known him most of my life."

Cherelle looked over at David admiringly, and her eyes sparkled with a joy that spread across her face. David caught her glance and winked at her. Cherelle mouthed the words: *I love you* and David mouthed them back.

"See what I mean, Cherelle? DC is all moonstruck like he's back in sixth grade."

"That's my king."

"And you are certainly his queen," Gus said.

Somehow, David managed to pry himself away from his aunts. He moseyed up to Gus and nudged him away from Cherelle. "Man, get away from my wife. You're standing way too close," David joked. He secured his arm around Cherelle's waist, pulled her to his side, and placed a wet, teasing peck on her neck. Looking up lovingly into David's eyes, Cherelle shuddered with aftershock vibrations. She couldn't imagine getting used to the chills David's touch caused her. She was like a giddy schoolgirl receiving attention from the opposite sex for the first time.

"How long are they gonna be here?" David whispered huskily into Cherelle's ear. The heat of his minty breath caused passionate prickles to radiate down Cherelle's spine to her lower back and up again. They were emphatic reminders of the sensuous arsenal David employed to completely disarm and undo her when they were alone. "You are terrible, Mr. Incorrigible," Cherelle whispered into his ear.

David laughed. "I know, but I'm so serious, though."

Moments later, he retreated to the family room where Gus was busy conversing with one of David's cousins.

David was grateful for all the attention and love the family was sharing, but he was truly ready for everyone to leave. Not because he wasn't happy to see them, but simply because he couldn't wait to have Cherelle all to himself again. The newfound level of passion they'd discovered and had been free to share the last two days was all David had thought about for the last few hours.

Leah noticed David's antsy gaze on more than one occasion. She was positive that she knew the cause. She'd planned to shuffle everyone out in a bit, but she didn't want to be too hasty. After all, some family members had traveled as far as Germany to attend the wedding celebration. David was a lovesick puppy. It brought Leah so much joy to see him happy in love.

"Okay, everyone, we are going to move the party to the hotel," Leah called out after she felt the family had visited long enough.

Thank You, Jesus! Past elation, David smirked. Cherelle tossed him a knowing look. It was ten p.m. David had secured several rooms for the family at a nearby hotel, and he'd paid for each of Joseph's sisters' arrangements. He'd loved the trio dearly since he was a boy. One would never have known they weren't his biological aunts. Joseph's sisters had treated David as if he were their blood nephew since they first met him, and Joseph always introduced David as his son. He'd never used the word stepson even though the two of them didn't share the last name.

David would miss the gang until he saw them again. At the moment, however, he had more delicious things on his mind. His aunts scurried to the kitchen to help Leah clean up.

"You guys can leave it, really. We have someone coming to clean tomorrow before we leave for our official honeymoon," David said.

David's aunts would have none of it. "Now, Punch, you know we can't leave a mess. And ain't no cleaning lady gon' clean better than we do anyway," Sue Ann said. "So just sit down and relax with Cherelle."

Joseph winked at David. It was his way of telling David to indulge his aunts. It made them feel useful and a part of everything that had taken place. It was their way of celebrating the union and the addition to the family.

David threw his hands up, "Okay, aunties."

"Yeah. Get your little butt on outta here," May said swatting him with a dish towel.

"I'd like a song from Cherelle while y'all women are cleaning," Sue Ann's husband, Wilbur, said.

"Oh, so, y'all men think y'all gone get a serenade while we in here cleanin'? Ain't that somethin'," Sue Ann joked.

Cherelle hadn't planned to sing. She'd done it at the wedding reception because while they'd been engaged, David had hinted a hundred times that he hoped she would sing for him at their reception. And she had. It tickled and perplexed David that Cherelle was relatively shy about her voice, as beautiful as it was. She had been a classically trained vocalist since her youth, and had studied voice and opera at Juilliard for two years. She seemed so confident and eager to share her talents in every area but her singing.

Cherelle opened her mouth to protest. "I don't know what I'd sing. I'm usually prepared before I sing something."

"Just sing something on your heart—anything," Wilbur said. The others in the room agreed. Cherelle wanted to decline.

"Sing for *me*, babe," David coaxed. The sexy timbre of his

voice sent vibrations through Cherelle. She nodded and closed her eyes. The women stopped moving in the kitchen, and the family gathered around loosely.

She sang Minnie Riperton's "Lovin' You," and David's chest inflated with pride from being the object of his beautiful wife's affection. Cherelle's meticulous ability to climb the high notes with perfect pitch made the hairs on the back of David's neck stand up and caused a sensuous vibration to pulse through him. He was standing directly in front of her when her eyes opened. Cherelle looked right into the eyes that told her things only she could hear. It seemed to David that he and Cherelle were alone, because he could no longer feel anyone else's presence or hear any of their voices, only his wife serenading him with the most sensuous song.

"Whoo!" one of David's cousins cheered. "Cousin Cherelle's voice is crazy beautiful!"

But David didn't hear a word. He embraced his wife and gave her a prelude to what he was saving for later, when everyone left. The family began clinking their glasses and tapping cups to encourage the newlyweds to continue kissing. But David didn't need any encouragement; he had Cherelle. She was all the motivation he needed tonight.

Joseph tapped him on the shoulder, and David and Cherelle pulled apart. Cherelle was embarrassed that she had lost herself in her husband's kiss so quickly. She was usually more reserved than David.

"Don't be shy now. You better enjoy all that romance while you can. You'll be wanting to clock him upside his head with a skillet in a few months," Aunt May teased Cherelle. The rest of the sisters agreed.

* * *

DAVID WAVED AGAIN as the family pulled off in the motor coach he'd rented for their stay. He shut and locked the door and rested his back against it. "Babe, I love my family dearly, but I couldn't *wait* for them to get outta here!" David laughed. "I ain't got *nothin'* but lovin' you on my mind. I felt like I was about to pass out!"

Cherelle stepped closer to David, grinning sheepishly. He pulled her flush against his body, and Cherelle let out a cooing sound. "I was thinking the same thing . . ."

The sound of a thousand boulders from heaven shook the house as thunder struck the sky and rain pelted the doors and windows. Startled, Cherelle pushed closer to David. He snaked his arms around her waist and dove in for a kiss. Cherelle let herself freely drift in an uninhibited space with him. In an instant, the power was forced out by the storm, leaving the couple in complete darkness. Cherelle pulled apart. "Babe, our power is out . . ."

"*Mrs.* Cole, I got all the power I need to do what I'm planning to do," David returned before locking his lips on hers again.

Chapter 10

Glow

Cherelle's vibrant, dark chocolate skin glowed. For the past six months, she'd been basking in the blessings of being Mrs. David Kent Cole, a title that came with being spoiled by a king. The couple had shared an exotic two-week honeymoon that included a week's stay on the private Vatuvara island in Fiji, a four-night stay at The Caves in Negril, Jamaica, and a three-night stay at the Escape in Tennessee. David had been a wonderful husband since the day they exchanged vows. He kept their date nights once a week, like he'd promised, despite his heavy schedule pastoring and serving as a board member of various community organizations. When Cherelle was on location in Toronto, Canada, for eight weeks filming another indie movie in which she had a lead role, David surprised her by showing up on the set. He flew there several times while she worked, so he could keep their fire burning. Cherelle had never felt so loved by a man in all her life, and David had never felt so free to love.

After six months of marital bliss, Cherelle was in full swing in her role as Dr. Cherelle Dupree, faith-focused psychologist and author with a few movies in between. For the last four weeks, she had been on tour with the Women Rising Conference, one of the largest annual Christian women's conferences in the country.

After she wrapped up her workshop, Waiting on God for Your Mate, she was on her feet as usual, answering the multitude of questions the women had. Several women admitted to feeling betrayed by God. A few of them had come to the microphone with the same story: they'd prayed for years, continued to serve in their churches or ministries, and remained celibate. And yet, God had still not blessed them with a mate.

Cherelle listened attentively as a woman named Destiny stood at the microphone in the room of one hundred and thirty women. Destiny was stylishly dressed in a pair of dark blue jeans, a royal purple ruffled top, and black leather ankle boots with spike heels. She had jet-black locs that crept down the front of her top. She was a shapely woman whom Cherelle guessed was in her mid-thirties.

"I just want to be honest, Dr. Cole . . ." the woman began.

"Please," Cherelle countered. "We're all here to be better women. Better women for Christ. Better women for ourselves and our families."

"Sometimes, I feel cheated. I have prayed for a baby—and a *husband* for years. I'm forty-two years old, and I feel like God has forgotten about me. I've been working in the church. I've been living right. I've been keeping myself faithfully for five years . . ." Destiny's voice shook as she tried to keep from shattering. Other women in the room mumbled in agreement. "Sometimes I feel like giving up. I hate to say that because I don't consider myself a quitter, but it's true. I want to please God . . . it's just that it seems that everyone else is finding their dreams except me . . . and I want it so badly," Destiny said.

Cherelle glanced around the room and saw the affirmation

of Destiny's words in many of the women's eyes. She took in a deep breath. She knew the feeling. Being married to her "swagalicious" husband for six months hadn't erased all her memories of years of loneliness and aching—the feeling that God had somehow abandoned her. The memories just seemed like a lifetime ago, as did the pain. Cherelle assumed that's how it was when God blessed you with something you'd been praying for. Your blessing would outshine any pain you encountered on your way to the blessing.

"Destiny, I hear you . . . and I *hear* you. I am not going to stand up here and give you a bunch of mumbo jumbo. I will only say that God is *faithful*. Even when it doesn't look like it, He is. I am proof. I once said the same things you just shared. Cried the same tears—before King David came along," Cherelle said. "I saved myself for a number of years after I learned that *not* saving myself *did not* and *could not* yield the outcome that I desired because the outcome I desired was God's outcome. And you can't get God's outcome without doing it *His* way. David and I stayed true to what God commands in terms of saving sex for marriage. And most importantly, we trusted Him through the process. And I couldn't be more blessed than I am. So, please, hold on. Keep praying. Keep trusting. Do not ever give up on God, because He sees you . . . and knows you . . . and loves you.

"I want to pray with you, and then I need to retire for the evening. I'm sorry, ladies. I need to make this the last question. I've been suffering from a killer headache. I think a little rest will do me some good," Cherelle said. She beckoned Destiny to the stage as she massaged her temples. She remembered not to make any ugly faces because the event was being recorded, and people were surely taking pictures. Cherelle smiled as Destiny made her way toward her.

The Q&A part of the workshop had run way over the

allotted hour. But Cherelle and the other presenters had seen God move so profoundly throughout the conference. They had promised one another to do all they could to ensure the women left the conference with renewed hope, peace, and strength to walk out their journeys.

Cherelle stepped down off the podium, and the other panelists followed. They gathered in a circle to pray. Cherelle hugged Destiny as the woman's tears fell. She spotted her mother-in-law, Leah, ushering women into the large prayer circle. Leah had volunteered to work as a hostess at the conference at Cherelle's suggestion. It had saved her a ton of money on registration prices, and it allowed her to spend time with Cherelle. Leah truly enjoyed having a daughter-in-law, and it made David feel especially blessed that the two had a wonderful relationship of their own.

Cherelle prayed fervently for the women, most of all for their faith. There was not a dry eye in the room when she finished. Leah was making her way to Cherelle, navigating through the crowd of women, when she saw Cherelle clutch her head. The women gasped as Cherelle collapsed with a thud.

"Call 911!" one of the panelists shouted.

"Is there an M.D. in the room?" another panelist asked on the microphone.

A doctor pushed her way through the crowd. Leah sighed with relief that there was a doctor among them. The young woman checked Cherelle's pulse and attempted to wake her.

"An ambulance is on the way," one of the conference hostesses said.

Washed in unmitigated fear, Leah felt choked by guilt. Earlier in the week, Cherelle had confided to her that she feared she might have an aneurysm. There was no other reasonable explanation for the extreme headaches she'd been having for the last two weeks. Something was wrong. Cherelle's mother, Eleanor, had suffered two aneurysms and a stroke. With that kind of family history, Leah had encouraged Cherelle to see a doctor right away. Cherelle assured Leah that she had a doctor's appointment the coming Monday, which was two days away.

The paramedics arrived within five minutes. Cherelle had come to after a minute, but she was disoriented. Leah told the paramedics about her and Cherelle's conversation. "I'm her mother-in-law. She's been complaining of headaches. She's supposed to see her doctor on Monday. She has a family history of aneurysms. She said she was worried about that," Leah volunteered.

"Can you tell me your name, ma'am?" a female paramedic asked Cherelle.

"Cherelle Dupree . . . uh . . . Cherelle Cole," Cherelle said, trying to shake off the dizziness.

The male paramedic looked back at Leah. "She's a newly-wed," Leah explained.

"Mrs. Cole, do you know what day it is?" the female paramedic questioned.

Disoriented, Cherelle responded with a confused look. "Um . . . no."

"Did she hit her head when she fell?" the young male paramedic asked.

Leah wrung her hands. "She could have. It happened so quickly. I'm not sure," she said.

"My head . . . uh . . . headache. My head hurts . . ."

They placed Cherelle on the gurney. "Lie back for me, Mrs. Cole," the female said gently.

"Could you be pregnant?" the male paramedic asked.

"No," Cherelle said. She had PCOS, which caused irregular cycles, and she hadn't had a cycle in over two months.

With her medical history, pregnancy was the least of her worries.

The paramedics moved expeditiously, and the women parted to give them room. Leah ran her hands through her honey-blonde bob before dialing David. Anxiety attacked her. She dreaded having to call him about this. Her guilt was multiplied because she should have been more direct with Cherelle when she learned that she had been having headaches. A part of Leah was relieved that David didn't answer his cell. His phone issued an auto-text:

> David: Hi, I'm in a meeting. I will return your call as soon as possible. Thank you.

Leah knew she could reach Deacon Lewis. Within seconds, Deacon Lewis conveyed the message to David, and he was burning up her cell.

"Ma, what's going on?" David asked too calmly for Leah to believe that he was.

"Cherelle's been taken to the hospital. She complained about having a headache earlier. She said she'd been having them for two weeks, but she promised me she had an appointment with her doctor on Monday, after the conference, so I didn't press her. She mentioned that she was a little afraid that she could have an aneurysm. I should have been more vocal, but I—"

"Ma, what happened?" David interrupted. It seemed to him that Leah was rambling.

"Cherelle passed out, Punch." Leah heard the catch in David's breath. "I saw her clutch her head like she was in pain, and then she just passed out."

"Why didn't she say something to me about the headaches? She knows her mom's situation. She can't be fooling around like this! She should have gone to the doctor as soon as she

78

suspected something was wrong!" David said. It took a lot to propel him out of his calm, always-in-control box. He was two feet out of the box already.

"Punch, calm down," Leah said.

"I am calm."

"No, you aren't. She'll be okay."

"Where are they taking my wife?" David asked his mother. His tone held more fear than annoyance, even though it didn't appear that way on the surface. Leah understood that and rattled off the name of the hospital.

"I'll be there in an hour and a half."

Leah didn't bother to ask David how he was going to make it there in an hour and a half; she just knew that he would be there when he said.

* * *

DAVID GOT behind the wheel instead of Deacon Lewis, who normally drove him. He wasted no time calling Maverick Kitts, a pilot he'd befriended over the last ten years. Maverick was now the owner of Maverick Private Charter Jets. When the two first met, Maverick worked as a pilot for another charter company. He and David had drummed up a conversation after a flight to New York, and Maverick spoke of his dream of owning his own charter company. After researching private jet charter companies and getting background details on Maverick, David decided that assisting Maverick would be a good investment. He helped to connect Maverick with a team that supported start-up businesses, and David also invested heavily. As a result, he received profits from the company yearly, which included a fractional jet card that allowed him to fly as much as he needed. Although he usually called the customer service line to schedule flights, he needed to talk to Maverick directly right now.

"Mav, I've got an emergency. Cherelle passed out, and it could be because of an aneurysm. I need to get to Chicago like right now. I'm on my way to the hangar. I need you to make that happen for me."

"I got you. Jackie will be ready to roll as soon as you get here," Maverick said. Jackie was one of the four pilots who flew for the small company, and David had been in her care on many flights.

After David hung up with Maverick, the screen on the Suburban's dashboard flashed a call from an unknown number. David answered hurriedly, thinking it might have been someone calling from the hospital about Cherelle. "Hello, this is David Kent Cole speaking."

"Dave, it's me. I need to talk to you. It's important . . ." Dominique's used-to-be-sweet-sounding voice filled his truck. Deacon Lewis shot an accusing glance at David.

David smacked his hand against the steering wheel. He couldn't believe she was doing this. She was stretching his patience. "Dominique, I don't want to be disrespectful, but it doesn't matter what you want! You and I are done! My wife is sick, and I don't have time for this! So please, for the last time, respect my life and my family, and don't contact me anymore," David said before disconnecting the call. He whacked the steering wheel again.

Dominique called right back, and David rejected the call. "Remember what I told you," Deacon Lewis said, warning him.

"It's done," David returned. He had other things on his mind.

Dominique was a non-factor.

* * *

ON BOARD THE PRIVATE JET, David's mind wandered to his woman. His wife. His everything. He prayed there was nothing seriously wrong with Cherelle—like an aneurysm. The two had talked about her staying on top of her health countless times because of her mother's condition. Why hadn't Cherelle confided in him about her headaches? Not one time had she mentioned having headaches when they'd spoken over the last few weeks. It was unlike them not to discuss important information with one another. David felt a tinge of betrayal. But his anger subsided as the strange, foreboding feeling of losing Cherelle pressed against his heart. For the duration of his flight, he prayed to rid himself of his worst fear.

* * *

DAVID ALMOST COLLIDED with Leah when he reached the hospital's emergency room. Cherelle had been taken back for an immediate MRI due to her history. David paced the floor with his hands jammed into his pockets.

"Punch, calm down," Leah said for the fourth time.

"I'm calm. I just want to know what's wrong with my wife. I can't believe she didn't mention anything about having headaches for the last two weeks. None of these conferences and book signings is more important than her health. Cherelle knows better."

"Punch, maybe she was afraid. You know how they say fear makes people avoidant? I don't know. Or maybe she honestly convinced herself that it wasn't a big deal."

"Well, if it weren't a big deal, we wouldn't be in an emergency room right now, would we?"

Leah knew when David was in one of his *moods*. She wasn't about to argue with him or attempt to convince him of anything. Everything he'd said was true, but it didn't matter now. Leah sat down and prayed that Cherelle wasn't in any medical danger. An hour passed before a doctor came to get David. Leah followed them. David turned to Leah and said, "I'll be back to get you, Ma."

Whatever was going on with his wife, he wanted the two of them to deal with it together first, before they added anyone else to the mix—even if it was his mother. He knew his mother's heart was in the right place, but he needed to be alone with his wife.

When David laid eyes on Cherelle's panic-stricken face, his heart paused. "Babe, what's the matter?" he asked.

"I'm scared . . ." Cherelle cried.

"What's going on, Kit? What did they say?"

"Hi, Mr. Cole, I'm Dr. Cleary," the doctor said, shaking David's hand. He was short and stout with brown hair streaked with grey. His brown eyes were puffy with bags, as if he hadn't slept in days. "The brain scan came back negative. There's no problem there. The headaches are probably due to hormonal changes. Her blood pressure was a little low. Mrs. Cole is about nine weeks pregnant. And we see two fetuses on the ultrasound. Due to her age, we consider this a high-risk pregnancy, but with adequate care, we can have a healthy pregnancy and delivery," the doctor said perfunctorily. David looked as if the doctor had spoken in a different language.

"She's *pregnant?* But I thought the PCOS—I thought—"

The kind, seasoned doctor spoke as if he were a part of the family. "*We* are definitely nine weeks along. Her pressure is abnormally low. It's not uncommon to experience dizziness or fainting during pregnancy. Mrs. Cole stated she'd been traveling a lot. And she didn't eat today. She's eating for *three* now, so that could have presented a bit of an imbalance . . . I've prescribed some prenatal vitamins for her to start taking right away.

"I've gotten in touch with Dr. Boatwright—Mrs. Cole's OB/GYN, and she'll take care of everything else on Monday. I understand she has an appointment with her primary care physician for a neurology referral. I don't think that's necessary anymore. If Mrs. Cole gets a little rest, she should be fine." He turned to Cherelle. "No need to worry so much. Women have late-in-life pregnancies each year, very successfully. I'm sure you'll be just fine," Dr. Cleary said sympathetically.

David's brow furrowed, and he stuffed his hands into his pockets again. "But what about the MRI? Can't that harm the babies?"

The doctor turned to David, "There's virtually no risk to the babies because the MRI doesn't use radiation, Mr. Cole. Please don't worry yourselves about that. I'm sure the babies will be fine. And congratulations. She can get dressed. Here are her discharge instructions," Dr. Cleary said, handing David a small packet of papers. He exited after shaking David's hand again.

David stepped closer to Cherelle and pulled her into his arms. She slumped against him and sobbed as if she'd been given a cancer diagnosis or some other terrible news. Confusion morphed into a streak of anger, then hurt-filled disappointment. A dark emotional cloud encompassed David. Why on earth was Cherelle acting this way about the news the doctor had given? David cupped Cherelle's face in his hands and spoke as calmly as he could. "Kit, babe, I need you to tell me what's with you. Please. Why do you seem so saddened by this?"

"David, I'm . . . I'm overwhelmed . . . I didn't think I would ever get pregnant. I had prepared for us to have a life without children. I'm forty-three years old—at an extremely high-risk age. There's so much that can go wrong with me and the babies. I'm just not ready for that. I don't want to go through that."

"Kit, what are you saying to me?" David took a step back from his wife and loosened his tie. He felt his past haunting him. He remembered Dominique telling him she didn't want to have his baby, and he could never forget that she murdered his child. Now, his wife didn't want his children.

"I-I—I don't know," Cherelle admitted.

David palmed the sides of his head. The woman he had given his whole heart to without reservation was driving a stake through it. This was the greatest blessing God had given them in their marriage yet, and Cherelle was rejecting him and their blessing.

He turned away from Cherelle and paced in the confined space. He raked his hands down his face a few times, trying to process it all. His past squeezed his neck tighter, reducing his ability to breathe. He loosened his tie even more and removed it. Then he undid the top buttons on his shirt. He rolled the tie into a ball and squeezed it in his right hand as he continued to pace in the small area.

David's innocuous act made Cherelle feel as though he was turning his back on her when she needed him most. Her tears flowed more steadily. She let out a whimper and gulped in air. David rushed to her and brought her hands to his lips and kissed them. It was a rote action. He was still stunned by her rejection. Then he heard the Spirit speaking to his heart. ***She's not rejecting you, David. She's afraid. You are her covering. You are her earthly king and protector. Soothe her fears.*** Those words were a balm to David's heart. The last few minutes with Cherelle had made him feel like the happily-ever-after with her had taken a wrong turn.

David pressed his lips to Cherelle's forehead. Then he affirmed their union. "I love you, babe. You are *everything* to me. I am so proud of you," he said, chasing Cherelle's eyes with his. "You have made me so very happy, Kit. You are carrying my life in your body, and I honor and adore you for that. God has blessed me tremendously—a double portion for anything I've ever lost. And He has truly restored my soul. There won't be anything wrong with our children. And there won't be anything wrong with you. You are going to have a healthy, natural delivery," David said gently, "because this is our blessing from none other than God. This is a time for celebration . . . not fear. I'm your *man*. I'm your husband. You are my wife. You are *mine*, and this is beautiful."

David felt the tension leaving Cherelle's body. He rubbed his hands gently over her back before untying the strings of the hospital gown so she could feel the warmth of his strong hands against her skin. He sat on the bed next to her and drew her into his arms. He stroked her hair and planted soft, wet kisses on her face and neck. "Let me take you back to your hotel, give you a bath and a massage, and show you just how happy you've made me, Kit," he whispered. Then he pulled Cherelle to her feet and placed his hands over her abdomen. He blessed her womb and thanked God for His manifold blessings, covering, and protection. David held his wife and nurtured her with his embrace.

"I've missed you so much. Have you missed your husband, Mrs. Cole?" David breathed seductively.

"Yes."

"Good."

* * *

DAVID DELIVERED on every romantic promise he made to his wife, causing her to relax and rejoice in the blessing God had placed in her womb. Cherelle awakened in his arms at six a.m. the next morning. Thoughts of her husband's loving, healing hands played softly in her mind. She looked up at David's handsome face and smiled because she hadn't expected him to be awake.

David greeted her with a kiss. "Good Morning, beautiful."

"Good morning, my king."

"How did you sleep?"

"Wonderfully. Peacefully."

"Glad I could be of assistance, Mrs. Cole."

"Me too."

David sat up against the headboard. "I've been thinking . . . this last time we were apart was different than the rest. I literally felt like I wasn't myself. I was more uptight—agitated, and I'm not usually that way."

"No, you aren't. What do you think was different?"

"I think I reached my threshold, babe."

"I don't understand, honey," Cherelle said.

"I don't want us to be away from each other like that again. A whole month is way too long. And I sure don't plan to do that anymore. Whatever we need to do in terms of coordinating our schedules so that we don't spend more than a week at a time apart needs to be done ASAP. I wasn't feeling that four-week stretch, babe."

David half-expected Cherelle to tell him that her schedule could be unpredictable, especially since the publishing company added book signing dates while she was still on tour. In addition, she was now the co-owner of a movie production company with director Asa Miles. But she remembered her pre-wedding conversation with her Aunt Jessie, her mother's sister. Jessie had been a staple in Cherelle's life since she was a little girl. Cherelle and Eleanor had lived with Jessie in Talla-hassee, Florida, until Cherelle went off to Juilliard in New York. *'You've got to be available to him, Cherelle. Don't ever let your career come before him. He's a man with a heavy burden on his shoulders because of his calling as a pastor. He needs you to be that place of solace. He doesn't need Dr. Cherelle Dupree, psychologist, author, actress, and film producer. He needs his wife. Don't leave room for any other woman to be to him what God called you to be.'*

"I'll make sure from now on that I have a few days' break every seven days, honey. And I will get with Maggie, the publicity manager at the publishing house, about syncing our schedules. I'm sure she and Ms. Greta can work something out," Cherelle said.

"Thank you. That means a lot to me, babe. I want us to be strong, especially now that we have kids on the way. I want us to *stay* solid. You are the most important thing in my life after Christ."

"I know. I love you, honey," Cherelle said.

"Love you. Are you hungry, babe?"

"No. I don't have an appetite. But I should probably eat anyway since there are *three* of us. What about you?"

"Well, since you took most of my energy last night, woman, I do need a little breakfast to replenish."

"Let's just order room service. You can get breakfast. And the twins and I will eat some of yours."

"Unh-uh, three on one ain't even fair. Y'all gotta order your own breakfasts. But I just might have a little dessert *before* breakfast," David teased, squeezing Cherelle close to his body and nibbling her ears playfully.

"So naughty . . ."

"I know."

Chapter 11

As Good As It Gets

It was DOC's annual Thanksgiving Day outreach program, orchestrated in conjunction with David's long-time friend and brother-in-law, Corey Perry, pastor of Greater Christian Center church. Together, the churches fed the homeless communities in the city. David helped to pack dinners to be delivered to several homeless shelters, as well as people living on the streets. The youth from both churches oversaw the event and did an awesome job of decorating the dining area. This year, they opted to have a theme. They selected a Hollywood theme and had a red carpet and shiny stars hanging from the ceiling. The tables were decorated with plasticware that looked like solid gold. Anyone in the neighborhood or surrounding areas could walk in, have a sit-down dinner, and feel special and valued.

The youth seemed to be extremely perky for five a.m. David observed a few of them laughing and chasing one another. He wondered how it would feel to watch his kids grow. It was surreal that he would finally be a father after serving as a surrogate father to a church full of young people. He was thankful to God for all the goodness in his life. He couldn't remember a time in his life when he'd felt this complete and satisfied. His church. His wife. His children. His family. Everything was good.

David was proud. He peeked in the kitchen at Gus, who was helping the head chef and other cooks with dinner and baked goods for dessert.

"How are we looking in here?" David asked.

Gus paused from basting one of the twenty-pound turkeys. "We're all good in here."

Gus made every effort to be in Michigan for David's Thanksgiving Day celebration. It was one of the things David felt God wanted him to do. Feed His people with His Word, and food His people literally.

"Was Cherelle feeling okay this morning?" Gus asked David.

"Yes, she's doing well. She just said she needed some more sleep. She'll be by later."

Gus put the turkey back in the oven and removed his apron. He followed David out of the kitchen, away from listening ears. "I can't believe you are going to have kids in just three more weeks, bro. And I finally get to be the Godfather. This is unreal!"

David's chest inflated with pride. "Alright, Don Corleone, watch it," he teased. "Man, I'm so ready! I'm looking at the youth, and I can't wait to watch Caleb and Chloe grow up," he said, imagining.

He and Cherelle had learned the sexes of the twins months earlier. They settled on naming their son Caleb Kent Cole and their daughter Chloe Eleanor Cole. The twins' nursery was decorated in a two-tone pink on one side and blue on the other.

Each space was decorated with each child in mind. A sports arena theme on one side for Caleb and a princess castle theme on the other for Chloe.

"Man, bro. I'm so proud of you. You have everything you've ever wanted," Gus said. Something in the way Gus spoke alerted David that his soul brother was sullen.

"What about you? You ready for a wife and babies?" David asked, knowing Gus's answer. But he hoped Gus had changed his mind. Gus didn't have to tell David why he didn't want a wife and kids.

Gus's upbringing in foster care caused him not to want to be a parent for fear of being a disappointment. In addition, he worked for the CIA in cybersecurity. He was used to not having any kind of routine, like normal people. He could be on the other side of the world at a moment's notice—especially since internet terrorism was on the rise in the U.S. His life wasn't exactly conducive to the whole white picket fence fantasy.

"Nah. I'm good with being a godfather," Gus returned honestly.

"You seeing anyone?"

"Not like what you might be praying for, bro," Gus admitted.

David knew his best friend often struggled with celibacy since he'd been saved. Gus had made up his mind. He didn't want to be married, which David knew would complicate his situation. "But you are *seeing* someone?"

"Bro, it's not anything like what you and Cherelle have. And I'm not proud of it. The need arises, and she's a means to an end. And I'm a means to an end for her. That's all there is to it," Gus said bluntly. "We have a mutually understood relationship. I wish I could say I was handling my walk differently, but the celibacy part of it has been a thorn in my side . . . for real."

"I get it, man. It takes a lot of prayer." Earlier in his walk with Christ, David had his share of setbacks before finally getting a grip. And then there was the whole Dominique debacle. Before that, however, David had proven for years that God was able to sustain him, even when it came to celibacy. He sincerely understood Gus, so he knew he had to reason with him a certain way. Gus was a man who'd lived a more dangerous life than the average person. He couldn't be verbally *beaten* into submission. He was a hard man with a hard heart at times. He had to be won with love—God's love.

"I know. I haven't given up. I'm praying every day, bro," Gus said, feeling like he'd let David down in some way.

"Keep on. I'm praying with you."

"Thanks, man."

David's cell serenaded him with Anthony Hamilton's "Giving You the Best of Me." It was a ringtone that only played when Cherelle called.

"Hey, babe, everything okay?" David said.

"Um . . . honey, I'm okay, but my water broke, and I'm having contractions. They're about fifteen minutes apart. I'm in labor. Lynn is already here. We're headed to the hospital."

With a wide smile, David said, "Okay, I'm on my way, babe! Gus, get my coat out of the office. Let's roll!"

* * *

Dr. Boatwright Pulled Caleb Kent Cole out first, and David realized that he'd watched way too many movies about birth. Unlike what he'd seen, Caleb didn't immediately cry when he entered the world. He was quiet. The doctor suctioned his airways, and Caleb coughed. The nurse quickly wrapped him and laid him in David's arms. "Thank you, Lord," David said, looking into Caleb's pale face. He and Cherelle had a minute of bonding time before one of the nurses took Caleb to clean and examine him.

"Cherelle, we need you to push," Dr. Boatwright coaxed warmly. "We've got to get Chloe out of there, and you're home free."

"Come on, babe, let's finish so you can rest. You're doing a great job, and you're so beautiful," David encouraged.

Cherelle grunted and pushed, "Ooh! It . . . hurts. It. Hurts!"

"I know, babe, but we're almost done," David said, squeezing Cherelle's hand.

Cherelle made a grizzly sound and pushed again. Two minutes later, she was holding another precious gift from God. And to David, it was like having a thousand Christmases. He couldn't stop praising God.

* * *

DAVID HELPED Cherelle by placing pillows behind her back so she could position the twins comfortably for nursing. While Cherelle nursed the twins, David sat next to her and stroked her hair. Watching her nurse his babies caused a sense of euphoria in David that he had never experienced in his entire life.

"Babe, I love you so much. You are *everything* to me, Kit. When God gave me you, He was showing me again just how much He loves *me*. You've given me my family, and nothing is better than this right here—what I have with you."

"I love you, honey," Cherelle said, meeting David's loving gaze. She returned her attention to Caleb and Chloe. "They're so precious," Cherelle said, listening to their soft coos.

David was full of emotion. Not one to openly display it, he couldn't contain it. His wife and children had changed him already. He couldn't thank and praise God enough for the miracle he'd witnessed in the delivery room. Just as he'd told Cherelle, her pregnancy and delivery were uncomplicated. She'd been active and healthy during her pregnancy, and David knew that was God's doing. Life was good. As good as it gets.

Chapter 12

Stormy Weather

David was on cloud nine as he left Zenobia's, an upscale gift shop downtown, where one-of-a-kind items were plentiful. After a stop at the jewelry store, he would have everything he needed for his perfectly planned weekend to celebrate his and Cherelle's *reunion*. His swag was re-injected with giddy anticipation. Today was Cherelle's six-week post-delivery check-up, and David was eager to get his wife back and get his love train rolling again. He was on his way to his car when his cell vibrated.

"Hey, babe, how did everything go at the appointment? David asked.

"Hey, honey! Everything's fine. You can have your wife back tonight," Cherelle teased.

David grinned mischievously. "Oh, I've been looking forward to that, babe. You have no idea," he said, getting into his truck and starting the engine.

Cherelle's voice dipped to a seductive whine. "I know. Me too, honey. I've missed you so much."

David eased into the heavy traffic. "I've missed you, too,

babe. Words can't even begin to describe how much I've been jonesin' for some Cherelle Cole," he said. His cheeks rose to a sucker-smile, and his voice was a steamy sweet cup of hot apple cider on a winter morning. "I was about to sign myself up for the Cherelle Cole withdrawal clinic," he continued.

"Well . . . tonight, King David, you can get your fix and have *all* the Cherelle Cole you want." Cherelle's voice was sultry and tempting.

"Oooh! Woman! You better stop talkin' to me like that while I'm drivin' before you make me crash my ride."

Tickled by David's sensual flirtation, Cherelle let loose bursts of giggles. "No . . . no . . . you be safe. But I still want you to think about me. And I picked out something pretty to wear out to dinner. Then, for the *after party*, I have this tantalizing little outfit that I think you'll love."

"I do. I will. I am," David said, repeating what he'd told her at their wedding when he confirmed his vows.

"I *do*. I *will*. I *am*," Cherelle returned.

"Babe, you've got me feeling like Simba, singing, 'I Just Can't *Wait* to Be King!'" David sang.

Cherelle erupted in sultry giggles again. "The feeling is mutual, King David." The purr of her voice had David all tied up in his feelings. "I'm headed over to the church to pick up the twins and drop them off at your mom's. Then I'm gonna head home and get ready for our date, my king. Are you going to tell me where you're taking me?" Cherelle queried.

"No way. It's a surprise, babe. Take your time, and I'll be home to pick you up at seven p.m. sharp."

"Yes, my king."

"See you in a few. I love you," David said.

"Love you . . ."

"Later, Mrs. Cole . . ."

* * *

DAVID WAITED WHILE PIERRE, his jeweler, boxed the diamond necklace he had picked out for Cherelle. Pierre's wife, Laina, who served as his assistant, handed him a beautiful gift bag covered in exotic flowers, and he slid the box inside and handed it to David.

"We love doing business with you, Pastor Cole. I hope Mrs. Cole loves this," Pierre said.

"Oh, I know she will. This will surely score me some brownie points."

"Someone around here needs to score some brownie points, too," Laina teased.

Pierre threw his hands up. "I give this woman everything, and she wants more," he said to David.

"When you asked me to marry you, you promised me the world," Laina said.

Pierre kissed his wife. "Yes, I did."

"You guys take care, and thanks again," David said as he exited the jewelry store.

As soon as he slid into his truck, he received a call from Dorsey, one of the workers at the church's nursery. "Hello, Dorsey, are the twins okay?"

"Uh . . . Pastor . . . First Lady hasn't picked them up yet . . . and they're getting a little antsy. I think they just miss you guys. We're supposed to close in fifteen minutes, but I can stay here and wait for her if there's a problem."

"She hasn't called you?"

"No, sir."

"Hmm . . . When I talked to her at three o'clock, she had just left the doctor's office. She was on her way then," David said. He looked at the clock. It read 6:15 p.m.

"She might have stopped to do some shopping or something," Dorsey offered.

"She wouldn't leave them there all that time. Do you have enough milk for them, Dorsey?"

"Yes, sir. I just fed them."

"Okay, I'm gonna call my mother and have her come pick them up so you can lock up and go home. She is supposed to keep them overnight tonight anyway."

"Yes, sir."

"Thanks, Dorsey."

"No problem, Pastor."

David's mind wandered back to the conversation he'd had with Cherelle. He was positive she hadn't mentioned anything about going anywhere before picking up the twins. When she'd called him earlier, she'd already taken care of her errands. Where was she? A sinkhole formed in David's stomach. Something was off. David felt it all through him. He dialed Cherelle's cell phone, and it rang until her voicemail came on. Then he texted her. There was no response. "Ma, have you heard from Cherelle?" David asked when his mother answered her cell.

"Not since earlier. She was supposed to be here by four. I figured she ran some errands or something."

"I need you to pick up the twins from the nursery at church."

"Joe and I are already on our way. Dorsey called a few minutes ago."

"Ma, it's not like Cherelle to leave the kids. She wouldn't do that. Something isn't right."

"Don't start worrying, Punch. Maybe she's shopping. You know how the phones act up in the malls. And it's easy to lose track of time when you've practically been in the house for six weeks, being a full-time mom. Cherelle's only been out of the house a few times since the twins were born."

David sighed. He wasn't listening anymore. "Okay, I'll call you later," he said. He pulled into a McDonald's parking lot and accessed the locator for Cherelle's phone, and discovered she was just a few blocks from the church at a nearby gas station. Maybe something was wrong with her phone. *That's probably why she hasn't called.*

David eased into the gas station lot. Cherelle's white Range Rover was still parked at the pump. It stuck out like a sore thumb in this neighborhood. David got out and hurried over. He pulled the unlocked door open. Cherelle's purse was on the passenger seat. David picked it up and went through it. Her phone was still in it. He grabbed her purse and walked into the gas station.

"Cherelle! Cherelle!" David shouted, searching the tiny gas mart. He hustled to the counter. "Hey, my wife's truck is parked at the pump. Have you seen a woman with—" He paused for a second, recalling exactly what clothes Cherelle put on before leaving the house that morning. "A bright red jacket—about waist length. She has on blue jeans and bright red knee boots—with high heels?" David asked. He had teased her about how sexy she looked for a doctor's appointment. "Her hair is natural—really big," David explained, gesturing by holding his hands out away from the sides of his head to demonstrate Cherelle's hairstyle. She had worn her hair in a blowout that morning.

The young boy at the counter shook his head. "Ain't no lady that looked like that came in here since I been here. That Range been sittin' there since I started my shift. I thought maybe it wouldn't start, and somebody was gonna get it towed or something. Don't nobody just leave they Range—not around here at least."

David held his phone up to the plexiglass to show the young man a picture of Cherelle holding the twins. "This is her. You haven't seen her at all today?"

The young man shook his head again. "Nah, I'd remember a lady that looked like that. She ain't came in here."

Sweat trickled down the back of David's neck. Everything in him told him something was wrong. "What time did you start your shift?" he asked.

"Uh . . . three o'clock. . . but I was a little late. I ain't get here 'til bout three twenty—or maybe a little after that."

"Who worked the shift before you?"

"Uh . . . Chris."

"What's your name, son?" David asked.

"I'm Brian."

"Brian, can you get in touch with Chris, please? I need to know if he saw my wife."

"I got you," Brian said. He dialed a number using the speaker phone so David could listen.

"Yo, Chris, did you see a chick driving a white Range come in here today?"

"Ooh yeah. It was this one fine chocolate honey wearing red. Had on these sexy-looking boots. Big hair. Big booty. She was gripping a Range."

David nodded to the young man.

"Uh . . . yeah. I think that's her. Hey . . . you on speaker, bruh. Her husband lookin' for her."

"Bruh! Why you just throw me under the bus, B?! I ain't tryin' to be in no mess, bruh. I ain't got nothin' to do with that, man. I mind my business," Chris said.

"Nothing to do with what, Chris?" David spoke loudly so that the disembodied voice could hear him.

"Look, man, I ain't no snitch. Keep me outta this," Chris said.

"Keep you out of *what*? My wife is missing! Her purse and phone were still in her truck," David said, tightening his hold on Cherelle's red satchel purse. "She was supposed to pick up our kids. She wouldn't just leave our babies. If you know something, I need you to tell me right now!"

Silence loomed on the other end. Just then, a customer came in. "Hey, Pastor Cole!"

David turned at the sound of his name. "Hi, Kurt." His response was hurried.

"Aw man, you a pastor?" Chris's disembodied voice came over the speaker.

"Yes. I pastor the church two blocks down. Disciples of Christ Ministries. Please tell me what you know," David pleaded.

"Aw, man. You *that* dude?"

David's reputation in the community was stellar. It was no secret how much he cared for the young people. "Yes! What do you know?!"

"Listen . . . I just don't want to be in nothin'"

"My wife is missing! I need you to tell me *anything* you know!"

Chris let out a heavy breath. "She got in a black Charger with some dudes, man."

A confused strain marred David's face. "What?!"

"It was some dudes from The Sect, man. That's all I know. She got in on her own. They wasn't roughin' her or nothin' I just figured she was one of they chicks, man."

David pressed his palms to the sides of his head before slamming his fist into the Plexiglas. The force shook the cigarettes and cigars down. "They took her! Call the police!"

David knew the criminal antics of The Sect all too well. Drugs. Prostitution. Anything illegal, The Sect was involved. They terrorized the people in the neighborhood. Although

David had managed to come to a peace agreement with the other gangs in the area, The Sect had made it clear that they didn't play by anyone else's rules. The gang recruited boys as young as eight to sell drugs.

"I need to see your surveillance video from earlier today!" David ordered as he dialed his good friend and mayor, Walter Kincaid's cell. He had to be careful now that he knew Cherelle's disappearance was a retaliatory move by The Sect. They'd warned David to stay out of their territory, dissuading kids from joining the gang.

"I gotta call the owner."

"I need to see that video now! I can't wait!" David spat.

The young man reluctantly opened the door and let David into the space behind the counter with him. Within fifteen minutes, the local police had arrived, along with Carlos Torres, head of the city's gang squad. Walter Kincaid had gotten the ball rolling. David had already seen what he needed to see and had a copy for himself.

Mayor Walter Kincaid met David at his home for a very private conversation after David had been interviewed by the police. "I'm using every resource I have, DC. I know you know that. Cherelle is my *family*. Just so you know, the Feds are going to lead because of the kidnapping," Walter said regretfully.

David nodded, grounded by too much emotion for words.

"Los doesn't think it's about ransom . . . he thinks it's revenge," Walter continued, referring to the conversation he'd had with the head of the gang squad.

David nodded solemnly. "I know. They sent me a note a while back letting me know that I was on their hit list. This is to teach me a lesson," David said, swallowing his emotion. He took a deep breath. "I've been threatened by gangs before, I didn't think too much about it, Walt, to tell you the truth. But I never imagined in all my days that someone would hurt my wife or my kids."

"This is not your fault. No one could have predicted this. It's like you said, you get threats all the time," Walter said.

David dragged his hands down his face. "I never thought it would come to this, Walt. I should have been ready. I could have gotten her a bodyguard or something. I've been in this game for a long time. When it was just me, I never worried about my safety all that much. But now that I have a family, I should have known."

"Don't do that, DC. We're on it. We've got the best of the best working on this. Los will find out something, and we'll go from there." David's bloodshot eyes met Walter's. He was beyond consolation; he'd failed at protecting his family, and for that, he couldn't forgive himself.

He thought about the way Eleanor had cursed him when he'd told her. She hated him even more now. He hated himself. At a time like this, he wanted to be with his babies, but he feared bringing the twins home until he knew it was absolutely safe to do so.

Under Gus's tutelage, Leah, Joseph, and the twins made a clandestine move to the Escape in Tennessee, where they were being protected by Gabriel Long and Aaron Mitchell, two members of the six-person, special forces-trained, private security team Gus had arranged to protect David and his family. The other four members, Julius Mitchell, who was Aaron Mitchell's older brother, Kedar Kennedy, Nelson Raymond, and Keenan Brock, were just outside of David's home in two separate vehicles, keeping watch—ready for anything that might occur.

Chapter 13

Say Goodbye

In the backseat of a black Charger with tinted windows, sandwiched between two men who couldn't have been older than twenty-five, Cherelle felt herself coming undone. "David!" she screamed. RIP, the young man on her left, who had a close crop fade with asymmetrical designs cut into both sides of his temples, pressed a Glock into Cherelle's side.

"Hey, calm down! Yo man ain't here!" RIP said.

Feeling the cool barrel of the gun on her skin where her mid-waist jacket and sweater had lifted, Cherelle shouted again, "Jesus! Jesus!"

RIP burst into laughter. "He ain't here neither!"

The rest of the young men in the car laughed, except for the one in the front passenger seat. He turned toward Cherelle and watched her every move. RIP met his eyes. "John-Two, why you lookin' at her like you thirsty, bruh? Jag said she's all *his.*"

John-Two shrugged and turned back around. He fixed his gaze on something on the outside of his passenger window.

They had given him the name John-Two because they already had a John in their crew—John, the driver. John-Two was the scope boy. He kept his eyes and ears peeled while John drove or while the others were handling business on the streets. He had a medium build and a cocoa complexion. He was known for being quiet and observant. But he was good with a weapon and his hands, if it came down to it.

John, the driver, was on the short side, about five-foot-four, with smooth dark skin covered with tattoos. He had a short fuse. RIP and Mellow, the two young men in the back of the Charger with Cherelle, had even shorter fuses.

Cherelle bent forward as far as the seatbelt would allow. They had cuffed her hands behind her back. It seemed like life itself was slipping from her. She had never felt this much dread before, nor had she ever experienced a panic attack of this magnitude. With tears streaming, Cherelle now knew she had made a fatal mistake. She couldn't stop shaking. Anxiety had wrapped its fingers around her heart and was destroying the soft, pliable organ with grinding squeezes. A sharp pain radiated in her chest. Then the smoke of a sudden, wrathful brushfire burned within, zapping her oxygen. Struggling to breathe, Cherelle gasped for air. Her eyes bucked from the stinging sensation of her tears.

She would never see her babies again—or David. *Lord, God, why?* She needed to see them one last time and say goodbye. David had told her a million times to be fully aware of her surroundings when she was in the neighborhood surrounding the church. '*Always be on guard. Pay attention to what's going on around you—watch people's moves. Make sure you know the number of people around you. Watch what everyone is doing. Don't allow anyone to get too close to you and scope out someplace you can run if you have to run.*' Cherelle hadn't done any of those things. And for that, she was going to die.

Finally, John, the driver, looked into the rearview mirror at RIP and Mellow. "Ya'll need to do somethin' bout her. I can't deal with all that noise while I'm tryna drive. Shut her up!"

"Hey, sit up and shut up!" RIP barked, yanking Cherelle by her hair.

Cherelle let out a yelp. "Oww!"

"Jag said hands-off that one. *Don't* rough her. Don't hurt her. He said to handle her with care," Mellow warned in a quiet command.

Mellow was the one who had initially approached Cherelle at the gas station. He had an innocent look about him, but it was mere camouflage for the monster he could be. Mellow's penetrating hazel eyes were disarming. His neat, sandy brown locs flowed to his shoulders and complemented his vanilla complexion. He was articulate and well-versed in a plethora of subject matters, as he'd completed three years of college and had been a registered nurse before Jag started paying him more money than he'd ever seen in his life. Mellow could charm the likes of anyone, especially when he wore a suit. But the reality of who he was lay just beneath the surface.

"What I'm 'sposed to do? John can't concentrate on driving with all this cryin' and screamin'," RIP countered.

John-Two turned toward them from the front passenger seat again. His eyes locked with Cherelle's, and he quickly turned back to the front. RIP was the meanest one of them all, but he wasn't crazy.

Jag was the new leader of The Sect, and he hadn't secured his position by playing nice. A body count ensued, which led to his rise up the ranks. Jag meant every word he spoke. When he gave an order, those who valued their lives followed it exactly.

RIP, whose real name was Craig Burton, had earned the name RIP because he was trigger-happy. Rest in peace was the only thing an enemy could do when RIP got out of hand. Ordinarily, Cherelle's outbursts would have caused him to unleash evil on her. But Mellow's warning had curtailed RIP's wicked propensities.

Mellow had been with Jag the longest, and Jag considered him loyal; he was trusted. When Jag wasn't around, Mellow called the shots on Jag's behalf. Mellow was known to make examples of people who didn't know how to *listen*. He was just as ruthless as Jag.

RIP pushed the gun hard into Cherelle's side again. He reveled in her pain. "You lucky," he sneered.

Cherelle prayed aloud. "In You, I put my trust, Oh, God. Let me not be ashamed. Your strength is made perfect in my weakness. You w-w—will n—never leave me . . . nor forsake me," she repeated, chanting.

John-Two turned to her again, his eyes fixed on her.

"I 'specially can't deal with that praying and stuff!" John, the driver, shouted with expletives following. "Come on, Mellow, man!"

Mellow sighed. Then, as quickly as the strike of a cobra, he grabbed Cherelle in a sleep-choke hold, pulling her body against him. Cherelle struggled against him momentarily, kicking as RIP held her legs. Then she went limp. In about thirty seconds, she moved, dazed. Mellow took a syringe from his pocket and shoved up Cherelle's jacket and sweater, exposing her arm.

RIP watched as Mellow injected a substance into her arm. He smiled and nodded at the way Mellow operated like a trained professional. Cherelle's limp body fell against Mellow. He pushed her off and adjusted her seatbelt so that her body was flat against the seat. He adjusted her head. "Y'all happy now?" Mellow asked.

Mellow lowered his window a couple of inches. He needed some air. They were on the freeway now and ghostly sounds came through the slit in the window followed by the rhythmic sound of tires bouncing over the worn, pothole-populated road. He would never mention it to the others, but all that praying had made him feel unnerved. He removed a JUUL and began vaping. "John-Two, put on some jazz or somethin'," he said.

Chapter 14

Twenty-Four Hours

Cherelle awakened in unfamiliar surroundings. She found herself lying on her side, cuffed at her ankles and wrists. She struggled to lift her head from the foam pillow, but she couldn't. "Da-vid. D—David . . ." she mumbled incoherently, feeling like she'd been spinning for days at a time in some abyss. Her eyelids were heavy with a mind of their own. They willed to close. And her brain, attempting to recover from the Special K cocktail Mellow had injected into her, was processing like an old mainframe computer, piecing information and thoughts together slowly, as she floated in a drug-induced stupor.

A thought ticked out. *They're not going to let me live.* She'd seen their faces. Knew their names. Why had they done this? In her mind, the incident replayed in slow motion. Cherelle had acted without thinking. The sinking feeling of death prevailed once she had gotten into the car with them.

* * *

WHEN THE TWO *young men approached Cherelle at the gas station, she had just thrown her purse on the passenger seat. When she shut the driver's door and turned around, they were already upon her. Mellow distracted her with conversation and offered to pump the gas. Initially, Cherelle was cautious, but then they'd addressed her as "First Lady." That was when she relaxed and let her guard down.*

Mellow spoke first. "Hello. Good afternoon, First Lady. How are you doing today? Let me pump that gas for you."

Cherelle turned slightly. "Hi . . . I can do it, but thank you," she'd said pleasantly.

"Oh, no. I got it. I was raised to be a gentleman," Mellow had said, gently taking the hose from Cherelle. He began pumping the gas. "How's Pastor Cole?"

"He's doing well . . . what's your name?"

"Oh, I'm sorry. I'm Mellow. But I don't wanna touch your hands and get you all dirty."

"Okay. No worries. How long have you been at DOC?" Cherelle had asked.

Mellow was quick on his feet. "I just joined a couple of months ago. Honestly, I haven't been going like I should. I got family stuff going on."

"Well, I hope you're able to get back soon," Cherelle had said, smiling warmly.

"I plan to."

RIP stood off to Cherelle's left, roaming his lustful eyes over her body. As soon as he heard the pump click and Mellow had replaced the hose. He closed in on Cherelle and pressed his Glock into her side. "If you want to see yo husband and babies again, you better follow me and Mellow to the car right there. If you try to run or scream or do anything to bring attention to yourself, I'm gonna empty this clip in you right here. And you ain't never gonna see your babies or yo' man again." His husky, evil voice had been laced with malice. All Cherelle could do was focus on the fact that they somehow had David and the twins. Her brain froze, and she was instantly paralyzed. RIP pushed his Glock into her side more forcefully. "Walk slow," he'd said. Mellow hurried ahead and slid into the back passenger seat.

In an out-of-body-like experience, Cherelle walked over to a black Charger with tinted windows. RIP opened the back door with one hand and kept the gun pushed into her side with the other. "Get in." Cherelle complied. In a moment, Mellow had handcuffed her and given the key to RIP. The Charger eased out of the gas station lot.

* * *

CHERELLE HEARD voices outside the door of the bedroom she was locked inside. Groggy, she attempted to prop herself up. A sensation of floating assailed her, and her depth perception was unreliable. As she tried to focus, the objects in the room seemed to be moving—shifting around her. The door. The dresser. The window. They all traveled toward her like neighborhood children, introducing themselves to the new kid, then went back to their respective places in the room.

This had to be some horrible Scream Theatre nightmare that had gone on too long. But it wasn't. This was not some movie. This was an account of the final hours of her life. She knew it. Somehow, she felt it. Cherelle didn't understand God's hand in this—she couldn't. But she was no longer afraid. "D—David . . . I love you . . . I . . . love you," she said. Holding her head up was a chore. She tried to sit up, but her body was heavier than her will to control it. She propped herself up on her elbow and stared at the door where the voices congregated.

She heard laughter. What were they discussing? What kind of sick monsters would do something like this? The door swung open, and Cherelle's eyes focused on the shadow of the figure that entered. Her heart jumped and fought. Was he the one who would do it? Was he the one who would kill her? Would he shoot her? Would he strangle her? How would he kill her? She wouldn't fight. She wouldn't scream. She wouldn't give him the satisfaction.

"My babies . . ." Cherelle mumbled. She imagined the smell of the twins' baby-soft skin, perfumed in baby lotions, and always the smell of milk on their breath. Precious little beings God had formed with His hands. The same hands that had created the entire universe. She could hear them cooing as she nursed them. She saw David's caramel face clearly as he sat on the edge of the bed, watching her nurse his children. She remembered the words he spoke. *'You have given me everything I've ever wanted in my life—you have given me my family. And I love you for it.'*

Oh, if she could just feel David's strong, safe arms around her one more time. If she could hold her babies, nurse them, and feel their faces on her breasts, as they found comfort in her bosom, knowing that they were loved beyond love itself. Knowing they were her gifts *from* God and her gifts *to* her husband.

David. Cherelle loved him with her whole heart and soul. Every part of her loved David Kent Cole. And she was sorry. She didn't do as he always told her. She didn't watch out. She hadn't been on guard. "Sorry, honey . . . not. . . your . . . fault."

The shadow drew closer until it formed into the man-monster. His skin was a deep brown, and he had jet-black hair full of silken waves that were pulled into a ponytail. Cherelle smelled him and was repulsed by his scent. How dare he do this to her! How dare he be the last person to see her alive. It was akin to disrespecting someone's grave. Intruding on a space one didn't belong in. Desecrating something sacred.

Jag sat next to her on the bed, and Cherelle tried to scoot away from him. She couldn't control her limbs; they were unruly, unrepentant children. Jag smelled of smoke—a mix of marijuana and cigars. The smell of liquor oozed from his pores. "First. Lady. Well, well, we finally meet. I'm Jag."

With all her strength, Cherelle formed the words and spoke them into the universe.

"Do it . . . kill me," she said.

A devilish, fiendish sound emanated from somewhere deep in his wretched soul into the air. That laugh. "Nah. Not yet," Jag said, stroking Cherelle's cheek. Repulsed by the intrusion, Cherelle withered. "Your man, your *king,* is bout to be taught a lesson," Jag continued with defiance and hatred, like a rebel soldier speaking ill of the existing regime. "He thinks he runs the city, huh? No! I—Jag Vincent—I run that city!" the foolish monster said, pointing to himself. "You call him king? Well, I'm gon' be your king tonight. And I'm gon' show the The Turn Around Preacher what it's like to get in my way. I'm gon' be the last king you ever know."

Cherelle disappeared into herself and prayed to her God. "Jesus . . . Jesus . . ." she repeated.

Chapter 15

And I Love Her

After settling Leah, Joe, and the twins at the Tennessee Escape, Gus arrived in Detroit a little after midnight, officially cutting his two-week vacation short. He sat in silence with David until four a.m., when David's body gave out from sheer emotional and physical exhaustion. Neither had spoken a word the entire time, but Gus knew what David was thinking, and he was hoping to persuade him otherwise.

David lay across his bed with his clothes and shoes on, having fallen asleep while praying. He was awakened by the Friday morning news at six a.m. A news anchor's harrowing report about the body of an African American female found in an abandoned warehouse that was scheduled to be demolished that morning jarred David out of his short sleep.

"This is your Friday Morning Edition breaking news story. The body of an African American woman was found in the Morgan Warehouse on Detroit's southwest side just hours ago. We're getting reports that the body matches the description of Cherelle Cole, wife of Detroit's megastar pastor and street evan-

gelist, Pastor David Cole, of Disciples of Christ Ministries. Mrs. Cherelle Cole was abducted from a gas station yesterday after-noon, just two blocks away from the church where her husband pastors.

"Mrs. Cole is a psychologist and author who recently stepped into the Hollywood scene and debuted her acting talents in the hit indie film, Status, and is up for a Star award for her role in the movie One of These Days, produced and directed by Detroit's own Asa Miles. Mrs. Cole co-produced the movie and has earned awards for three screenplays. She is the primary consultant of the city's youth task force and is the city's co-liaison for the president's urban task force, along with her husband, Pastor David Cole.

"Cherelle Cole and Pastor David Cole were married in a celebrity-filled ceremony last year and recently became the parents of twins—a boy and a girl: Caleb Kent Cole and Chloe Eleanor Cole. Again, I want to stress that the identity of the body has not been officially confirmed. We will keep you updated as this sad story unfolds."

David was up on his feet, standing in front of the flat screen that hung over the fireplace in his and Cherelle's master bedroom.

"No! No! Baby, no!" David shouted. He tore out of the room and down the steps, tripping and sliding down the last few. He snatched his truck keys from a wall hook in the kitchen and rushed out the front door.

"DC!" Gus shouted. Tugging a sweatshirt over his head, Gus bolted down the stairs after David, but David was already outside. Gus flew out the front door in hot pursuit. The truck was in motion, and Gus pulled on the locked handle. His feet left the ground as David skidded out of the driveway.

"It's not her!" Gus shouted, letting go of the handle.

Chapter 16

No Turning Back

David sat across from Gus at his kitchen island, fighting to keep his eyes open. The hollow sound of the house haunted him; he folded his arms and rested his head. He'd been sitting in the same spot for the last five hours. He wanted and needed to hold his babies, but he thought it better that he stay away from them for the time being, and Gus agreed. It was too dangerous. They weren't sure how or when The Sect would strike again, especially since there were at least two factions of The Sect. There was no way to be certain as to which faction was responsible for Cherelle's abduction.

David grieved for the family of Charlotte Meyers, the woman found earlier that morning. She was an elementary school teacher who hadn't come home the night before. Her husband was being held as a suspect, and David couldn't fathom how a man could hurt the other half of himself. That's what Cherelle was to him. It had become more apparent to David that Cherelle was his perfect mate from God. He had never felt the comfort and oneness he shared with Cherelle with anyone else.

David's heavy eyes stared blankly. "She's *everything* to me, Gus. Everything," he mumbled, dragging his hand down his face.

"I know, bro," Gus said.

"If they've hurt Kit, I may as well be dead because I don't want to do life without her. I asked God why He would give her to me and then just snatch her away like this. I don't understand."

"Did you get an answer?"

"No."

"Well, let's pray that she is still alive, bro. No matter what it looks like."

David wanted to accept that. He wanted to believe that the love of his life and mother of his sweet little babies was coming home some kind of way, but something had him doubting. There was a part of him that understood The Sect had to make good on their promise. That was the way things worked on the streets. He watched the time on the clock shuffle to 3:17 p.m. It was the exact time Cherelle was abducted the day before.

"Gus, bro, I need you to help me get my wife back," David said.

"DC, you don't know what you're asking."

David banged his fist on the marble counter. Coffee leaped from inside the cup, just as angry as David. "Yes, I do! I know that you know people who can get her back, man . . ."

"DC, the people I know who do things like that are not CIA agents. They are people whom the government contracts with sometimes when they need certain things done. They ain't law-abiding citizens, DC. They are not going to go around and knock on doors and pass out fliers! These people can be heartless machines. They go into situations and eliminate everyone and everything that is not an asset. That could be an innocent person—a child, even. It's nothing nice, DC. You want everything you've worked for your whole life to be destroyed with that kind of blood on your hands, bro? Because I don't think you do. If we get into something like that, there's no turning back, bro."

"I want my wife back," David said grimly. And I want her back now! I don't care how it's done. I. Don't. Care. I've never asked you for anything, Gus. I just need her back, man." David turned and sulked away. He stalked up the stairs and slammed his fist into the wall leading to his bedroom. The drywall caved in from the force of his anger and gave way to a gaping hole.

How HAD it come to this? Twenty-four hours ago, David had trusted and relied on God to bring Cherelle back. Now, he was willing to trust men. He was in love with God, and yet he was in love with his wife. He wanted Cherelle back, and he couldn't quell the hostility he held toward his Father now. He'd been praying. His entire church congregation and all his family and friends were praying. He couldn't keep doing it this way. Every hour that went by made him less and less confident that Cherelle would be found alive—if at all. He didn't want to wait any longer.

David opened his laptop and signed into one of his bank accounts. He scanned his financials, then moved a large sum of money from one account to another. He realized that Gus would be forced to do what he'd asked him. All their lives, David had been the one person Gus could count on. At the age of twelve, David had welcomed Gus into his home, and he'd become a part of his family. They shared a bond that was beyond friendship. They were brothers in every sense, and David trusted that his soul brother would come through for him now.

Gus had been a CIA agent for over seventeen years and had a stellar reputation with the agency. Doing what David wanted could end Gus's career if anyone ever found out. It boiled down to hiring some sort of hit man. And then there was the simple truth David couldn't ignore. They would be acting outside of God's will. David knew he should be an example for Gus, who'd only been a Christian for a few years. Instead, here he was demonstrating a lack of trust in God. But all he could think about was getting his wife back.

David cried out to God. "Why did you let them take my soul from me?! I love you. I have loved you. Why?!" His rough tenor voice reverberated. He waited for an answer to be pressed into his spirit. A word. A sign. Something. But he was met with silence.

* * *

EARLY SATURDAY MORNING, David awoke with a start. In a nightmare, he had relived Thursday afternoon, and it left him with an odd feeling, like he was dying. He tried to shake the feeling off by showering. It was the first time he'd bathed since Cherelle's abduction, and it did nothing to rid him of the dreadful feelings pulsing through every part of him.

For the last twenty years of his life, David had prayed every morning upon waking. Today, he refused. He pushed every thought about praying out of his mind so that he could distance himself from what he intended to do. He couldn't talk to his Father right now, because he had already made up his mind.

He ignored the sorrow overwhelming his spirit. He ignored the pain of separation from God. He ignored it all so that he could do what he'd decided. It was nearing forty-eight hours. He couldn't wait any longer. He wouldn't.

Gus was on one of his three cell phones when David entered the kitchen. He'd made breakfast: Bacon, eggs, and toast. He pivoted as David sat on a stool at the island. He slid David the plate he'd prepared for him. David pushed the plate away, and Gus exchanged it for a cup of straight black coffee, which David readily accepted. He grimaced from the heat when he swallowed his first sip. It was Saturday, the one day of the week he and Cherelle usually shared lazy mornings. It was their custom to stay in bed until noon—at least before the twins had been born. Saturday was their day for each other. Cherelle's absence was David's ruination.

"I moved some money—about two hundred fifty thousand. I can get more—I have more," David said when Gus ended his call.

Gus took the stool opposite David. He held David in a steely stare. He'd resigned himself to the ungodly task David had requested. He loved David that much. He owed David that much.

"No. It's taken care of. That was my contact on the phone. I don't want you in this, bro. Leave your money where it is for now. We're done with this conversation—forever. It never happened. And just know, there are no guarantees," Gus spoke matter-of-factly.

David nodded. He couldn't miss the pained expression on Gus's face.

"I'm going to check on the guys," Gus said. He pulled a hoodie over his head, stuffed his feet into a pair of snow boots, and headed out the door to the car, where the private security team was posted.

A question rested on David's heart and caused him to weep. **Do you love her more than you trust Me?**

Chapter 17

On The Third Day

David tossed in his bed. His lean, muscular legs were tangled in the sheets. He kicked at the covers to loosen himself from the snake that had coiled around him. Freeing himself, he turned on his side, then his stomach. Then he turned onto his back, refusing to open his eyes. Several hours ago, he'd taken an over-the-counter sleep aid for the first time in his life. But the Lord hadn't allowed him to rest. His body and spirit were restless, and it wasn't solely because of Cherelle's abduction.

He sat up slowly against the headboard, feeling an eerie cold. He shivered as his sweat-soaked t-shirt clung to him. Feeling a draft, he staggered to the bedroom window, thinking maybe he'd opened it for fresh air and had forgotten to close it. The securely locked window was decorated with frost. David peered through a tiny space that hadn't surrendered to the cold temperatures. He stared out onto the beauty of his two-acre property that was blanketed with fresh white snow. He pressed his forehead to the window and imagined Cherelle outside making a snow angel. She had made him promise that they would both make one as soon as there was enough snow. This would have been the perfect morning for them to do it. With all her sophistication and prissiness, David marveled at the fact that there was a sincere innocence about Cherelle. She was everything a man would want in a wife, yet everything he never expected. And all those unexpected blessings made him love her more.

David slow-walked into Cherelle's boutique-style closet. Large as a bedroom with wall-to-wall white oak shelves, glass cabinets, and gold clothes racks, it was painted in a hot pink color. David had spied on one of Cherelle's social media decorating accounts to get a feel for what she liked. He passed the information to the interior decorators he'd hired to decorate their home in a week-long frenzy, and they had successfully duplicated the designs Cherelle loved. Two huge white crystal chandeliers lit the room, and David inhaled the scents of jasmine, lavender, and chamomile. Something caught his attention, and he walked over and removed a dress from a golden hook near Cherelle's extravagant gold dressing table that looked like it belonged to a queen in a fairytale story.

David discarded the satin hanger and held the dress in his hands. It was the dress Cherelle had planned to wear on the date he'd planned for them the day she was abducted. It was David's favorite dress—a royal blue Roberto Cavalli wrap dress that fit Cherelle expertly. She often teased him that he would get bored with her if she kept wearing the same dresses when they went out, but David had his favorites, and this dress was his main one. Cherelle had wanted him to be happy on their special night, so she hadn't bothered to purchase a new dress. She had another new purchase in mind instead.

David realized that although he and Cherelle had only been married a short time, she had never ceased to be *unselfish*. She was one of the most selfless people he knew. His wife had the uncanny ability to consistently make him feel that he was her priority—like he was king, and yet place God above everything. He was so in love with her. He held the dress to his face and inhaled it, rubbing it softly across his skin.

On one of the two center islands, David spotted the lingerie Cherelle had laid out for their return home. He picked up the powder-blue, lace teddy and viewed the tag absently. Three hundred and fifty-seven dollars. A La Perla special. David shook his head and cracked a pained smile. Then tears sprang from his wearied eyes. How many times had he jokingly told Cherelle he didn't need all the expensive lingerie? And how many times had she surprised him anyway? Her heart had always longed to please his, and David longed to hold her at this very moment. To feel her softness against him and smell her hair. To enjoy the sound of her girlish laugh. To hear her call him king one more time.

David dropped to his knees and wept profusely. His voice boomed through the space as he prayed. "Bring her back, Lord! I need her back. She is my everything . . . but . . . there is no one above You—no one! Not the children. Not Cherelle. No one. There is only You, Oh God! There is only You!" Psalm 46:10 came to David while he was still praying. ***Be still and know that I am God.*** It rang true in David's soul. "Forgive me! I am a wretch! Forgive me, Father."

Chapter 18

Plan in Motion

D avid sat in the steam shower for over an hour. Afterward, he made his way to the kitchen, where Gus had prepared cream of tomato soup and homemade cornbread. David finished his soup and ate a second helping of cornbread. It was his first meal in three days. He had to give it to Gus; he was an outstanding cook. Gus and Cherelle frequently swapped recipes while David designated himself their taste-tester.

"I know you said *not* to talk about this anymore, but . . ." David started. He figured there was no opportune moment to have the conversation they needed to have.

Gus let his spoon thump against the edge of the old-fashioned, wooden soup bowl with a wide handle and sighed. David had already broken a rule by speaking on things that were never to be spoken of again. "What is it, bro?" The twitch of Gus's right eye revealed his agitation.

"As much as I want her back—as much as I *need* her back, I need to trust God on this, man. I've prayed, and He wants me to trust Him. I've got to trust Him."

Gus shot up from his seat, pointing. "Are you freakin' serious?! I told you to be sure this is the way you wanted to go, bro! Gus' pale white face flushed red. He gripped his head in his hands and paced. "When I made that call yesterday, I set a plan in motion! You can't just change your mind. It doesn't work that way. Even if this guy and the people who work for him are just gaining information from people who know something about what happened to Cherelle, or who might have been involved—they don't get to just walk away. That's not how it works, DC! I told you that! Who knows what's already occurred!"

David raked his hand down his face. At this impasse, words were pointless. Gus was right. He'd put everything important to him on the line for David, and now he was backing out. Gus brushed past David, bumping him out of his way. He grabbed his coat from the parlor and stuffed his bare feet into his boots. When Gus opened the front door, Deacon Lewis was standing there with his hand raised to press the doorbell.

Deacon Lewis gave Gus a military nod. "Young Gus," Deacon Lewis greeted.

"Hey, Deac," Gus said, finding it difficult to tamp down his anger. Gus was so red, Deacon Lewis had to know something was wrong.

Deacon Lewis lowered his voice. "How's he doing?"

"As good as he can be, I guess. I need to take a walk," Gus said flatly. He felt around in his pocket for his "emergency" cigarette and lighter. He had quit smoking a few years ago when he'd gotten saved, but now he needed the nicotine.

"Don't be too long. Today's first Sunday. I brought communion," Deacon Lewis said, holding up a recyclable bag.

"Okay. Be back in a few," Gus said.

"Son! It's me. Brought communion," Deacon Lewis called out.

David stepped into view as Deacon Lewis walked toward

the kitchen. They embraced when Deacon Lewis was within arm's reach. "Hey, Old Man," David said solemnly. Deacon Lewis held David in a fatherly embrace and gave him a few firm pats on the back. When the two pulled apart, David noticed the puddles in Deacon Lewis's eyes.

"I've come to love her like my own daughter . . . she gave me my grandkids. My heart sho nuff broken," Deacon Lewis admitted.

David nodded. "I know, Old Man. The Lord has given me peace—no matter what the outcome. But I want my baby back. I feel like there is a hole in my soul."

Instead of talking, Deacon Lewis prayed over David. When he was done, the two sat and drank coffee together. Gus returned thirty minutes later, and Deacon Lewis gathered them for prayer. Standing in a circle next to the kitchen table, Gus looked up at David and said sincerely, "I'm sorry, bro. Forgive me." He was always the one to apologize first whenever they had any kind of disagreement.

"No, I'm sorry. It was all on me. Forgive *me*," David returned.

Deacon Lewis eyed them curiously before praying and handing them their communion packets. When they were done, Deacon Lewis smacked his hand up against his head lightly. "Almost forgot. That little Tate girl worried me to death about bringing a gift to you," he said, looking in his coat pocket. "It's a letter. And I hope it's appropriate. It's sealed up, so I couldn't read it first. You know how these young girls are some-times. I think she's got a little crush on you, son. She asked me ten million questions. 'When was I going to see you? How long would I be with you?' All kinds of questions. When I told her *today*, she even asked me if I was sure." Deacon Lewis shook his head. "She sumthin' else I tell ya." He handed David the letter. David read it and tossed Gus a look. Gus took the letter from

David. Most of the letter was from Sharia Tate, and it was appropriate, but the last sentence was in a different script. *May have info. Will be in touch tonight.*

"They know something. I hope to God Sharia's brother Rico had nothing to do with Kit being taken. I—" David started. His cell buzzed on the counter. He snatched it up and answered in a single motion. "This is David Kent Cole." Gus motioned for David to put the call on speaker.

"Good afternoon, Pastor Cole, this is Rico."

David slammed his fist on the counter. "Where is my wife?! If you've hurt her, I swear I will kill you!"

The cool voice on the other end was unperturbed. "Aye, slow your roll. Pump yo brakes, man of God. I ain't got nothin' to do with that part of The Sect. I told you I got a little sister. I don't roll like that. But I got a dude on my team who is loyal to me; he says the last place your wife was is this address: 7802 Glen Road, near Holland, Ohio. I'm on a burner, so don't bother calling me back. You understand how things work in the streets, don't you, Pastor Cole? This is an *anonymous* tip. Any mention of me or Sharia puts our lives in danger—then you and I *will* have a problem. I know you understand that. Sharia is still acting like a little lady. Thanks," Rico said and disconnected the call.

Chapter 19

Fragile

Wrapped in a blanket, Cherelle was escorted out of a sprawling ranch that sat on twenty acres of farmland. The nearest neighbors were several miles away in each direction. FBI agent Mya Shelton covered Cherelle's head with her bureau jacket. Agent Shelton could feel Cherelle shaking hard from sheer exhaustion as she walked on unsteady legs. She spoke soothingly into Cherelle's ear and kept her arm belted around Cherelle's waist. "Mrs. Cole, I'm going to be walking with you the whole time. We are going to walk outside. You will hear lots of voices. But I won't let you go. I'm going to be right next to you." Still in shock, Cherelle's breathing quickened, but she gave no verbal response. "I'm going to help you into an ambulance where your husband will be waiting for you. He's going to ride with you to the hospital. You're safe now," Agent Shelton reassured Cherelle. The team in place had agreed to bend the rules for David. Gus's connections extended far.

Cherelle felt the cold concrete through the thin slippers.

She felt the whipping of the winter wind on her lower extremities. She kept her head down with her fingers tightly pinching the jacket in place over her head so that she could not be seen.

"There are lots of reporters in the distance. Keep your head down. I'm going to guide you. Don't worry," Agent Shelton said. Cherelle's teeth clattered together; she couldn't stop the insufferable shaking of her body. Agent Shelton continued to coach Cherelle, comforting her along the way. "Just a little farther . . . Okay . . . step up, but keep your head low," she said. Cherelle followed Agent Shelton's directions and heard the ambulance door slam shut behind her. David reached out and pulled the jacket from Cherelle's head as if she were an apparition that had to be validated with his eyes.

"Jesus!" David said just above a whisper. He pulled Cherelle to his chest, squeezing her. Cherelle locked her arms around David's neck and squeezed. Then she let out a loud wail and sobbed against his chest. David felt his heart restart as if he had been jolted with a defibrillator. He held Cherelle close and wept into her hair. God had brought her back.

THE TRIAGE NURSE entered the room with a blood pressure reader on a rolling cart. She was a tall woman with perceptive gray eyes and strawberry-blonde hair. Her waif figure seemed to be lost in her purple scrubs. With a friendly demeanor that was genuine and trustworthy, she acknowledged Cherelle and then David. "Hi, I'm Nurse Barnett. I need to get a little information from you," she spoke in a southern drawl.

With her chin tucked into her chest, Cherelle responded in a barely audible voice. "I—I—need a rape kit, please."

The words fell slowly on David like volcanic ash, then

penetrated the first layer of his skin, and the next before burning tiny holes all over his body and finally scorching his heart. David pinched his bottom lip between his teeth to keep from screaming out in frustration. In a moment, he was flush with fire pricks of emotion. He squeezed Cherelle's hand and said the only words that came to mind. "I love you. You're mine, and I'm yours. Nothing else matters." Cherelle's resolve splintered, and her sobs rang out in the small space. She lay her head on David's shoulder and released almost four full days of trauma.

* * *

DAVID REFUSED to leave Cherelle's side. He sat through the rape examination and the FBI interview, trying to control a rage he thought he had conquered years ago. When he and Cherelle were left alone for the first time since she'd been rescued, the words she spoke broke David's heart.

"I'm . . . so . . . sorry . . ." Cherelle cried, unable to look her husband in his eyes.

David wrapped his arms around her. "No, Kit. Please, don't say that. You've done *nothing* wrong, babe. You are strong and courageous, and you are *my* rose. You will *always* be my rose. Whatever storm we have to go through, we'll do it together. I will be right here with you."

The emotional shattering that broke Cherelle into pieces by the minute simultaneously broke David. They were one. The same deep blow Cherelle felt in her soul, David felt in his. But she was *alive*. That was his blessing. Cherelle was alive. God had answered his prayer and brought her back home.

"They . . . hurt me . . . they hurt me," Cherelle cried to her husband.

"I'm right here, babe. No one will ever hurt you again," he

said. Explosive firestorms raged in David's heart. At any given moment, he could combust. How could he praise God for his wife's return and yet be angry with Him? He didn't quite understand it, but the emotions were real. More real than he'd ever felt.

Chapter 20

Miracle

After an overnight stay at the hospital, Cherelle was released. David had already arranged for her mother, Eleanor, and her mother's sister, Jessie, to meet the couple at the Tennessee Escape, where the rest of the family was waiting in anticipation of Cherelle's return.

When David, Cherelle, Kedar, and Julius stepped off Misty, one of the private charter planes Maverick Kitts owned, Gus and Keenen were waiting to escort David and Cherelle to the Escape. The two had flown ahead with Nelson to Tennessee to make sure the Escape was secure for Cherelle's return.

"Hey, my favorite person," Gus said, hugging Cherelle. He kissed her forehead. "I missed you, sis," he said, buffering the emotion rising within. "Let me introduce you to Keenan Brock, but we all call him K-9. He's going to be around to make sure you guys are safe. You'll meet the rest of the team at the Escape," he said to Cherelle.

Cherelle leaned into David and nodded as her eyes

followed Keenen's height. He was at least six feet four inches tall with rich, dark chocolate skin that was silky smooth. Built like the Rock, he was a formidable opponent, dressed in all-black combat gear. He sported a salt-and-pepper beard with a low fade haircut that was also sprinkled with salt and pepper. Keenen reached out and shook Cherelle's hand, and she reciprocated with a flimsy shake in return. Last night at the hospital, she'd met Kedar and Julius, who bore a strong resemblance to David. Though none of the other men looked as intimidating as Keenen.

"Thank you again for protecting my family and me," David said, following up with a firm handshake. He sensed that Cherelle was uncomfortable with having all the different men around, but it was necessary for her and the twins' safety. He'd never take any chances again. With his left arm around her waist, David pulled Cherelle closer to him.

Two specially outfitted black Suburbans were parked nearby. Gus addressed Kedar. "You're gonna flip and ride with Keenen," he said. "Julius and I will escort my family, and you guys will cover."

"Got it," Kedar said and headed to the second SUV with Keenen. Gus slid behind the wheel of the first SUV. Julius waited and carefully scoped the area as David helped Cherelle into the backseat and scooted in after her. Confident that everyone was secure, Julius closed the door behind David and got into the front passenger seat.

The sound of jazz piped through the speakers of the SUV, but the melodic infusion of musical notes was not enough to soothe what bubbled hotly underneath David's placid surface. He was in a battle with his own demons, but he drew Cherelle close to his side, and she burrowed herself underneath his arms and closed her eyes. David threaded his fingers through hers and stroked her hand with his thumb. Just to touch her, inhale the scent of her, and have her so close to him that he knew the steady pattern of her breathing was a blessing. Every inhaled and exhaled breath of Cherelle's gave David a second chance at life. He allowed the thought to settle deep in his spirit to help override the swell of vengefulness that arrested every cell in his body.

Gus relayed the message that Cherelle's brother, Corey, had arrived and was waiting at the Escape as well. David had forewarned the family to give Cherelle the space she needed once she arrived. He wanted her to rest. It had been an excruciating four-day ordeal, and he didn't want to overwhelm her. She'd been through enough.

*　*　*

DAVID EXPLAINED to Cherelle that the family was waiting inside as he helped her out of the truck. "You don't have to talk to anyone or do anything, babe. You can just go right to bed if you want. They just wanted to be here when you came home," David whispered to his wife. Cherelle nodded. They stood on the porch for a moment, hand-in-hand, reassuring one another with their eyes. David felt his wife's anxiety, and he wanted her to feel at peace in her own home. "You ready?" he asked, feeling the tremor in her hands. She nodded again, and he hoped the family would truly give her space once they'd had a chance to hug her and see her for themselves.

David opened the right side of the massive French doors, and Leah embraced Cherelle and pulled her over the threshold. "Oh, sweetheart . . . I'm so happy to see you," Leah cried as she squeezed Cherelle, relieved for her and David's sake. Joseph put his arms around the two. Full of gratitude to God and the prayers of her family, Cherelle hugged Leah slackly because her body was fatigued. She felt like she couldn't be on her feet any longer.

Eleanor and Aunt Jessie were next. Full of tears, Eleanor took Cherelle's hands in hers and said, "I knew God would bring you back. You are the only thing I have left in this world, Cherelle."

Aunt Jessie hugged Cherelle and kissed her on the cheek. "Bless you, my beautiful niece. Oh, I love you. God is so good."

Corey was next in line. Cherelle bawled on him, crying so hard she shook. "I love you, girl," Corey said. His tears flowed freely with his sister's. He'd been plagued with the fear of losing her after he'd already lost their father to cancer five years ago. Corey sucked in a long, gulping breath and squeezed his sister and patted her back. "I'm so glad you're okay."

Cherelle pulled apart from her brother and said, "My babies?"

"They're asleep in their nursery. They're fine, Cherelle," Corey returned.

Cherelle turned to David. "I want my babies . . ." she said, dazed.

"Okay. Yes, babe," David said. He took Cherelle's hand and led her upstairs to the nursery, where Chloe and Caleb lay together in Caleb's baby bed. Cherelle took hurried steps to where the twins slept as peacefully as if they knew they were being guarded by angels. Cherelle picked them up and walked over to her plush, purple rocking glider and sat. "I—I just want to hold them for a while, honey," she said weakly.

"Okay, take your time. I'm right here." David said, claiming the second rocking glider next to her. He was thankful that they had decided to create a nursery for the twins at the Escape as well as their home in Detroit. Having a nursery here made everything convenient for Cherelle.

She was a beautiful vision before David, with each of his

babies in her arms. Her eyes and tender touches were full of the love she had for their children. No other woman could ever be to him what Cherelle was. She was his everything. David praised God for this miracle. His wife had been found alive after four long days. But underneath his praise, a dark part of him vied for lordship. That part of him wanted to hurt someone. Wanted to kill.

* * *

DAVID SUPPRESSED his angry urgings as he washed Cherelle's hair. He lathered each section, pulling his fingers through gently while massaging her scalp until calm settled over her and him. He smiled when he thought about how often Cherelle teased him about his hair *fetish*.

He thought one of the sexiest and alluring things about a woman was her hair. And there was no woman sexier and more alluring to him than Cherelle. He loved her. His soul loved her. Another layer of his heart peeled back to reveal the depth of the love he felt for Cherelle, as he performed this simple act with the same care as he handled their newborn babies. Every touch of David's fingertips on Cherelle's scalp solidified his love for her.

The familiar aromas of Cherelle's natural hair products brought David back from the dead. Taking care of her in this fashion was a ritual he welcomed. A precious task that just days ago, he had begged God for the chance to do again. With a grateful heart, David recognized that all the incidental but intimate moments he and Cherelle had shared throughout their relatively new marriage were larger than life itself.

Those memories were the most valuable assets he possessed. He had never appreciated time and togetherness the way he did right now. They were heavenly gifts he would never take for granted again. He would cherish Cherelle every day and let her know that she was his everything, no matter what those monsters had done to her. She was his, and she was *home*.

Chapter 21

Home

David sat in his recliner in the massive sitting room of his and Cherelle's master suite. Not wanting to disturb her with his restlessness, he had opted to lounge in the sitting room where he could give her some space while keeping an eye on her. A knock on their bedroom door tugged David out of a light nod. He unraveled himself from the oversized, chunky-knit throw blanket. He stood and stretched and then walked drowsily toward the door and swung it open. Eleanor stood before him, leaning on her cane, her lips pursed tightly, her eyes lasering into him.

"I'm taking Cherelle back to Florida. She'll be safer at Jessie's with me—in a different environment that will be less stressful."

Was Eleanor seriously talking about taking his wife away from him to Florida or anywhere else after he'd just spent the last four days of his life in total anguish over her abduction? David was too exhausted to blow a gasket. After considering his response, he spoke resolutely in a low voice that was measured with patience so as not to incite what would surely become the biggest family feud in history. "Cherelle is staying here with me. She's safe *here*." The soft, matter-of-fact tone David used was a precursor to something more verbally aggressive, but there was no way Eleanor could have known that. She didn't know David well enough.

Eleanor pointed a shaking forefinger at David, and her icy, strained voice lashed him. "This is no time to be selfish! My daughter has been through enough because of you! She needs to be away to get herself together. She can't do it here. You should understand that!"

David stepped out into the hallway and closed the bedroom door behind him so as not to awaken Cherelle. "Lower your voice . . ." he commanded.

"I will not!" Eleanor roared.

The elevation of Eleanor's voice caused Leah, Gus, Corey, and Aunt Jessie to end their conversation in the kitchen. Gus stopped stirring the stew that was on the stove and washed his hands quickly. Tucked in a padded carrier that was strapped around him, Chloe squirmed and fidgeted on his chest. Gus rubbed circles on Chloe's back and stroked her head lightly, in awe that a child so small, barely seven weeks old, could pick up on his tension so innately.

Standing on the bridge overlooking the two-story family room. With heightened senses, David could hear every sound in the room below, from the crackle of the fireplace to the hum of the refrigerator in the kitchen, to the sound of Gus's bare feet strumming across the porcelain floor toward the staircase. David forced his anger down to a tolerable level. Eleanor had hit him with a low blow just as she'd intended. He shook his head disapprovingly. Whatever anger or ill feelings she had harbored against him since he and Cherelle became engaged were now full-blown. It was neither subtle nor concealed. And David was too burdened and too regretful to care. He pinched his bottom lip with his teeth, unconsciously penetrating the soft flesh.

Eleanor stood as straight as she could, placing herself on equal footing with David. "She's coming back to Florida with me!"

"No! Cherelle *Cole* isn't going anywhere! She is right where she belongs," David said back. He took a long, labored breath before saying, "We are *one*! Whatever we go through, whatever we have to get through, we will do it *together*! You are a guest in my house, and I respect you because you are my wife's mother. You gave her life, and for that, I am eternally grateful. But if you came here with any agenda that's in opposition to supporting us as *one*, you can leave now! I mean it!"

"Cherelle is coming back with us! I'm going to pack her bags so that she and my grandchildren *can live* in peace!"

Caleb's cries filled the kitchen and family room. Seconds later, Chloe melded her cry with her brother's. "Eleanor, stop it! You have no right!" Aunt Jessie yelled, hurrying up the stairs toward the two.

"Cherelle! Cherelle!" Eleanor shouted, attempting to bypass David.

His solid frame blocked her path. "Leave her alone! She needs to rest!"

The twins' cries soared to higher levels, as did the arguing. The palatial estate became a battlefield of voices, combatting each other for air space.

"My daughter is coming with me!"

"You are out of order! I am not going to let you disrespect me in my own house! I want you out of here!"

"You are going to be the death of her!" Eleanor screamed,

and her open hand cracked against David's right cheek, stunning him.

With Caleb cradled in the crook of her elbow, Leah bounded up the steps to where David and Eleanor stood. Gus was right behind her. "That's enough, Eleanor!" Leah shouted. Her anger matched David's. Couldn't Eleanor see that he'd suffered just as much as Cherelle had? "You've got no right to do this! This is wickedness!" Leah continued.

The commotion had awakened Joseph. "Lee!" Joseph called, hurrying up the staircase.

David clenched his fists at his sides. His body shook as he fought to tamp down the violent current that flowed through him. The weight of the last few days had robbed him of all sensibility and diplomacy. He and Cherelle had been violated in the most heinous way, and now Eleanor was violating him in his own home. Gus appeared right next to David, forever his protector.

"DC . . ." Gus probed with a hand on David's shoulder.

David stood as still as a wax statue, allowing his guilt to flow freely through him and out. Cherelle was home. Nothing else mattered. He spoke through gritted teeth. "I want you out of my house. First thing in the morning," he said to Eleanor. He turned to Gus and said, "Call Mav and make the arrangements." A single tear slid down his face.

A weak but angelic sound penetrated the cries of the battlefield. "David . . ." Cherelle called softly. She stood in the doorway surveying the battleground where the soldiers had gathered to wage war. In an instant, the softest part of David floated to the surface. He turned to address his wife. "Yes, babe?" His voice was wrapped in a tender blanket of love and serenity.

"The babies . . . they're hungry," Cherelle said.

Gus lifted Chloe out of the carrier and handed her to

David. He knew that would help to calm Chole and David. Leah moved forward with Caleb and handed him to David as well. David carried them both while attempting to soothe their cries. Corey cut through the battlefield with two bottles in tow; he handed them to Cherelle. He had intended to stay out of the melee, but his spirit sided with David. Cherelle lifted Chloe from David's arms so that they each held one twin, and she gripped David's hand with her free hand. She looked right at her mother and said, "Mama, I'm staying with my husband. Good night."

* * *

CHERELLE FED the twins one last time before she eased under the covers for bed, and David placed the sleeping duo in a double bassinet next to his and Cherelle's bed. He wasn't sure if they would sleep long enough to allow Cherelle to get some rest, but he hoped they would. Gus brought up a cup of Chamomile tea with a splash of honey. Cherelle took her last sip and snuggled under the covers on her stomach.

David sat on the edge of the bed, rubbing Cherelle's back. "Honey?" Cherelle mumbled into the pillow underneath her

"Yes, babe?"

"I want everyone to go. I can't do this with them here. Please . . ." Cherelle turned to him with eyes that were heavy and haunted with dark circles. "I'm sorry."

David stroked her hair and lifted her chin. "No, babe. Don't apologize. I understand. I'll take care of it, okay? But I will have to fly back to the city in a few days—and I'll fly right back. It's the church's anniversary, sweetheart. I need to be there for just a few hours. Gus and the security team will be here with you while I'm gone. I trust Gus with my life. You and the kids will be safe here."

"Okay . . ." Cherelle nodded. At least everyone else would be gone soon. She hadn't left the bedroom except to interrupt the family war that had ensued earlier. And she wouldn't have done that if the twins hadn't needed to be fed. She wished she could shrink somewhere and be alone. David sat next to her until she drifted off into a deep sleep, truly resting for the first time since her abduction.

Chapter 22

Kill

With Cherelle in a deep, sound sleep and the Escape quiet, David attempted to purge the evil that had infiltrated his soul. In his lower-level fitness room, he attacked a heavy punching bag. It was a stand-in for the men he wanted to kill with his hands. Gus held the bag as steadily as he could while it absorbed the brunt of David's ire. It had been years since Gus heard his brother use swear words, and David had spewed enough of them to make up for it. He pounded the bag relentlessly, hitting it with everything he had. Punch by punch, David destroyed his enemies. He'd been at it for a while, and Gus wondered when he'd tire.

David stumbled and hugged the punching bag for support. Breathing heavily, he held on to it like it had the power to save him from his misery. Then, after a few moments, he released the bag reluctantly and staggered before dropping to his knees. "Arrgh!" David roared. His eyes stung with tears. He sat on his butt and scooted until his back was pressed up against the wall. He brought his knees up to his chest and rested his head on his forearms. He tried to slow his heart rate down by repeatedly inhaling and exhaling deep breaths. He wanted to calm himself and get rid of the sharp pain in his head and his heart.

Gus squatted down in front of David and removed his boxing gloves. He walked over to the see-through mini fridge, pulled out a bottle of water, and handed it to David. David gulped it down at once, and Gus noticed the steady flow of tears in his eyes. He waited for David to share all that had him burdened.

David flexed his hands and squeezed his eyes shut. He took the bottom of his tank and wiped his face, but his tears continued to trickle. "Bro," David said, staring into Gus' eyes, "they *raped* my baby . . . they . . . raped my baby." David pinched his bottom lip with his teeth and shook his head incredulously. "I wasn't there to protect her! They put their hands on my *wife*," David continued hoarsely. "She is the best thing that ever happened to me, and they hurt her because of me!" David grunted as a sudden onslaught of shooting pains created fireworks in his skull that he hadn't felt in a long time since his recovery. He palmed the sides of his head with his fists and grimaced. The pain was a reminder that he'd survived being shot in the head two years ago. The headaches sometimes came with the territory, but the pain tonight was colossal.

Gus's right eye twitched as he shared his brother's anger. "They won't get away with this!" he assured David. Gus stood up and began pacing. He had to move when his anger was out of control. In his peripheral vision, he saw movement from David, and he stopped suddenly.

David held his hands out in front of him, and they shook with the evil he wanted to inflict. "I want to kill every last person who had something to do with it."

"They've got five people in custody. None of the guys who abducted Cherelle were on the premises when the Feds raided it. But I promise you, every single one of them will be brought to justice—one way or another. You have my word, bro. I promise you," Gus said.

"I can't begin to tell you how torn I am. One part of me is rejoicing, and the other part of me wants to kill. I have never felt this much hatred and evil in my life. I sat and listened to the whole interview, bro. What they did to my baby . . ." David squeezed his eyes shut and grunted again. His gut churned from just thinking about Cherelle detailing the abuse she endured for three and a half days. "I. Am. So. Angry. And my heart hurts for her. I've never seen her do anything against anyone intentionally. She is so loving and kind—the sweetest angel. So, what purpose did this serve?" David asked. "I shouldn't be questioning God at a time like this, but . . ."

"DC, they took seventeen young women—some as young as thirteen—out of that house where Cherelle was held. All those young women were saved from being sex-trafficked because of Cherelle—because we were looking for Cherelle. If we hadn't gotten that tip, those young women would be God knows where by now. People's daughters and sisters would be gone forever. I know that's no consolation, and it doesn't take away the pain of what you feel right now—or what Cherelle must be going through. But you told me that all things worked together for good to them that love God and are called according to His purpose. Now I know you and Cherelle both love God, and I know both of you are called according to His purpose. So, this evil, wicked thing that happened will ultimately work for you guys' good. That's Scripture, bro."

"I know," David said, covering his face with his hand.

Chapter 23

Nightmares

David did exactly as Cherelle had asked and sent everyone home the very next day. Eleanor had insisted on making her own arrangements, and she and Aunt Jessie left before the rest of the family. David was glad she was gone. He didn't need any more negative vibes. His only regret was that he'd had to call Deacon Lewis and tell him to cancel his trip down because Cherelle didn't want to see anyone. But he was willing to do whatever it took to help Cherelle feel comfortable and begin to heal.

Nelson and Keenen met with David and Cherelle to explain how the security team would handle the family's errands and visitors. The team came with their own set of rules, which made David feel as though some of the freedoms he'd been accustomed to enjoying were being stripped away. Having the assurance that his family was being protected was a blessing. But as a man who prided himself on being private, the thought of having someone around him twenty-four seven was exasperating. Gus wouldn't tell him how much it was costing.

He'd only said that people owed him favors and that the team was being well compensated.

Now that David had sent the family away, he and Cherelle were alone with the twins. David propped two pillows behind Cherelle's back as she bottle-fed Caleb and Chloe. Before she resumed breastfeeding her babies, she wanted to make sure her body was free of any traces of the drugs those monsters had injected into her.

Scooting in bed next to Cherelle, David admired her strength. It had only been two days since she'd been back, and she'd stepped back into her motherly duties as if nothing had happened. Like she hadn't been snatched out of his life for four of the most grueling days he'd ever lived through.

In his opinion, Cherelle was holding up well, evidently better than he was. He felt just a modicum of remorse for the way he'd spoken to Eleanor, but he meant every word he'd said. He would never let anyone, or anything, come between him and Cherelle ever again. Eleanor had to know that wasn't an option.

The heaviness of the last few days pressed David into a deep slumber. Hours later, he turned over in bed, and the spot where Cherelle had lain next to him with the twins was empty. He sat up against the headboard and tried to gather his faculties. The twins' bassinette was empty. The only sound in the room came from the crackling of the two-way, clear-glass fireplace in front of their bed.

Through the glass, David spotted Cherelle's slumped body in the soaking tub in the bathroom. He struggled out of bed, feeling as if he'd been drugged. Staggering toward the master bathroom, he called out to her. "Kit . . ." Cherelle's head hung limply with her chin pressed into her chest. David couldn't tell if she was breathing or not. In a panic, he thudded across the hardwood floor into the master bathroom. "Kit!" he yelled, shaking Cherelle. Water splashed onto his t-shirt and pajama bottoms, and the stone tile. Cherelle awakened and pulled out of David's grasp. "No . . . no . . . no!" she cried, fighting him.

"Babe, it's me. It's me, babe! Kit!"

Cherelle scanned the opulent bath, confirming her surroundings. She leaned back again and rested her head on the cushioned headrest of the soaking tub. "I'm tired, honey. I'm tired."

David nodded. "Okay . . . I'm here. Let's get you to bed."

* * *

DAVID SAT and cried before God, then passed out on the sofa in the family room on the first level. A clangorous shriek tore through the seven-bedroom estate. "No! Please don't! No! David, help me!" Cherelle screamed from upstairs. Catapulted out of his sleep, David popped up straight like a Jack-in-the-Box toy. It took only seconds for him to spring from the sofa. He bounded up the stairs two at a time.

"David, help! David! Don't let them do this! Please don't let them touch me!" Cherelle's voice was a screeching siren as she fought hard against her attackers. David! Nooo!" she screamed. A loud, horrific howl followed.

The piercing shriek caused a gripping tightness in David's chest. He squeezed his eyes shut repeatedly and tried to blink away the pain. He felt it throughout his entire being. He panted, ignoring it, and rushed to the bed where Cherelle bucked and kicked like a wild stallion. David was forced to approach her from behind and secure her arms. He grabbed her, and the howling continued. The godforsaken sounds caused his chest to cave.

"Kit! Kit! Wake up, babe! Kit!" David shouted. Holding Cherelle from behind, he pinned her arms across her chest with his left arm and held her head steady with his right hand to keep her from head-butting him. His shortness of breath caused him to feel dizzy. "God, I need You!" David shouted. Cherelle screamed and cried for minutes before the bucking slowed.

David continued to hold her body steady as her legs slowly transitioned from hard, rough kicks to gallops, to soft, sleep-kicks. David's tears came as he spoke hoarsely in Cherelle's ear. "Kit . . . I'm right here, babe. I'm right here. I've got you . . . you are safe with me, babe. I'm right here." His reassuring response turned into a chant that slowly brought peace to Cherelle's spirit. Without awakening, her body relaxed against his, and he held her, rocking her into a space where there was nothing but peace. David spread his fingers against Cherelle's soft, chocolate face and wiped the wetness. He let his tears fall into her hair and nuzzled his nose in the crook of her neck.

Then, in the darkness of the night, he let go of his failure, crying openly. Cherelle had fallen back to a peaceful sleep, but David was awake and tormented by his wife's screams for help. She had called for him while they'd assaulted her. She'd screamed for *him*. She'd pleaded for his help. He had been looking for her, praying for her safety. But he hadn't been there to protect her from those wicked monsters. How could they have defiled his rose? David contemplated with bitterness. His heart broke for the second time and disintegrated in his chest. He felt the burning heat of a stress headache pummel all his thoughts.

Caleb's cries echoed from down the hall. In usual fashion, Chloe's cries followed. David didn't want to leave Cherelle. He needed to be near her more than she probably needed the comfort of him. But the twins' cries would eventually wake her, and she needed to rest. Sleep was a well-deserved luxury that David didn't want to deny her.

He heard stirring in the house, and then a voice. "Pastor

Cole, I've returned. I thought you might need some more rest tonight. Chloe and Caleb are okay," Marie Everly, David's Tennessee housekeeper and cook, called out in her honey-laden southern drawl. She had been working for David since he purchased the Escape years ago.

Highly recommended to him by his realtor at the time, Marie kept the home cleaned, dusted, and stocked with food in preparation for his visits to Tennessee. She also served as his unofficial property manager while he was away in Michigan. David hadn't had to do much convincing to get her to agree to act as his and Cherelle's part-time nanny. Marie loved babies. Having been a domestic worker for over thirty years, she had cared for plenty of children, despite not having any of her own.

David thanked God for Marie; he hadn't even heard her enter the house, nor did he know how long she'd been there. But she was right on time. He pictured her face, the color of cocoa, and her round body, moving around in the twins' nursery, calming them with hymns as she scooped them into her arms. She was around the same age as his mother, and she showered love on his babies like a grandmother would.

But right now, David relished the feeling of holding Cherelle in his arms. And he never wanted to let her go again. If he could, he would spend his last breath right next to her. His heart couldn't have been more filled with her than it was. Like a never-ending waterfall, it overflowed with his love for her.

Chapter 24

Truth

The banquet room of Disciples of Christ Ministries was decked out extravagantly with blue and silver tulle that crisscrossed and swooped from point to point on the ceiling. Beautiful glass centerpieces filled with silver branches and all manner of blue flowers decorated each table, surrounded by tea-light candles. David's heart swelled with gratitude and pride. He scanned the room and appreciated all the faithful members who had worked so hard to make DOC's tenth-anniversary celebration a success. He sneaked glances at his cell phone periodically to ensure he didn't miss any texts from Cherelle.

He struggled with a tinge of guilt for leaving her alone so soon. But this was the church's anniversary celebration; he needed to be here for his congregation. This was a celebration of God's faithfulness to DOC. David had drilled that into the heads of all the committee members. It was a night to celebrate the goodness God had shown them. For that reason, there was no way he could cancel or not be present. Nelson and Keenen were protecting Cherelle, and Gus was also there to make Cherelle feel more comfortable while David was away.

As David moved about, greeting members of his congregation, he had the distinct feeling that someone—more than likely Pastor Clint—had cautioned the members not to ask him anything about Cherelle. A few members told him they were lifting him and his family in prayer, but that had been the extent of the conversation concerning Cherelle. That in itself was rare, considering the fact that he was in a church full of inquisitive young adults.

David had penned a loving message on the church's website and all his social media accounts, letting the congregation know that Cherelle was home safe and thanking them for their prayers. He couldn't wait to get back to her this evening. He felt an ache just being away from her for a few hours, even though he knew she was tucked away safely. Gus insisted that David and his family retain the six-man security team until he felt it was no longer necessary. David had no idea when that would be, but with Gus's background, he trusted him implicitly. Aaron and Gabriel were assigned to Leah and Joseph, while Julius and Kedar stayed close to David without drawing too much attention. They'd been discreet all evening, allowing David to interact with his church members but not venturing too far away from him.

David had simply introduced them as friends. Julius seemed to be the more sociable of the two. He fell into easy small talk with all the people who approached David during the evening. He even smiled when some of the attendees commented that he and David resembled one another. The two shared the same honey-brown complexion, dark-colored eyes, and the same strong jawline. Observant and dutiful, Julius managed to do his job with pleasantness.

Kedar, on the other hand, would never in his life win a

social butterfly award. David discerned that being sociable wasn't one of Kedar's strengths. The man barely spoke, and when he did, it was in short messages and codes. Even when the gorgeous likes of Lailah Augustus, one of the attorneys for the church's scholarship foundation, approached the table to greet David, Kedar didn't warm up one iota. He shook her hand perfunctorily, but never flashed a tooth, let alone a smile.

He was as rigid as a sentinel on duty. Kedar didn't seem to notice Lailah's café au lait skin, amber eyes, and curvy figure. And if he did notice, David couldn't tell. Most of the time, after meeting Lailah, men usually asked David a million questions about her, including if he would be willing to put in a good word on their behalf. Lailah was quite the looker, but Kedar Kennedy was strictly business. David expected nothing less from anyone Gus dealt with.

After many accolades and a feast of prime rib, stuffed mushrooms, and loaded potatoes, DOC's anniversary celebration came to a close. As usual, David was one of the last people to leave the church. As soon as he could make it back to his office to change out of his tux into a tracksuit, he would head to the airport where Maverick was waiting to fly him and his two-man security crew back to Tennessee. David texted Cherelle; he didn't get a response back, so he phoned Gus.

"Hey, bro, what's happening? How's Kit? And how are my babies doing?" David asked.

"Cherelle is asleep. She fed Chloe and Caleb about a half-hour ago. And both of them are in their swings right now listening to Mozart and watching their godfather bake a German chocolate cake for their mommy—actually, the cake is done. I'm making the icing."

David ignored Gus's ribbing about baking a cake for his wife. He'd punch him later in person. "Did Kit eat dinner?"

"Yep. And she had seconds. I made crab cakes, grilled asparagus, and shrimp pasta."

"That's good. She needs to eat. She's been picking over stuff for the last few days."

"Well, she ate pretty well tonight, and all is quiet around here. How'd the anniversary banquet go?"

"It was beautiful, man. The love in the room for Christ, and for me and my family, was just mind-blowing. The Lord never ceases to amaze me," David said.

"Sounds good. I have to leave tomorrow for business. You'll be in good hands with the guys."

"Okay, bet. Thanks, bro. For everything."

"Nah. Don't thank me. This is family," Gus said.

David nodded. Gus was right. They were family. "I'm getting ready to get out of here. I'll check back in before take-off, and again when we're on our way to the house."

"Alright."

David looked up and saw Mother Ludlow approaching him. She wiped her hands on her apron. She must have been supervising in the kitchen all evening, right down to the clean-up. She was a faithful member who worked tirelessly in the Lord's house. Her plump body strolled toward him, carrying something in her hands, as she strutted on her eighty-four-year-old legs. Julius and Kedar took a relaxed stance.

"Pastor Cole, I wanted to bless you with this salve I made. Well, it's for First Lady. It heals all manner of wounds, Pastor. And it'll get rid of scars too. I made it so it would be sweet-smelling, 'cause I know First Lady loves garden scents. The Lord put it on my heart to make this especially for her."

"Yes, ma'am. Thank you so much. We really appreciate it," David said, taking the jar from Mother Ludlow's aged hands that were both strong and weathered, with seasons of wrinkles.

David hugged her and allowed himself to rest in the hug as if he were hugging his long-deceased Grandma Rose.

"God's gonna make everything alright, Pastor," Mother Ludlow said when the two pulled apart. She held David's hand.

"I know," David said. As far as he was concerned, everything was already alright. Cherelle was home. The wounds and scars Cherelle had were all emotional. He wished the salve could miraculously heal those wounds.

* * *

STEPPING out into the whipping cold of the Michigan winter, David felt the below-zero, stinging wind chill at the same time as he noticed Dominique walking towards him at a furious pace. She was toting something. Kedar and Julius had already drawn their weapons. "Stop. Right. There," Kedar warned. David had a feeling Kedar wasn't one to repeat himself without engaging in swift retaliation.

"Put your guns down!" Dominique shouted, shifting the bundle on her hip that was covered with two blankets. She shielded the bundle with her arm. Kedar and Julius did no such thing. "Dave! Tell them to stop aiming at my baby!"

The guns were aimed at Dominique, not the bundle she was carrying. David bit his lip to keep from swearing. He stretched his arm out and lowered it, signaling to Kedar and Julius. They only complied after scanning the area thoroughly. David stepped away from the two and closed the space between him and Dominique. He lit into her right away. No more playing nice. "Woman, I have asked you to stay away from this edifice and from me and my wife! I don't have the time nor the patience to keep dealing with your calls, your texts, this crap right here—you showing up here—none of it!"

Frost floated from Dominique's lips. "Can we go somewhere out of this cold and talk, Dave? Just for a few minutes? Please?"

Veins sprouted on David's forehead. "No!" David roared. "There's nothing to talk about. I have nothing to say to you. Just go!" David pivoted, walking toward the car that was waiting to take him to the airport. He had to get home to his wife and children. Kedar opened the door of the sedan for David.

"This is your son! This is your *son*, Dave!"

David snapped around. "You're a liar! You *killed* my baby!"

Dominique's voice splintered as she walked closer to David. "No, I didn't, Dave! I couldn't. Don't you remember that day you called for me after your accident? I came to your home, and you asked me about the baby—"

"And you said, 'No—no baby'!"

"I never *said* I had an abortion, Dave! You assumed that I'd had an abortion, and you went crazy, yelling and knocking things over! I only led you to believe that because I was scared and confused. I didn't know what I was going to do. I was being hounded by the press almost every day. And I didn't know what Brent was going to do to me. And you were in no position to protect me! I had to protect my baby!"

Brent King, Dominique's disgruntled former lover and ex-narcotics officer, had ordered a hit on her two years ago. He had nearly killed David in the process. David was immediately overcome with a sudden headache that was ten thousand times more painful than his worst head trauma headache. His anger was so fierce that he could no longer feel the freezing temperature.

"Dominique, you are the biggest liar! What are you trying to do? What do you want from me?!"

"Dave, I'm trying to tell you that you have a son—this is your son," Dominique said, clutching the bundle. "Did you even look at me that day? Don't you remember I never took my coat off? I was four months pregnant with our son. I wore an oversized sweater and a coat. Even though I was hardly showing, I knew you'd be able to tell if I had taken my coat off. I moved away to Chicago to have my baby in peace after all that had happened. If you get us out of this cold, I will show you that he's yours," Dominique said, struggling to swallow. "You can do a DNA test. You can do whatever you want. This is *your* son, Dave . . ."

David's memory wasn't what it used to be because of the shooting, but now he remembered that day. He recalled that afternoon, Dominique's petite frame looked curvier than he remembered—even with her coat on, her face was fuller. Her skin glowed just like Cherelle's when she was *pregnant*. A sickening, suffocating heat pulsed through David.

"Come on," David relented. He motioned to Dominique. "Get in."

Kedar opened the back door of the sedan, and Dominique and David scooted inside. Kedar shut the door behind them before taking his place in the passenger seat. Julius was already behind the wheel.

"Can we have some privacy?" David asked.

Kedar turned to face David. "No. Under no circumstances," he said with no expression at all. He checked the rearview and the side view mirrors methodically.

"I need some privacy. Can you two just step out of the car for a moment?" David asked.

Kedar twisted his body and turned to David again. "No. Those are our orders from Mr. Merrick."

Dominique ignored their conversation and removed the blankets that were covering the child. "There you are, sweetie. Were you getting too hot?" Dominique cooed at the child. Groggy, the child mumbled something as he opened his heavy eyelids before they closed right back. Dominique untied the hood string on the child's navy blue snowsuit and slid off the hood. She removed a small red knit hat that had a fireman's symbol on it. Then she unzipped his snowsuit. David watched how lovingly Dominique did those mundane tasks in such a motherly way, and he was reminded of Cherelle.

"How old is he?"

"Twenty-two months—he'll be two on March twenty-fourth. Do the math, Dave. I wouldn't lie to you about something like this. Here . . ." Dominique said, handing the child to David. He bore the same caramel-colored skin as David's, and he shared David's jet-black features and coarse, curly hair. He looked like David.

"Hey, how are you doing, little guy?" David asked, placing the child on his right thigh, supporting the weight of his little body with his arm. The groggy, handsome little boy was limp in David's arms. His eyes fluttered open and then closed.

"Do you know who that is?" Dominique asked the toddler.

The child's head turned slowly from David to Dominique at the sound of her voice. His eyes fluttered open again. He looked back and forth between the two before he returned to his sleep.

"That's your father. You know that?"

"I don't trust you, Dominique," David said flatly. "And you know why. What is it that you really want, huh? This just seems so unreal. What reason would you have to wait until *after* I'm married to tell me this—if it's true? And how could I ever trust you enough to believe *anything* you say?"

"Dave, what *reason* would I have to lie to you about something like this when you can just do a paternity test?"

Sweat beaded on David's forehead and neck. None of this could be true. But if any of it was, it would turn his world upside down. The first thing that came to his mind was

Cherelle. He couldn't hurt her now with this. She was too fragile. He was too fragile. The mention of having a paternity test and the outcome validating that the child he was holding was his made David's gut churn, and his equilibrium spin out of control. He touched the window button and cracked it just a tinge to avoid putting too much cold air on the child. His cell phone rang. He knew from the ringtone that it was Cherelle. He shifted the child to his other thigh, unclipped his phone from his belt, and answered it. "Hey, babe. Are you okay? Gus said you were sleeping."

Dominique watched David's stiff disposition soften. There was a marked change in his tone; it was tender and honey-dipped. Unlike the way he'd been talking to her.

"I smelled something baking. It woke me up," Cherelle mumbled robotically.

"I'm not surprised. Gus is over there pouring on the charm, cooking all your favorite stuff," David kidded.

"I think he's trying to take good care of me because you're not here."

David smiled. "I know. He better. I'll be home in a few hours. Are you getting enough rest?"

Cherelle sounded like she was drained of all her energy. "Yes. Just wanted to get a piece of cake."

"Do you need me to get anything for you on my way home? Some Reese's Pieces? Ice cream?" David asked.

"No. Gus brought both with him. I'm gonna go back to bed while the twins are occupied with Gus. See you soon, honey."

"Okay. I love you, babe," David said, staring at the sleeping child that might very well be his son.

"Love you too. Be safe," Cherelle returned.

"Will do."

Dominique had turned sullen. "I wanted you to know that you had a son. What you do with that information is up to you,

Dave. We've got to go," she said, reaching for the child. She cuddled the child and kissed his cheek tenderly. David watched Dominique with a discerning eye as she put the child's hat and snowsuit on again. He studied her body language and her breathing. He wondered what she was thinking. Then it dawned on him that if this child was his, he had unknowingly been neglecting him emotionally and financially for almost two years. The thought left him feeling disgusted.

"Can I send you some money electronically until we get everything straightened out?"

"I didn't come for your money, Dave. We'll be fine. I just wanted you to know . . ."

"Please, just let me do something. I feel like I need to do something. I wish you hadn't done this—waited to tell me this, Dominique."

"Dave, I did what I had to do to protect *him*. I'm coming to you now because it's the right thing to do. I basically grew up without my father. He wasn't there for me when I needed him most. I didn't want the same for our son. Let me know when and where you want to do the paternity test, and we'll be there."

She handed David a business card that read: *ACE Tactical Training. Proprietor: Anthony Street.* It had a Chicago address and phone number. "This is where I'm staying. It's my dad's place. We reconnected after everything happened here, and he's been helping us out. My cell number is on the back," Dominique said. She reached for the door handle, and David opened it. He got out first so that he could assist her. Dominique handed the child to him before she stepped out into the cold herself. Kedar exited the car as well, but put a little distance between himself and them.

"Where are you parked?" David asked.

"I'm right over there," Dominique said, gesturing with her

head. David walked by her side, still holding the child snugly. Dominique reached the midnight blue Lexus SUV and took the child from David. She opened the back passenger door and removed the blankets from the child's head. David stood there as she bent over and buckled the child into his car seat. She tugged the straps to make sure the child was secure. Then she stood to face David again. Her eyes were brimming with tears. David followed Dominique around to the driver's side and opened the door for her.

"I'll be in touch," he said.

Dominique nodded instead of a verbal response. She hated for David to see her broken. She got in and started the engine with a push of a button, looking straight ahead. David turned away, then turned back suddenly.

"Hey!" David said, causing Dominique to lower her window. "What's his name?"

"*David* Anthony Street."

Chapter 25

Pieces

David and his two man security crew arrived at the large iron gate that led to his gated Tennessee estate at three a.m. Nelson was staked out near the entrance. Julius signaled to him that everything was okay by flashing the car's bright lights before opening the gate with the remote.

"I don't want Gus to know what you overheard tonight. I need time to talk to my wife first—when I think she can handle it. She's been through hell already," David said when Julius pulled into the circular driveway. He was sure the security team knew most of the details regarding Cherelle's abduction and rescue. Every major news station in the country had been reporting about the ordeal.

"We get paid to protect you, not report on you," Kedar said flatly, but an outpouring of understanding was in his eyes.

David went inside and spoke with Gus briefly before going upstairs to shower. He kissed Chloe and Caleb, who were sleeping in their bassinet without a care in the world. Then he slid into bed. He kissed Cherelle on the cheek, and she mumbled "Good night" before drifting back to sleep. David contemplated how David Anthony would change all their lives.

* * *

WHEN DAVID AWAKENED LATE the next morning, Cherelle was feeding the twins. He must have been sleeping like a log. Gus was gone, and Marie was back. He lay in bed with Cherelle and the twins for a while, then went downstairs to his office to pray. He needed time to sit in God's presence and release everything that was weighing him down. Checking his cell phone, he saw a string of pictures from a number he didn't recognize initially. They were all photos of little David Anthony. Special moments in his life, beginning with the day he was born. The sparkle in Dominique's eyes in some of the photos told a different story of the woman David knew all too well, yet not at all. In the photos, Dominique appeared soft and motherly. Loving. Goofy. David Anthony had changed her.

David sighed and nursed his cup of coffee. He knew he needed to sit down with Cherelle and tell her he had another child. He couldn't think of any reasons why Dominique would lie about something that could be proven so easily. It had to be true. But now wasn't the time to break Cherelle's heart. And knowing that he had fathered a child with Dominique would surely suck the remaining life out of her. David couldn't do that to his wife right now. He'd take a paternity test first, so at least he could present Cherelle with the facts before engaging in all the necessary conversations about joint custody and visitation schedules.

David pushed away from his live-edge, wood slab desk, and kneeled and prayed. He found it hard to concentrate on anything except the child who was about to change his and Cherelle's lives. He cursed the very day he'd ever laid eyes on

Dominique Antoinette Street. She'd brought nothing but chaos to his life. First the shooting, and now this. The sin of falling sexually with her was still strangling his life. But it wasn't David Anthony's fault. He was as much David's as Chloe and Caleb were. David's heart had already yielded to the strong possibility that he was the child's father. His heart had already opened to loving him.

David contacted a DNA testing lab in the Tennessee area. He needed a place that would operate with absolute discretion. Someplace where he wouldn't have to worry about anything getting out to the press or anyone else before he had a chance to talk with Cherelle. He set up an appointment for two days away. He planned to call Dominique with instructions soon. He had a nagging feeling that he should sit down and talk to Cherelle about the situation today, but he dismissed it. They needed time. He especially needed time to figure it all out. When he sat for longer than he should have, he finally phoned Dominique.

"Hey, Dave," Dominique greeted on what seemed like the first ring. Perhaps she'd been waiting for his call.

"Hey ... um ... I—"

"Dave, I'm sorry," Dominique interrupted. "I'm really sorry that I'm dumping all this on you after what you've just been through. And I am sincerely happy that your wife is back home safe. I don't want you to think that I'm just insensitive to everything that's been going on with you and your family, you know. I—I just didn't know when the right time would be. I tried to get in contact with you several times. I wanted us to sit down and talk this through. I didn't want to just spring it on you the way I did. My life is different now. I'm not the same woman."

"You know how I feel about life, Dominique. When something happens that you're not prepared for, you just have to deal with it and move forward. I want to be a good father to my son and provide everything that he's entitled to. No different than the twins."

"I don't want to go through court or anything like that, Dave. I've been keeping a low profile for a reason. I want DA—that's what I call David Anthony—to be safe. I'm not asking you for anything. This is not about money for me. I want you to understand that."

"Dominique, what do you guys need?"

"Right now, we're okay, Dave. Really."

"What do you mean by *right now?*

"Well, as you probably read in the papers, after everything happened, I resigned from the force. I had a nice little stash in my 401K, so we've been kinda making it off that. The only thing that's been a burden is our medical bills. But like I said, we're good for now. I plan to start working with my dad soon. DA and I have been living at my dad's place. It's a converted loft warehouse. There are three other loft apartments in the building and a few small businesses, but my dad's place has a secure private entrance. He's no longer a police officer; he now owns a tactical training company, and he's been dabbling in real estate with his girlfriend for the past few years. He seems to be doing quite well for himself, and we're getting to know each other again. He's been a great help to DA and me."

David took in everything Dominique said. As far as he was concerned, having to live with someone else put her and his son in a vulnerable position if there were ever a disagreement of some sort. If she were financially solvent, she would have a place for herself and their child. "Dominique, I will reimburse you for all your medical bills and any doctor appointments. I'll text you one of my email addresses. Just copy everything, scan it, and email the bills to me. After we've done the paternity test, I can add David Anthony to my health insurance. That should take a huge burden off you financially. What about a nanny or someone to give you a break sometimes?"

Dominique chuckled. "A nanny? That's not something that has ever crossed my mind, Dave."

"Well, there's no harm in getting a little help. I'm not talking about a situation where someone else is raising my son; I'm talking about giving you a break to do some adulting."

"I have a babysitter I use sometimes. I found her through an online service, and I did an extensive background check. She's a young college student. But honestly, I haven't been out that much without DA. My dad chips in when it's conducive to his schedule," Dominique said.

"Well, look into getting someone to help out. And let me know. I'll take care of it. What about rent? Is your father charging you something?"

"No. Dad's not charging me right now. He understands my situation. He's letting me get back on my feet. But I've been taking care of the utilities here."

David calculated numbers in his head. "Okay . . . um . . . why don't you give me your bank account info so I can do a wire transfer today. I'm texting you all the info I need from you right now."

"I got it," Dominique said after a few moments.

"Have you set up a college fund for him yet?" David asked, opening a file on his computer.

"To tell you the truth, Dave, we've just been living. I know it's something I need to do soon, but my money has been channeled to our day-to-day stuff."

"I'll get one started right away. I have Chloe and Caleb's college fund set up through a stock account. I control it myself. I'll add DA," David said. He was being practical. Doing what he did best. He was a problem solver. He couldn't get stuck on the what-ifs.

"Dave, I don't want you doing all this out of guilt. And I'd rather you wait until we do a DNA test so that you can feel comfortable and confident that DA is yours. I know he's yours, but I want you to have the proof before you start investing money and time. I'm okay. I can take care of him. I've been doing it by myself all this time," Dominique said.

"That was your *choice*, Dominique," David scolded. "You deprived him of his father, and you deprived me of my son—for whatever reason. You took something away from both of us."

Dominique humbled herself. "Dave, I apologize. I wasn't implying anything or accusing you of not being present. You're right."

"Whatever is done is done. Let's move forward. I made the appointment for the DNA test. I hope you can exercise discretion until everything is complete."

Dominique bit her tongue to keep from saying what she wanted to say. Besides, David was being more than gracious, considering the circumstances. "I have no problem with that," she said. One thing Dominique knew about David Kent Cole was that he was a man of integrity. He would always do the right thing. She expected nothing less of him.

"I have charter plane service through a company a friend of mine owns. He will fly you guys to Tennessee for the DNA test and back to Chicago," David said. He refrained from telling Dominique that he and his family were living in Tennessee for the time being. "Transportation to and from the airport and the facility has already been taken care of. I'll send you the details short—ly."

David heard a light rap on his office door. "Honey . . . we need some things . . ." Cherelle said through the door, stopping David mid-sentence. She rarely disturbed him when he was in his office with the door closed because she assumed that he was either studying or praying.

"Come on in, babe," David said.

Cherelle zombie-shuffled into the room. Her pajama top was soiled with milk, and her uncombed hair was pulled back into a messy ponytail. She hadn't taken any interest in self-care since she'd been home. She spoke hesitantly. "I'm sorry. I didn't know you were on the phone—I didn't know you were busy," she apologized distantly.

"I'm never too busy for you, you know that," David said lovingly. "What can I do for you, my queen?" he asked.

"We need more diapers and formula," she said.

"Okay. I got it. Anything else, babe?" David asked. He looked her over and decided he would have Marie braid her hair and maybe have a nail tech come to the house to give her a manicure and pedicure to make her feel special.

"No."

"Okay. Let me wrap up this call, and I'll take care of it, babe."

Cherelle nodded and shuffled back out. The monsters had robbed her of all vibrancy. David felt the twisting of a knife in his heart. He turned his attention back to Dominique, realizing he'd been rude by not asking her to hold on while he spoke to Cherelle. "Excuse me, I'm sorry about that," he apologized to Dominique.

"Oh, no problem. I expect to get put on hold for 'the queen,'" Dominique blurted before she could catch herself.

David didn't miss the jab, and he quickly moved to nip the animosity in the bud. "Dominique, let me set you straight right now with your little sarcastic remark. If you want us to stay civil as we raise DA, I suggest that you keep any unflattering remarks about my *wife* to yourself. Cherelle is my wife, and I honor her. And you and everyone else around me will respect her. I'll forward you the transportation details, and I'll see you and DA on Friday," David said before pressing the end-call button. It was better to just walk away from a confrontation or anything else that was going to pull him out of his square. He had enough to deal with right now, and his main priority was taking care of Cherelle.

He was aware that he could easily go from zero to sixty in two seconds when it came to Cherelle and his kids, especially after all that had transpired. He knew that Dominique wasn't going to make life smooth for him and Cherelle. That one snide comment she'd just made let him know that it would be a bumpy road for the next eighteen years or so. He was convinced that Dominique was pleased about disrupting his life and tearing his little fairytale story to pieces. He had a feeling she was just getting started, like the pulling back of the ocean before a tsunami. But he would never view David Anthony as a burden. He was his son. He was a Cole. And David loved him already.

Tell Cherelle.

David heard the imperative again and brushed it aside. He couldn't tell her right now.

Chapter 26

Now

David held the paternity test results, pinched between his fingers. He stared at the page until his eyes blurred. There was a ninety-nine point nine-nine percent chance that David Anthony Street was his son. As shattering as the thought was, he had prepared himself for this revelation. Dominique had been right about one thing: it made no sense to lie to him about being David Anthony's father when all he had to do was get a paternity test. And now the results confirmed everything David expected and everything he feared in the same breath. It wasn't difficult to love his child and be a real father to his child, but it was difficult to hurt the woman he loved.

He dreaded the day he'd have to tell Cherelle that the past he thought he'd put behind him was no longer his past. It was his present and his future. Like a curse, he, Cherelle, and Dominique would be inextricably linked because of David Anthony, and it would leave a scar on Cherelle's heart. Yes, David knew Cherelle would love David Anthony like he was hers. She was that kind of woman. But having Dominique in their lives for any length of time would leave a bitter stain on their fairy tale.

Holding Caleb in his arms, feeding him, David couldn't help but think of David Anthony; he'd missed nearly two years of his life. He'd missed holding and loving David Anthony the way he was holding Caleb right now. He'd missed being one of the first persons to welcome David Anthony into the world and pray over him. Now, he had to make up for lost time.

He would do things right. Little David Anthony would know that no matter what his family situation was, he was loved by his father beyond measure and that his life was a blessing despite the situation surrounding his birth. David would make sure that his oldest son grew up with confidence and security in the knowledge that he loved him. He would do all he could to include him in the family he'd built with Cherelle.

David stood and shifted Caleb from the cradle of his arms to his chest. He patted Caleb's back lightly, coaxing a tiny burp from him. "Good job, man," David said, rubbing soothing circles on Caleb's back. He kissed Caleb's sweet face as he stared out the window into his future. He'd call Dominique and start visits with David Anthony right away.

* * *

Today, Keenen and Aaron served as security for David. Aaron drove, and Keenen watched. After Aaron circled the block a few times and Keenen had thoroughly surveyed the area, Aaron pulled the SUV into the nearest parking space in front of a warehouse loft in downtown Chicago as David sat in the back-seat, struggling with a somersaulting stomach. He'd spoken on stages all over the country and had been in the presence of presidents and numerous dignitaries, but none of those events had prepared him for his first real encounter with his nearly two-year-old son. David let out a sigh that sounded more like a grunt.

"You good back there?" Keenen asked without taking his eyes off a young man with shoulder-length locs, who was walking nearby, toting a brown leather backpack. The young man appeared to be scouting the surroundings as well.

David hesitated. "Uh. . . yeah . . . I think I'm good."

"Think?" Keenen asked, turning to face David. In the short time he'd been serving as part of David's security detail, he'd never known David to be uncertain of anything. David was quite the opposite. Always definitive. Always planning meticulously, possessing an air of confidence that few men did.

David flicked his wrist and glanced at his watch. They were half an hour early. "I need another cup of coffee," he said.

Aaron hid a smile as he maneuvered out of the parking spot and headed to where he'd spotted a coffee shop a few blocks away. Magic potion in hand, David drank slowly and relaxed his shoulders. That one cup of straight black coffee cut his nerves instantly and filled him with calm. Aaron exited the vehicle and met Dominique at the private entrance of the converted work-live warehouse. They took the private elevator up to the penthouse loft.

The team had already gone over procedures with David; Aaron would go in to scout and make sure the place was secure, while David remained with Keenen until Aaron gave the okay. Then Keenen would remain inside with David throughout the visit. That was the part David didn't agree with. Cherelle's abduction had upended their lives significantly. Moving forward, they had to handle their lives differently, with the caution that came from knowing that someone could be waiting to harm them at any time. Gus's little security team was a large part of that 'differently.' Though necessary for his safety and the safety of his family, David hated the intrusiveness of it all. He was never left alone without a "handler," as he jokingly called them, unless he was at home. Those were their orders. They weren't budging, and Gus wasn't budging.

* * *

Dominique, David, David Anthony, and Keenen rode the private elevator to the penthouse loft. Dominique took the liberty of introducing David Anthony to their guests.

"DA, this is David, your father, and this is Mr. Keenen, his friend. Say hi," she said.

David Anthony clung to Dominique as he rested on her hip, but he did extend a cordial salutation. "Hi," he said softly, waving his small hand at David and Keenen.

"Are you afraid?" Dominique asked David Anthony, but it was she who was nervous.

David Anthony shook his head from side to side, but he didn't release his hold on Dominique. He eyed David and Keenen with curiosity and apprehension.

"Hello. How are you doing? It's nice to meet you, DA," David said.

"It sure is," Keenen agreed and smiled. Cognizant of the fact that his height and stature were intimidating, he attempted to be as friendly as possible to put little David Anthony at ease. David Anthony mumbled something inaudible into Dominique's shoulder. The elevator stopped and opened right into the foyer area of the penthouse loft. A myriad of original artworks hung on the exposed brick gallery wall and served as the focal point for the main entrance.

The high-end pad was not what David expected of a woman who claimed to be struggling with money. He looked around observantly, noting everything. It had a three-story open floor plan with a gourmet kitchen that contained wall-to-wall marble and high-end appliances. Both the living room and dining room areas were lavishly decorated with furniture that looked as if it had been custom-made.

Various art pieces accented the sofa and end tables, and some were set strategically in a few museum-like pedestal display cases. David knew from experience that a glamorous, polished look like this was the work of an interior design company. He had been in quite a few luxuriously impressive homes and hotels in his life, and this place was near the top of the list for its level of grandeur.

"This is a pretty nice place," David said. He wondered if Dominique had lied about "getting by" and the medical bills and everything else she'd told him. It was impossible to fully trust a woman like her. Not that it mattered. It was his responsibility to provide for his son. David Anthony was his, and he had a right to the same standard of living as the twins.

"I'm sure my dad would thank you. This entire building belongs to him. He got it for a steal during the recession, and he's since been able to add lots of value with renovations that have brought in a few commercial tenants. Let's sit in the living room area," Dominique said, directing David. Keenen looked toward the kitchen, where there was a breakfast/dining room area.

"If it's okay, I'll sit over here," Keenen said to Dominique.

"Sure. That'll be fine," Dominique responded. And Keenen slipped away to the spot he'd chosen for himself, allowing David some space.

"Hey, guy. You're getting heavy. Mommy's gonna have to put you down, okay?" Dominique said to David Anthony.

David Anthony nodded, and Dominique placed him on his feet. "I pway wit toys," he said. It was a question.

"You sure can, but remember, you have company. David came to see *you*."

"Yep," David nodded. "And I brought you a couple of things," he said, almost forgetting the large tote bag he was holding.

David Anthony's eyes brightened. "You have toys?"

"I sure do," David said. He took off his jacket and placed the tote on the floor. He bent down and pulled out a fire engine and a few large toddler-friendly cardboard books, one happened to have a fireman on the cover.

David Anthony went straight for the firetruck. "fiwer truck, Mommy!"

"Nice! You can add that to your ever-growing collection," Dominique said, chuckling. She gave him a big approving smile before saying, "What do you say when someone gives you something, DA?"

David Anthony took his eyes off the truck for a second and turned to David. "Thankchu," he said.

"You are very welcome. Do you mind if I play with you?" David asked.

"Yes! Fiwer trucks!" David Anthony exclaimed before running over to his play area, which was littered with toys. The space was set off in a corner with a huge window. It was David Anthony's own little spot in the loft.

Amazed, David said, "Wow. He seems to know a lot of words for an almost two-year-old, and he speaks so clearly," David said to Dominique as they followed David Anthony to the play area.

"Yes, he knows a lot of words for his age. Too many some days. He can get on a roll and will talk you to death," Dominique laughed. "I read to him a lot. And we watch educational shows once a day for about an hour. He's pretty smart."

"You've done an awesome job," David said. It was hard to

remain angry with her. His son was healthy, energetic, and seemingly advanced for a child his age. And David could tell that the handsome tyke was kind by the way he responded to his request to play with him.

David got on his knees and indulged David Anthony in play. The two became fast friends. While Dominique prepared lunch, the two Davids played together as if they'd already known each other. Then David read the fire truck book to David Anthony just before it was time for his daily nap.

Dominique reentered the living room after having placed David Anthony in his fire engine bed on the third level of the penthouse. David had fallen into a light nod. With his head lying on the back of the sofa cushion, and his mouth wide open, he snored.

"I see you're just as whipped as DA," Dominique said.

The sound of her voice woke David out of his nap. He shook off the sleepy dust and sat up straight. "I think he wore me out," David said, yawning.

"Yes, a twenty-two-month-old with a ton of energy and an inquisitive mind will do it every time."

"How long does he usually nap?"

"I only let him sleep an hour and a half, so it doesn't interfere with him going to sleep at bedtime, which is at eight o'clock. We have a very regimented life."

"That's good," David said.

"You must be missing out on a lot of sleep these days, Dave. Two newborns? I can't imagine," Dominique said as the two slipped into an easygoing conversation.

David smiled at the thought. "Sleep is a precious commodity that I don't get a lot of these days, but the three gifts God has given me in the form of my children are more precious than sleep. I am blessed to be a father three times over, so I won't complain. I have everything I need—a beautiful wife and three kids. I couldn't ask for more."

Dominique went silent. She paused from folding David Anthony's laundry for a split second. Her easy-going conversation with David had come to a complete halt at the mention of Cherelle.

David changed the topic of discussion. "So, your father has a real estate business and a tactical training business?"

"Yes. This is his official residence. But he spends most of his time at Nanette's place. Nanette Crowley is his girlfriend," Dominique explained. "She's a big-time real estate agent. He practically lives with her. And you think this place is nice? Nanette's place is unbelievable. She has a penthouse loft in the West Loop area. DA and I being here really isn't inconveniencing my dad. He told me he was hardly ever here anyway."

"I'm glad that he helped you out. My son is somewhere safe, and he's being well taken care of. That means a lot to me."

Dominque stared at David with an unreadable expression. "Is there something on your mind?" David asked sincerely.

"No," Dominique said. But there was plenty on her mind, and it was best that she didn't speak on any of it right now.

David hoped he hadn't overstayed his welcome. But he at least wanted to stay until David Anthony was up from his nap. He wanted to say goodbye to him before he headed back to Tennessee.

"Listen, I don't want to overstay my welcome or prevent you from doing anything you had planned to do. I was hoping to spend a little more time with my son before I have to head back home."

Again, an unreadable expression was fixed on Dominique's face. Then, as if she realized it, she smiled humbly. "Dave, it's fine. Really. Spend as much time as you like with DA. I didn't make any plans today because I expected you to be here. And

I'm glad that you're here," Dominique said with a distinct softness. "He needs a father in his life. That's important to me."

"Thank you. It's important for me to be in his life and spend real quality time with him. My schedule is still hectic, but I want him to know that I will always make time for him, no matter what."

"I know you will, Dave."

David was sure Dominique spoke from a place of sincerity and appreciativeness; it was evident in the way her eyes met his. Maybe she *had* changed.

Chapter 27

Laughter

The sound of David Anthony's fun-filled screeches and laughter caused David to relax and forget about everything else but enjoying time with his son. He was having way more fun than David Anthony as the two played in a ball pit at a local Chuck E. Cheese pizza eatery with a kids' play area and games. Surprised that David had climbed into the pit, Dominique snapped pictures of him and David Anthony with her cell phone and let them have their time together. The establishment was fairly empty because it was an early morning weekday. Kedar and Julius were David's handlers today. Dominique had forgotten they were there until she spotted Kedar speaking with one of the employees. There were only three other families there. All three had small children around DA's age. Dominique felt guilty that DA wasn't around other children regularly.

She watched David interact with David Anthony, and another side of the man she once loved revealed itself. It was a wonderful, admirable side. During the time they'd dated, she'd never seen David interact with small children. However, he had told her on several occasions that he looked forward to becoming a father one day. He had seemed downright giddy about the prospect of having children. Even when she had first told him she was pregnant on that fateful night, he jumped right into father mode. He'd wanted her to keep the baby. He'd wanted to be a father.

Judging by the way he lost himself so completely while playing with David Anthony, Dominique concluded that David was the perfect father. She had always known he would be. Recognizing the nurturing way he played with David Anthony and engaged him in conversations as if he were a seven-year-old, instead of a two-year-old, Dominique knew David was meant for fatherhood. It came naturally to him. No one would have known that he'd met his son just two months ago. It was like David had always been in David Anthony's life.

Dominique placed a large, number-two-shaped candle on top of the cake she'd had specially made for David Anthony. It was decorated with an image of a fire engine and a fireman's hat with his name on it. She lit the candle and smiled proudly. David Anthony would love his birthday cake.

"Ticks, Mommy! Ticks!" David Anthony shouted as he ran toward Dominique with a long string of tickets in his hand that David had won playing various games. David trailed behind him, holding the end of the ticket string so that David Anthony wouldn't trip and fall over them.

Dominique turned away from the cake. "Wow! Good job!" she encouraged. "You guys have a billion tickets. You should be able to get a nice prize with those."

"Fiwer cake!" David Anthony beamed when he caught a glimpse of his birthday cake. "Ooh . . . fiwer truck!"

"This is for you, birthday boy! How old are you? Count for

me," Dominique said. She bent down in front of David Anthony and held up two fingers.

David Anthony touched each one. "One. Two," he counted. Dominique scooped him up in her arms and kissed him. "Yes! Look at you! You are so smart!" she said. She sat down with David Anthony on her lap.

Happy that Dominique was pleased with his success, David Anthony's face spread into a wide smile. "I two!" he said to David.

"Yes, you are, buddy! Give me a high-five!"

David Anthony stretched his hand out and gave David a high-five, then said, "Yaay!" and clapped for himself.

"Come here, buddy," David said. He reached across and lifted David Anthony across the table onto his lap. "I'm gonna hold you so we can sing Happy Birthday to you," David said.

"Ooh, wait!" Dominque said. "He needs his birthday hat!" She reached down into the shopping bag she'd brought and pulled out a new plastic fireman's hat. Then she and David sang to David Anthony, and he blew out his candle all by himself.

After pizza, cake, and playing some more, David Anthony was down for his midday nap. David laid him across his lap while he finished another slice of pizza.

"Dave, how many slices of pizza have you eaten?" Dominique teased.

"Huh? David talked with his mouth full. "This is only my third slice," he said, holding up three fingers.

"I don't know about that," Dominique said, eyeing the pizza tray that had only two slices left. She twisted her lips and said, "I only ate *one* slice, and that pizza is almost gone."

"DA must have eaten the rest of those slices. You know he has a big appetite," David said innocently, before bursting into a laugh.

Dominique couldn't help herself. She joined David in laughter. "You should be ashamed of yourself for eating all that baby's pizza, Dave."

"By the time he wakes up, he will want a peanut butter and jelly sandwich, woman. He ain't gonna be thinking about pizza. Plus, I just bought him two new fire trucks. So, I might as well take one of these, and you can have the last one—just in case you get hungry later." David picked up one of the last two slices.

Dominique rolled her eyes playfully. "I might as well go ahead and eat it now before you gobble it down. You act like you haven't eaten in days. Is your wife feeding you at home?" Dominique joked, then just as quickly she said, "I'm sorry. It was just a joke." She wanted to be careful not to offend him.

David shook his head. "It's cool," he said, smiling. "No harm taken. She feeds me very well, it's just that at home I eat more healthily. It's good for a man to pig out every once in a while—especially if he's celebrating."

Dominique chuckled. "Oh, so you're gonna blame your bad eating habits on a two-year-old?"

"Of course, that's what any respectable man would do," David said with a laugh.

Dominique twisted her lips. "I guess."

David reached into his jacket pocket and pulled out an envelope. He slid it across the table to Dominique.

"What's this?"

"That's for you. For the party and everything else."

Dominique slid the envelope back to David. "I already took care of everything, Dave. I had planned to do this with him way back at the beginning of the year. No other kids were invited, so the cost was minimal. I'm just glad that you were able to celebrate with us."

"Dominique, take it." This time, David held it out to her.

They were in a spot near the back, away from the other patrons, so he wasn't worried about anyone seeing him.

Dominique took the envelope and opened it. It contained a stack of crisp bills.

"Whoa . . ." she said before looking back at David. "You don't have to do this. Just taking care of the medical bills was enough. You've bought him clothes, toys, and stuff he doesn't even need," she joked. "You've already given me money for him for the month. DA doesn't need anything else, Dave. Seriously." Dominique had been adamant about not going through the court system. She wanted to maintain a low profile. And David was more than satisfied with that decision, considering he hadn't told Cherelle about David Anthony yet. He had come up with a monthly amount of child support he thought was fair, and Dominque had readily agreed to it.

"Dominique, that's not for DA. That's for you. Now that I'm a father of three with a set of twins who are only a few months old, I know what good parenting looks like. I know the sacrifices that have to be made, whether it's sleep or time to yourself. You are raising my son without my physical help for most of the week. Yes, I have been coming once a week to see him, but I can't be here every night to give him a bath and tuck him in, or read him a story and give him medicine if he gets sick in the middle of the night. That's crappy, but it's our situation. It is what it is. You're doing most of the direct parenting on your own. And I recognize that it's no easy task. So, this is just to show my appreciation for you doing that for my son. And most of all, for exercising discretion while I work things out with my family. I fully intend for David Anthony to take my last name as soon as possible."

"Thank you," Dominique said. She didn't know all the particulars of David's relationship with his wife, but she had assessed from his general conversations that Cherelle didn't know about David Anthony. David had never divulged anything to Dominique about his family and home life—especially the reason why he hadn't told his wife about his other son. But Dominique knew David was an upstanding man, so whatever his reason was, it had to be valid. Besides, she already had what she wanted.

Chapter 28

Salve

David lay in the dark, listening to the flow of water as Cherelle took a shower. He was past exhaustion. Two months of lying and sneaking around had taken their toll on him. Now that Dominique was back in his life because of David Anthony, the old habits he'd developed when he dated her were taking over again. The lying. The sneaking. Not to mention his hiding the knowledge of his son. There was something about Dominique that seemed to bulldoze everything David stood for. Even though they were co-parenting amicably, Dominique brought out the worst in him. Deception had disrupted his life to the nth degree.

He'd just returned from Chicago, celebrating David Anthony's second birthday. He wanted his oldest son to be comfortable with him, so when the time came for David Anthony to come home with him and meet Cherelle, Chloe, and Caleb, it would be a smooth transition. Once David Anthony trusted David completely without Dominique around, it would be easier for him to adjust to Cherelle and the twins.

David heard music playing faintly. He listened for clues of

crying or anything abnormal. He couldn't sleep until Cherelle was next to him in bed. He had become masterful at identifying the change in sounds, like the spray of the water when Cherelle moved around in the shower, or when she padded from place to place in the master bathroom. The weekend was finally here, and he'd made plans to spend it with her and the twins. He had arranged for Pastor Clint to preach this Sunday so that he could be home with his family in Tennessee. But all the flying and lying during the week was catching up with him.

David's eyelids drooped as he waited for Cherelle to get out of the shower. He tried to shake off the lethargy, but he struggled to keep his eyes open. He took his phone out of the nightstand drawer and scrolled through the pics he and Dominique had taken during David Anthony's birthday outing. His face brightened with fatherly pride, and he chuckled when he recalled that David Anthony hadn't been afraid of the larger-than-life mouse at the Chuck E. Cheese establishment. While some of the other kids his age cried and were fearful, David Anthony pointed the creature out, saying, "Moussse. Big Moussse!" He had been intent on touching the huge thing.

"That's that Cole blood!" David had joked with Dominique. "Ain't scared of nothin' and nobody!"

David placed his cell phone on top of the nightstand. He could still hear music playing, but something was amiss. He got up and went into the master bathroom. Cherelle sat on the marble shower bench with her head against the wall, staring blankly. Slits of red covered her dark brown skin like a pattern. David eased the glass shower door open and turned off the water.

There were scratches all over Cherelle's body where she had scrubbed her skin so hard with a loofa sponge that it had bled.

"Kit?"

Cherelle continued to stare off into nothingness with forlorn eyes, unable to acknowledge her husband's presence.

"Kit?" David repeated as he lifted an oversized body towel from the towel warmer rack and stepped into the colossal shower. Taking extra care, he pulled Cherelle up by her hands and wrapped the towel around her. She flinched and stiffened from the body contact. He led her out of the shower by her hand and avoided getting too close, aware that she had an adverse reaction every time he was physically near her.

He grabbed her big, fluffy, purple robe and helped her put it on. Then he led her out of the bathroom and into their bedroom, where he sat next to her on their bed. Instinct caused him to take Cherelle's hands in his and kiss them. It was a non-sexual sign of affection. He was unsure what to do or say at the moment. He only wanted his wife to know that he was there to support her through the trauma she was experiencing. But Cherelle snatched her hands from David's grasp and locked him out of her world, and his heart crumbled.

"Why are you hurting yourself, babe? I love you. Please don't hurt yourself," David pleaded quietly, looking into his wife's absent eyes. "You're mine and I'm yours. That's all that matters, Kit. That's all that matters. I love you."

"I can't do this anymore, honey. I can't . . ." Cherelle said finally.

"I'm with you . . . I'm right here for you. Let's get you some help, babe. Let's talk to someone who can help us get through this."

Cherelle scooted away from David and stood up. She shook her head. "No . . . I can't. I can't..." she cried. She couldn't relive it again. There was no way she could ever talk about them again. Not with a therapist. Not with David. Not with anyone.

"*Cherelle, please.* We need help, babe." David's plea sent

Cherelle into a fearful hysteria, and she backed away from him and screamed as if he were leading her to her death.

"No! Don't make me! Don't make me!" she repeated.

David surrendered immediately. He threw up his hands and backed away from his wife to give her some indication that he was dropping the argument. "Okay, babe . . . okay . . . okay," he spoke calmly. "Just let me pray for you."

DAVID STAYED AWAKE LONG after Cherelle had gone to sleep. He was grateful that after she had calmed down, she allowed him to cover her scars with the salve Mother Ludlow had given him months ago. He wanted Cherelle to be whole again. She refused to see a therapist, but David knew he needed to see someone. They were both scarred.

Chapter 29

Kiss of Death

I t was Marie's weekend off. David bathed and fed the twins while Cherelle slept. The little sleepyheads went right back to sleep after eating. David had become an expert at handling them. He made sure the baby monitor was on in the nursery, then he peeked in on Cherelle. She was still knocked out in the same sleeping position she'd been in the last time he'd checked on her. That was a good thing.

As David trotted down the stairs of his Tennessee escape, he heard Gus on the phone. Whenever Gus was in town, he felt it his supreme duty to make a special dish for Cherelle. "Zuri, I'm sorry! That's not what I meant!" Gus explained uselessly.

David heard a female voice among pots clinking and clanging. The female voice shouted back from the speaker of Gus's cell phone. "You said we were going to be transparent, so let me give you some transparency. If you don't want me to call you anymore, I won't. But if you think you are going to call me when you feel like it, or when you're bored or whatever, you can delete my number right now and forget you ever met me!

Do you understand me?! Just because I'm a Christian doesn't mean you get to walk all over me! As a matter of fact, I don't feel like talking to you anymore. Call me when you grow up—or not!" the voice said. Then, there was a telltale silence that let David know the call had been disconnected.

"Ugggh!" Gus grunted with his fists balled. "Darn it!"

David looked curiously at Gus, who prided himself on not having women problems. Gus turned to face David.

"Hey, bro. Sorry if I woke you," Gus said.

"Nah. You didn't wake me. I remembered you were coming over to cook for *my* wife," David joked. He walked to the counter and turned on the monitor receiver. "I just fed the sleepyheads. So . . . was that the '*arrangement*' woman you told me about?"

Gus dragged an open palm down his face and shook his head. "No. I stopped seeing her last year. That was Zuri. Totally different ballgame."

David's mouth spread, and his straight white teeth gleamed. It was the first authentically goofy smile Gus had seen from him since before Cherelle's abduction. "You keepin' secrets?" David asked.

"Nah, bro, it's just . . . I mean, Zuri and I . . . we're not involved like that. At first, it was just us hanging out—she was like one of the guys. I met her at the health food market. She's a normal woman with a normal life—not like mine.

"Hmm . . . I see . . ." David said, mimicking a therapist.

Gus smirked. "You know you're really irritating, right?" he said to David.

"Well, I got that from you."

"Whatever, bro."

"So, tell me about Zuri. How does she look? What does she do for a living? What is she doing with you?" David laughed.

"Oh, you're full of jokes, bro."

David walked over to the stove and lifted the lid off the pot. "This smells good."

"It's my famous taco soup. It's one of Cherelle's favorites. She loves it."

"Uh-huh. Stop stalling. What's up with Zuri?"

"First of all, she's beautiful—milk chocolate. You know I *love* chocolate," Gus said, winking. "Body by God Himself!" he teased. "And she's got a *normal* job as a social worker at one of the local soup kitchens. She's saved and committed to Christ, and filled with just the kind of sass I like. She's played a pivotal role in helping me understand the Word more clearly."

David widened his eyes and feigned offense. "So, what did you do to make her go off on you? From what I heard, you need to *man up!*" David joked.

Gus threw an oven mitt at him. "Shut up, bro. And she didn't say 'man up', she said 'grow up,'" Gus laughed.

David chuckled. "Same thing. Man up. Grow up. Same thing."

"And it's what I *didn't* do that made her go off," Gus said.

"Do tell."

"Well, things were going pretty smoothly for a while. I can honestly say for the first time in my life, I felt like a woman was my best friend. Yeah, Zuri was like my best friend."

David stared incredulously, and Gus laughed. "She wasn't taking your place, bro. It was just that I could talk to her about anything—life, doubts about Christ, my struggles as a Christian man. She was just a good sounding board."

With bugged eyes, David feigned offense again. This time, he held his hand over his heart and looked up as if he were praying.

"You know you're real stupid, bro," Gus said.

"I'm just saying . . . you could have talked to your brother about that. So, what happened?"

"Like I said, everything was going great. Then one night after Zuri and I had gone to dinner, I kissed her."

"The kiss of *death!*" David said. He slapped a hand against his knee and howled.

"Aw, shut up, bro!"

"Wait. Let me finish the story for you," David said. "I know *exactly* what happened after that. I got this. Trust me," David said, nodding. "You kissed her, and it changed your little *friend-ship*. You were feeling her; she was feeling you. But you— you're scared to death. You *love* her and it scares you."

Gus's smile was gone. He sighed. "That's sorta what happened, I guess. I don't know about all that love stuff, bro. But after that kiss, I knew for sure that I was getting in too deep. And I pulled back so I could get my head on straight— just figure this thing out. But she took it as me playing with her emotions—after we'd talked about honesty and transparency. Now, I'm not sure what I should do."

"First, you gotta let go of your past, man. Then you need to call Zuri up and tell her the truth about where you come from —foster care—the loss of your mother—everything. Just come clean. Tell her how you feel about her. Heck, tell her you're scared. But tell her you *love* her. Life is short, bro."

"What makes you think I love her?"

"It's easy. If you didn't love her, you wouldn't be *afraid* of her. You want more from her than just her body. She makes you feel things you've never felt with a woman before. That's how it was with Cherelle and me. She made me feel things so powerful that I wanted to be away from her just as much as I wanted to be near her.

Gus contemplated, doubtful about stepping out on a limb with a woman. Life was less complicated when relationships with women were fluid. No expectations. No commitments. And yet, that wasn't God's way. He knew that for sure. He was going to have to straighten up and fly right sooner rather than later. And maybe it was time for him to heal.

Chapter 30

Falling Down

David sat in his Friday evening leadership meeting, completely distracted. To someone sitting at the end of the twenty-four-person conference table, it probably looked like David was taking copious notes on what was being said. In reality, he had scribbled *Kit,* Cherelle's nickname, a gazillion times. He was breaking one of his own meeting rules: *Be physically and mentally present.* But he couldn't do anything but focus on Cherelle. She'd been deteriorating before his eyes. He had taken to *making* her drink protein shakes every day because his housekeeper and nanny, Marie, kept confessing that Cherelle was hardly eating. He didn't need Marie to tell him that because it was obvious that Cherelle had lost at least twenty-five pounds.

David's new life had him commuting between Michigan and Tennessee three to four times a week, never spending a night away from Cherelle. Now, Chicago was in the rotation at least once a week so that he could visit David Anthony. His body and mind were worn out. He planned to bring Cherelle back to Michigan soon so they could start the process of regaining normalcy. He'd kept Cherelle sheltered away at their Tennessee property ever since the abduction four months ago.

"Pastor?" Greta called out, forcing David out of his daydream.

"Yes, ma'am? I'm sorry. What did you say?"

"I said, 'Was there anything else you wanted to add to the policy and procedures manual for the daycare center?'"

"Uh . . . no . . . I'm going to leave all of that up to JoAnna and her team."

"Okay, I will get it printed up right away."

"Noted. Thank you," David said. Then an incoming text message stole his attention.

Emergency

The team was well aware that David's no cell phone use during meetings policy had been bent and stretched since the abduction. He'd plainly told everyone that he didn't want to set a double standard but that it would be necessary for him to have his phone on at all times from now on. Of course, his leadership team understood and had gotten used to him placing his phone on the table in front of him and periodically glancing at it.

"Team, can we take a five-minute break? I need to return a call." They agreed readily, and some filed out of the room. David went to his office.

"Hey, what's going on, Nik?" he said when he closed his office door. Dominique was crying so hard that David couldn't understand a word she was saying. "Nik, breathe . . ."

"I—I left Tasha here so I could go buy groceries. And she let my baby fall down the stairs! His head . . . is gushing, Dave. He's bleeding!" Dominique cried.

"Dominique, where are you?"

"We're at the hospital near the loft." David Anthony wailed in the background.

"Dominique, what's happening?"

"They're trying to stitch his head, I'm right here with him!"

"I'll be there shortly. Try and calm down."

The wailing screeched to a crescendo. "I gotta go! I gotta go!" Dominique shouted. The cell disconnected.

David's next call was to the charter service to re-route his flight to Chicago instead of Tennessee.

* * *

UPON HIS ARRIVAL at the hospital, David had a déjà vu moment. He reminisced about the night he and Cherelle discovered they were having twins. That night, he had feared losing his wife, only to find out that God had given him a double blessing. The memory made David smile and relieved some of the tension he felt.

Turning another corner, he searched for Dominique and David Anthony. He was just about to reconfirm the directions the receptionist had given him when he spotted Dominique down the hall talking with someone. He called out to her, and she turned. David jogged to her.

"How's he doing?" he asked.

"He's good . . ." Dominique said weakly. There was fear in her eyes.

David looked between Dominique and the woman she was talking to. "What's going on?"

Dominique stiffened. "This is the hospital social worker; she wants to talk to me about what happened to DA."

David nodded. "Okay."

"Are you his father?" the hospital social worker asked.

"He's a friend of mine," Dominique interjected quickly, just as David opened his mouth to answer the woman. It was the first time anyone had asked him if he was David Anthony's father. He had been a second away from telling the worker the truth. He was grateful for Dominique's save. What if someone were to overhear him? Cherelle had no knowledge of David Anthony, and David sure didn't want her to find out from anyone else.

"Were you there at the home when the *fall* occurred?" the worker questioned.

David was thrown off by the woman's accusatory tone. He stood confused for a moment until his brain registered what was happening. "No. I was in a meeting. I just arrived."

"You can join us if you'd like. I'm Rebecca Morang, one of the hospital social workers," the woman said. David shook her hand, and she reciprocated. She was an African American woman, just a few inches taller than Dominique, with a stocky build. She sported a short, gray afro, and David guessed the woman was in her mid-fifties. "If you would follow me this way, please," she said. Her serious face was devoid of warmth.

Dominique eyed David with worry as they followed the woman. David placed his hand on her back in a reassuring manner and shook his head. "No worries," he whispered.

Dominique wasn't convinced. She took a deep breath and swallowed hard, as tears crept down her face. "These people try to take kids away from their parents," she whispered back.

David and Dominique sat down and waited for Ms. Morang to conduct the interview.

"I'd like to be honest with you both. The reason why I'm speaking with you is because one of the nurses didn't feel comfortable with your story, Ms. Street. It is our job to protect the children we treat at this hospital and refer some cases to child protective services if we deem it necessary," Ms. Morang said.

"I told them the truth!" Dominique rebutted as her leg bounced up and down from nervousness.

David placed a hand on Dominique's leg and then quickly removed it. Unbothered by Ms. Morang's explanation, David reassured Dominique. "Calm down. Just answer her questions and tell her exactly what happened," he said.

Ms. Morang inspected David. She noticed his professionalism and calm demeanor. He radiated a good vibe. "Ms. Street, why don't you walk me through what happened again."

Dominique scooted to the edge of her seat and swiped at her tears. "I left DA with the sitter I've been using for several months while I went grocery shopping. I got a call from her an hour later, saying he'd fallen. At the time, I was right around the corner, so I made it home within a few minutes. His head was bleeding. She said it was an accident. We live in a loft, and he tumbled down the staircase. She's really good with him, and he loves her. I guess she just wasn't paying attention at the time. I just want to hold my baby. No one hurt him. I love him! It was an accident! Can I please just be with my son?!" Dominque cried. David pulled a tissue from the Kleenex box on Ms. Morang's desk and handed it to Dominique. She blew her nose and broke down crying again.

Ms. Morang continued to question and double-question Dominique like a trained interrogator.

Ms. Street, do you have any reason to believe that David may have been pushed?"

"No."

"How do you discipline David when he doesn't behave?"

"I talk to him and tell him what I want him to do, and he does it. He's a good boy."

"Has David ever received any kind of injury as a result of discipline?"

Dominique shook. "No. Never."

David rubbed circles on Dominique's back. "Everything's fine. Calm down," he said. He directed his attention to Ms.

Morang. "Ms. Morang, we understand that you have to do your job in order to keep children safe, and we really appreciate that. Today has been unusually rough for Ms. Street. She left to do errands and came back to a child who was bleeding profusely because he had taken a hard tumble down the stairs. She's a first-time mother, so that was very frightening for her. Then, when she got to the hospital, she had to listen to her son scream as the doctors cared for him and stitched him up.

"She wasn't able to be there for him and comfort him because the doctors had to do what was necessary. After the medical professionals finally got him taken care of and settled, Ms. Street was prevented from seeing her son because she had to meet with you—which we totally understand. But it doesn't negate the fact that she's tired, stressed out, and frustrated. It's late, and she just wants to go home with her son and get some rest. We can call the sitter, and you can talk with her directly so that you can feel comfortable allowing Ms. Street to leave with her son," David reasoned. He felt like a complete heel for not acknowledging that David Anthony was his son, too. Ms. Morang relented only after she had spoken to the sitter herself.

By the time David, Dominique, and David Anthony made it back to Dominique's loft, it was past midnight, and David felt like he had run a marathon. David Anthony slept soundly on David. They'd given him children's Tylenol at the hospital and had fitted him with a small neck brace for the sprain. He'd been fashioned with dissolving stitches, and luckily, he had no signs of a concussion. Dominique took off her coat and tossed it over her red accent chair that looked like a woman's high-heeled shoe. She quickly spun her hair into a loose, sloppy bun and pinned it on top of her head. "Give him to me, I'll lay him down upstairs," she whispered, afraid to awaken David Anthony. The poor thing had never cried so much since he'd been alive.

"No . . . I want to hold him," David whispered in return, rubbing David Anthony's back. The toddler slept contentedly as David held him. His little limbs hung like those of a worn-out rag doll as he lay against David. David kissed the top of his head and eased his little jacket and shoes off, then his own.

He rested against the back cushion of Dominique's extra-deep sofa and closed his eyes for all but three minutes before they snapped open. *Darnit!* He'd forgotten one not-so-minor detail. He should have been home in Tennessee two hours ago. Now, he had to call Cherelle and explain why he wasn't. He moved gingerly to avoid waking up David Anthony. He retrieved his cell and made the call. There was a burning nervousness in his gut as he formulated his excuse. *Liar.*

Marie answered.

"Hello, Marie, is Mrs. Cole awake?"

"Yes and no," Marie whispered. She's been moving around here like a ghost."

"Please put her on the phone."

"Yes, sir."

Four minutes ticked by while David waited for Cherelle to come to the phone.

Cherelle spoke without feeling. "Hi, honey," she said.

"Hey, babe. How are you feeling?

"Ok."

"How are my babies doing?"

"Ok."

Trying to get Cherelle to engage in a conversation beyond one to two-word answers was like pulling teeth nowadays. "Hey, babe, I just wanted to let you know that I'm not going to be able to make it back tonight. I'm sorry, I should have called you earlier to let you know I had a lot of business to take care of. I'm going to get some rest, and I'll be back tomorrow afternoon."

"Ok. See you tomorrow," Cherelle said. The old Cherelle would have asked if something was wrong—if he had missed his flight, or if he was just too tired to make the trip tonight. But the post-abduction Cherelle was just a woman who looked like David's wife. She didn't have any of Cherelle's personality or nuances.

Tell her about David Anthony.

"Okay, I love you, babe," David said, ignoring what was in his heart.

"Love you," Cherelle returned, sounding like a computer-generated customer service representative who pretended to have human emotion but didn't.

David manipulated his way out of his dress shirt by shifting David Anthony skillfully without waking him. He made himself comfortable on the extra-deep sofa that felt like a bed. David Anthony snored lightly against his chest, and David treasured the privilege of loving another little blessing from God, in the form of a handsome little two-year-old, who had proven to be as resilient as his father.

The sparkling city lights of Chicago poured in through the set of floor-to-ceiling windows and illuminated the dark space. David surveyed the modern warehouse-style loft, scrutinizing the details. Everything looked like a hazard to him now. Like the low metal rail in the loft area. David Anthony could get a running start and flip over that easily—or climb over—right to his death. Then, there was the elevator to the third floor. What if he were to somehow get squeezed in the door? Was there even a safety mechanism for the thing? And what about the chrome and glass rectangular dining table with the sharp corners? David Anthony could accidentally run into that thing and put another gash in his head or worse, injure an eye. And the steel and metal steps up to the loft were just too steep. Even though he noticed that Dominique had a child gate at the top and bottom of the stairs, those things weren't foolproof. This place was just too dangerous. And where was David Anthony supposed to run and play with reckless abandon like little boys should? This was a warehouse loft with no backyard.

David spoke softly into the darkness. "I want you to hire someone reputable to help you with DA. You need some help. And Tasha has got to *go*. He could have broken his neck today. This place is hardly kid-friendly as it is, so she should have been watching him more closely."

Dominique unraveled in an instant, bawling out her failure. "I'm trying to be a good mom! I was only gone for a little bit—to buy groceries. I was trying to get everything ready for the week."

David's heart welled with compassion. Dominique *was* doing a good job with David Anthony on her own. She didn't have the benefit of Joe and Leah Montgomery as grandparents or a godfather like Gus, or even the benefit of having David there to co-parent with her twenty-four seven. Still holding onto David Anthony, David leaned in Dominique's direction, reached out to her, and pulled her closer to him. He rested his free arm around Dominique's shoulders. "Hey . . . listen . . . I'm here to *help* you. I'm not criticizing you. You are doing a great job, Nik. You're a very good mom. Shh . . ." David said as he comforted her. The moonlight cast a glow on him and his other family.

* * *

DAVID WAS AWAKENED by David Anthony tapping his hand with a sippy cup.

"Wake up! Wake up! Juice!"

David turned over and faced the little guy. He yawned and tried to shake off his sluggishness. "Hey, man," David said, reaching for David Anthony. "I guess you're feeling better, huh?"

"Wake up. Juice?" David Anthony repeated, holding a Mickey Mouse sippy cup that was the shape of Mickey Mouse's head. He tried to place it in David's hands.

David stood up and scooped David Anthony into his arms. "Come on, buddy."

Dominique walked over to the sofa where David stood holding David Anthony. She reached for the sippy cup. "DA, first of all, I said, 'wait.' Secondly, you're supposed to say, *Please*," she said.

"Mommy, pwease. Juice?"

"You woke David up. I told you to let him sleep."

"Da-bid. Not sleep," David Anthony said, shaking his head back and forth.

David chuckled. "No, I'm not sleeping anymore . . . and from now on, I'm *Daddy* to you. Say, Daddy."

"Da-dee."

"Yes, Daddy. That's good. That's who I am. *Daddy*."

"Da-dee," David Anthony repeated.

"Good," David said, kissing David Anthony on the cheek.

Dominique's shoulders tightened. She tried to relax as she walked into the kitchen area. David followed her to the counter, where she had placed the stack of pancakes she'd made for breakfast. "Can you put him in his chair for me, please, Dave?"

David strapped David Anthony into the high chair, and Dominique set a plate with one pancake in front of him. She'd cut it into smaller triangles so that he could pick them up with his hands. She put a small dipping container filled with maple syrup next to his plate and tied a bib around his neck. "What do you say?" she asked.

"Thankchu," David Anthony said, kicking his feet as he picked up one of the pancake triangles.

"Dip," Dominique instructed.

"Dip," David Anthony repeated as he dipped the triangle into the syrup. He brought it to his mouth, and maple syrup dripped down his chin. He touched his chin. "Sticky," he said.

Dominique took a wet wipe and wiped his chin. "Yes, it is."

"Juice mommeee!"

"No, *David Anthony,* you have to wait. You eat your food first, remember?" David Anthony scrunched up his little face and poked out his lip. "Fix your face, that's rude," Dominique said.

"Wude?"

"Yes. Rude."

"Sowee."

"Okay,"

David's mind wandered back to what had been bothering him all night. "Have you thought about moving someplace where he can run around more?" he asked Dominique.

"Yes, but affordability is the key, Dave. I can't just jump up and do stuff. I'm living off my savings. We've talked about this."

"This place is nice, Nik. But it's not nice for a two-year-old boy."

"I'm doing my best, Dave."

"Don't be defensive. I'm just thinking of what's best for him. Why don't you look at some places that will be a better fit for *him,* and let me work out the financial details, okay?"

Dominique ignored the offer but still wanted to remain cordial. "Would you like some pancakes? And would uh . . . Kedar and Julius like to eat?" she asked.

David had explained the night before that since Cherelle's

abduction, the family had 24-hour security. With all that had occurred, he'd forgotten about his two-person crew outside until Dominique mentioned them. He had tried to get them to come inside last night, but they'd refused. He hoped his witness for Christ hadn't been muddied by what it looked like was going on in his life.

He was sure Kedar and Julius had filled Nelson and the rest of the crew in on the whole Dominique and David Anthony situation. However, this sneaking around didn't look good. David wondered what the security team thought of him. "Yes, I could eat, and I'm sure Kedar and Julius would appreciate the gesture. I'll text them, then I'll get my bag and take a shower."

"You can shower in my room upstairs, Dave. And the guys can use the one in the guest room down here."

David nodded. "That sounds good. I'm going to spend a little more time with DA after I shower and eat, and then I need to head out around three so that I can be home by five. I need to get home to my babies."

Dominique kept her feelings in check and made sure not to display any unflattering facial expressions. She was quite sure when David said the word 'babies,' he was talking about Cherelle, too. That pricked her nerves. A combination of envy and jealousy swirled in her gut.

Chapter 31

Touched

Cherelle stood at the kitchen sink washing the twins' baby bottles and nipples. Marie entered with her purse slung over her shoulder.

"I would have done that for you, Mrs. Cole," Marie said, retrieving her coat from the coat closet. "I won't be gone long." Her soft brown face was empathetic.

Cherelle stared out the window, focusing on nothing. "It's fine," she said.

"I have a doctor's appointment, but I'll return in a few hours. The pot roast is in the crockpot. It's already done. The twins should be waking from their naps in about an hour. Get a little rest while they're sleeping, okay?" Marie said like a loving mother. "I'll wash and braid your hair when I return."

Cherelle turned away from the window, finally making eye contact with Marie. "Thank you," she said politely, wishing Marie would leave so she could cry in peace.

"Eat something. The roast is good for you. I used all fresh vegetables—just the way you like," Marie continued.

"Thank you," Cherelle said again, hoping Marie would take the hint.

"Well, I'd better hurry . . ."

Cherelle leaned against the counter and sobbed the minute Marie shut the door. Oh, how she ached. A foul, ungodly energy had settled over her, and she couldn't shake it. She'd prayed, but the black cloud prevailed. It was suffocating. The day she was abducted was still fresh in her mind, along with every single time one of them had defiled her; she couldn't move beyond it.

She prepared herself a cup of tea and sat at the kitchen table with the Bible David had placed next to her cookbooks. She opened it and glided her hands over the thin pages. *You are my refuge and my shield; I have put my hope in your word.* She closed her eyes and tried to remember a time when she felt *normal*. When she wasn't afraid to go outside. When she wanted to be around people. When she desired her husband and didn't feel dirty every time he so much as brushed past her unintentionally.

She had taken to sleeping close to the edge of her side of the bed, fearful that David might want her. The truth was, she couldn't stand his touch anymore—not even his loving, non-sexual gestures of affection, like kissing her on her forehead or cheek, hugging her, or holding her hand. She just didn't want to be *touched*. David had acknowledged the boundaries without saying so, and he made every effort to avoid making her feel uneasy or causing her any distress. But the emotional separation from Cherelle was another blow for him.

Acts that were once ritualistic, like kissing his wife goodbye before he left in the mornings, or giving her a hug when he returned home, unsettled her now. David understood the whys, but that knowledge didn't make it any less traumatizing. In the deepest of her heart, Cherelle hated that she had isolated herself from her husband. She was appreciative that he was a considerate and patient man because there was nothing she could do to curtail the repulsion she felt.

If only she could find joy in something. Being saved didn't seem to be enough to make her feel whole again or exempt her from feelings of worthlessness. She wanted to joy in her babies, but that had become difficult as well. The numbness she felt within was turning her to stone. She was numb and yet wracked with pain. It was a cruel contradiction.

Cooing sounds echoed from the baby monitor on the kitchen island, and Cherelle knew one of her sleepyheads was awake. *Had an hour passed that quickly?* She moved as fast as she could, preparing two bottles. She wiped her face with her hands and rubbed the remainder of the wetness on her jeans. She didn't want to be a mother right now. She didn't want to be a wife. She wanted to go somewhere and just—" The sound of aggravated cries inched in volume, and Cherelle hurried up the stairs.

Entering the twins' nursery, she placed their bottles on top of a giant grey ottoman designed like an elephant with an upward-pointing trunk. It sat in front of the twins' swing/sway do-dads. She could feed them both at the same time this way and then let the gentle swaying of the machine comfort them while she tried to pull herself together. She checked to make sure both their diapers were dry, then she lifted Chloe from her bed and placed her in her swing before placing Caleb in his. Chloe always seemed to be the most demanding of the two, and Caleb followed her lead. Their cries continued, and Cherelle felt a migraine coming. "Shhh . . ." she said.

She sat on the large, round elephant ottoman in front of the swings and attempted to feed the twins, but neither was cooperative. They turned their little faces from side to side in protest and continued to rattle Cherelle with angry cries. She turned the music and the sway device on to no avail. It seemed that they screamed louder. Her head pulsated. "Shhh . . . come on, you guys . . . calm down." They wanted to be held, but she couldn't right now. Cherelle stood. "Please . . . stop it . . ." Anxiety strangled her, and she felt her chest tighten. She rubbed her sweaty palms on her jeans as her head throbbed.

Cherelle scurried out of the nursery and into her master bath, where she emptied the contents of a powdered aspirin packet on her tongue and washed it down with water. The monitor in the bedroom shrieked, amplifying Chloe and Caleb's rage. Cherelle stared at her image in the mirror. She looked horrible, with her hair frizzed and unkempt. Her once curvy shape was now lithe and subsequently lost in a pair of old, sagging jeans, and one of David's tattered car-washing t-shirts that needed to be discarded. She splashed water on her face, closed her eyes, and counted to ten. She leaned her head back and tried to regulate her breathing enough to thwart the panic attack. But then he was there.

Cherelle felt him behind her before she opened her eyes. His very presence made her skin crawl. *How in the world had he found her here?* She snapped her eyes open and turned simultaneously. She let out a horrified scream before Jag grabbed her by her neck and choked her, forcing her against the counter. "Call me King!" he demanded. Cherelle tried prying his fingers away, but he was too strong. Jag tightened his grip on her neck, and his evil stare willed her to die. He squeezed harder, and his nails sliced into her skin. The strength of his grip cut off her oxygen. "I said, call me King!" he insisted as he choked her. Cherelle struggled as her feet left the cool marble tile and dangled in the air before she blacked out.

"Wake up, First Lady . . ." RIP said, trailing his finger down Cherelle's cheek. "Jag ain't here now."

Cherelle awakened on top of her bed. Her heart hammered

against her chest when she realized RIP and several of the other monsters had surrounded her. Perched over her, RIP eyed her with a menacing grin across his face. "You know what I been dyin' to find out?" RIP asked Cherelle. She sat up and inched away from him. "I been dyin' to find out why Jag been so stingy lately, keepin' you all to himself. Matter of fact, we all been dyin' to find out. Ain't that right, fellas?" he asked. And the monsters agreed. "But lucky for me, Jag had to take care of some business and he ain't gon' be back for a good little while . . ." RIP said, placing a knee on the bed. Cherelle felt the mattress give in to his weight. *Where was David?* Propelled by fear and adrenaline, she jumped up and sprinted into the bathroom, knocking RIP off balance. She grabbed David's Japanese straight razor and unfolded it from its handle in one motion.

None of them chased after her, but their laughter filled the room. Then Chloe and Caleb's angry screeches boomed through the monitor in the bedroom, overpowering the raucous laughter of the monsters. Cherelle edged to the opening of the bathroom door and peered into the bedroom. The monsters were gone, and she was confused and paralyzed by what had just happened to her. One deafening screech from Chloe sent her running to the nursery with the blade in her right hand. She plopped down on the elephant ottoman and screamed. *Had they really been here? No. How could they? What was happening to her?* Afraid to touch the twins, Cherelle bawled.

THE FIRST THING David heard when he opened the front door was the twins' wailing. He could hear them throughout the two-story foyer and through the monitor that sat on the counter in the kitchen. "Marie!" David called out. "Kit!" Alarm set in, even though he knew the house had been secure the whole time he'd been away. He'd spoken to Nelson three times. All had been quiet there. David took off his coat and tossed it on the family room sofa. The twins' cries were different. Something was wrong. "Marie!" David shouted. "What in the—" Another wail and what sounded like one of the twins choking caused David to hurry up the stairs to the nursery.

Dazed and unaware, Cherelle rocked feverishly on the ottoman. A steady pour of tears flowed down her face, and she sobbed softly. Keenly assessing the situation, David focused his attention on his straight-blade razor that Cherelle held in her hand as a weapon. He took his foot and slowly pushed the ottoman away from the twins. He needed space to subdue her if necessary. The first thing he had to do was get the blade out of her hand. David squatted down cautiously in front of her and inched his hand toward her wrist. "Let it go, Kit," David said in a non-threatening voice. He applied a slight pressure to Cherelle's wrist. He felt her hand flex, but she didn't let go of the blade. "*Cherelle*, give it to me right now."

"Oh, my goodness!" Marie shouted.

"Get them out of here!" David said to Marie without turning to face her. He shook Cherelle's wrist. "Cherelle. Let. It. Go." Cherelle's blank stare was haunting. "Cherelle! Let it go now!" David said, applying more pressure to her wrist. He felt her loosen her grip on the blade. David slipped his hands over hers and eased the blade out of her hand. He closed it and placed it in his pocket. Somewhat relieved, He cupped Cherelle's face in his hands, forcing her to look at him. "Cherelle, babe, I need you . . . to tell me what's happening. What were you doing?" Cherelle shivered as if she were outside in freezing conditions. David steadied her with his hands on her shoulders. "What were you doing with my razor, Cherelle?" he asked her calmly.

She looked through David, not at him. His fear and frustration bubbled together, and he grunted. He didn't want to believe what he thought he'd seen. Cupping her face again, he said, "Cherelle, I need you to talk to me. I—I need to know you're okay. Talk to me!" David pleaded. "I need to know why you were sitting in front of my babies with a razor in your hand."

Cherelle's mind scattered in different directions. She tried to find the words to reassure David, but the shock of everything that had happened to her just a few minutes ago, which didn't happen at all, was eating away at her sanity. Her silence destroyed David's resolve, and for a moment, he regretted loving her. He shook off the unwelcome feeling and leaned his forehead against hers. He didn't want it to be true—what he'd just seen. Cherelle wanted to come out of the dark place and explain what had just occurred, but she couldn't find her voice. David pushed back and sat in front of her. His voice quivered. "Cherelle, were you going to hurt my babies? Were you trying to hurt my babies?! Tell me right now!" he shouted.

The force of David's voice snapped Cherelle out of that place, and she coughed as if she'd been drowning. "No . . . th— they were trying to hurt me again!" she said.

"The twins?" David asked incredulously. Cherelle didn't know what to say. How could she tell him that they had been here? "Who was trying to hurt you again, Cherelle? Who!" David said impatiently.

"Jag and RIP and t—the rest of them. They were here—and they were going to rape me again . . . and I had to defend m— myself!" Cherelle broke and wailed.

David rose and pulled his wife into his arms. She stiffened, but she didn't pull away. David let his tears fall. "We need help, Lord. We need Your help . . ." he whispered.

* * *

PEACE RETURNED to David's home once Cherelle was asleep, and the twins were snuggled happily in his arms. He kissed both of their sleeping little faces before he placed them in their beds. Significant changes had to be made now that David was certain Cherelle was having a mental breakdown. He'd talked to Norma over the phone, and she'd given him instructions. They both decided that taking Cherelle to a hospital right now would be more traumatizing for her because of her fear of talking to a therapist. He'd removed all medicines from the medicine cabinets and locked them away in the second safe in his office. Norma had explained that hallucinations were sometimes a byproduct of Post-Traumatic Stress Disorder. They settled on monitoring her closely and not leaving her alone.

Marie folded the twins' clothes in the laundry room. She hummed a sweet song and seemed to be joyful about taking care of the twins' miniature fashions. David stood in the doorway.

"Ms. Marie, I want to talk to you about what happened earlier . . ."

"Pastor Cole, I'm so sorry—I had no idea that Mrs. Cole was on the verge of a—"

"From now on, she cannot be left alone for *any* reason," David interrupted. "If you need to go somewhere or you need time off, please just let me know so that I can have someone here—inside the house. I need to know that she's safe and that my kids are safe when I'm away."

"Yes, sir. I understand."

"Thank you for everything you do around here. I appreciate it. And I'm glad you're here to help us," David said.

"You're welcome, Pastor Cole. And I know everything is going to be just fine with Mrs. Cole."

Chapter 32

The Long Haul

David shook hands with Dr. Sylvester Buckley, a psychologist in the Metro Detroit area. It was the first time in his life that he'd ever been to any type of counseling outside of marriage counseling. But he was desperate, living with a zombie. There was nothing he could do to help Cherelle. He'd tried everything to no avail. That was the one thing that was killing him day by day, robbing him of his sleep, and making him feel like an utter failure. Having Cherelle back like this was almost as traumatic as her abduction. She was living with him and sleeping next to him, but she wasn't there. She wasn't alive anymore.

Cherelle's nightmares were occurring at least three times a week now, and understandably so, she'd slipped into depression. David felt terrible for lying to her by omission, but he knew the news about David Anthony would break her. She'd been through enough already. When she was doing better than she was now, they'd talk.

Cherelle was still refusing to see a therapist, but David

knew she needed one. He paid Marie to "babysit" her whenever he was away or had the twins on an outing. He'd read up on PTSD. Cherelle met all the criteria. He was certain she was suffering from a nervous breakdown. In addition, she was dealing with postpartum depression.

David hated it when it even crossed his mind that someone had *touched* his wife, abused his wife. He was enraged enough to kill. He'd walked with God for a long time, and he knew how to control his temper—his flesh. But he didn't want to. He wanted to kill whenever he thought of those thugs hurting Cherelle.

"Good afternoon, Pastor Cole, it's nice to finally meet you in person," Dr. Buckley said. He gripped David's hand and gave him a firm handshake. The two made direct eye contact. Dr. Buckley was dressed casually in a pair of khakis and a polo shirt. He was a poster guy for middle age, suave and debonair. The sprinkles of gray in his beard made him look like a sage, and David hoped he was.

"You too. You came with very high recommendations from Debra Martin. She's married to a good friend of mine."

Dr. Buckley nodded. "It's nice when people say uplifting things about you," he said, smiling. "Have a seat, please. Let's get started."

David sat down. "Sure," he said. They'd already spoken at length via a secure virtual connection and gotten some preliminary background information out of the way. Dr. Buckley was attempting to accommodate a growing number of clients who wanted virtual therapy. It was new ground for him, but he wanted to appease his clients. "So . . . um . . . like I told you . . . I'm not sure what to do right now. Cherelle's been back about four months now . . . but she's been like the walking dead." David's voice wavered. "She's there, but she barely speaks—

even to the kids. It's like she's just existing. I don't know what else to do to try and bring her back. I've fasted. I've prayed. I've done everything I know to do spiritually and naturally. And nothing's changed."

"Severe trauma affects people differently. Sometimes it takes months—or years for a person to return to normal. If there is such a thing after an event like what happened to Cherelle," Dr. Buckley returned.

"She's empty, and so . . . I'm empty. I love her so much. To see her like this every day is a heavy weight to bear. I don't know how much more I can take. I feel more helpless now than I did when she was missing for four days. When she was gone, I knew I couldn't do anything. She's back with me now, but I can't reach her. I can't even touch my wife. I don't even put my hands on her—in any kind of way now. Because she . . ." David paused, swallowing the lump in his throat. "She flinches whenever I come near her—and that's not us. I understand it, I do. But it's hard to take." David sniffed in and swallowed hard. He looked away, suppressing the pain.

"Yes, it is," Dr. Buckley agreed. "You've been extremely resilient, and your wife has been strong too. But this is a long process, David. This is not something that is going to be resolved quickly. It takes time to heal from physical and emotional trauma. If it were a quick process, I wouldn't have a job," Dr. Buckley said lightheartedly. "I always tell my clients that being *here*, coming to see me, tells me you're committed. And that's all it takes—along with a little patience. But tell me more about the emotional and physical distance you've been experiencing."

"The truth is, I've been handling not having any physical intimacy with Cherelle. From the very beginning, I expected this to be the case, and I understand it. I can't imagine the trauma she's been through, and is still going through. If I even think about it, it sends me to a place I don't want to be emotionally. I believe I have the resolve to get through this because I know that it's just a matter of time before we return to our normal intimate routine. And as beautiful as our intimacy is—or was—we have a friendship that surpasses our physicality.

"What's really killing me is the emotional distance—not being able to just *talk* with her and reach that sacred place within her. Cherelle is truly my best friend. I used to look forward to coming home, telling her about my day, listening to her talk about hers, eating dinner together, and just enjoying our closeness. Now, it's like I'm living with someone who looks like my wife and sounds like my wife, but isn't."

"Are you saying that she doesn't talk to you at all?"

"If I don't initiate conversation, no, she won't, Doc. In the beginning, she spoke one or two words if she said something. Now, she doesn't say *anything*. She responds, but her affect is completely flat—even with the twins. She doesn't even talk to them anymore; she just feeds them and changes their diapers like a robot. And they need stimulation and interaction at the stage they're in now. I'm so thankful for our housekeeper, Marie, who also serves as a nanny. I don't know what I'd do without her."

Dr. Buckley jotted down a note and said, "David, what is it that you want from Cherelle right now, considering all that's happened?"

David sat back in his chair and rubbed his temples. He shifted and let out a sigh. "I don't know," he said hesitantly. "When I realized Cherelle had been abducted, my prayer was: 'Lord, bring my wife back.' Now that she's home—physically if nothing else—I find myself praying that same prayer: 'Lord, bring my wife back.' Nothing I've done—including praying has broken down the wall that was created by the assault. I just don't know how much longer I can take it, without having a meltdown myself."

"Have you been tempted by another woman?" Dr. Buckley asked.

"No. I have—" David started.

Dr. Buckley put up a lone finger to silence David. "This is not something I want you to respond to abruptly, David. I want you to hear me out. *Then* you can respond. Even though you've been going about your regular duties as a husband, as a father, *and* as a pastor, I want you to know that right now, you are most vulnerable."

David interrupted Dr. Buckley. "Why are you telling me this? I don't want another woman. I'm not even thinking about another woman. I want my wife back. That's the truth," David said, annoyed by Dr. Buckley's pursuit of a matter he felt was unnecessary.

"David, I'm positive you feel that way, but you just said a few minutes ago that you weren't sure how much longer you could take it. What is 'it'? Did you mean the emotional separation from Cherelle, or did you mean both the emotional *and* physical separation?"

Noticeably agitated, David said, "I was talking about the emotional separation. Like I told you, I can deal with the physical separation. I understand what she's been through. I don't even want to make love to her if it can't be like it was before everything happened." He could not bring himself to say the word *rape*. "I don't want our intimacy forced. I can wait. I believe Cherelle knows that," David said with finality.

"You know, David, when we tell ourselves we can't 'take it anymore,' the brain begins to look for ways to avoid experiencing what's causing the pain. That's why sometimes, when couples go through traumatic events like losing a child, or something such as your wife's abduction and assault, divorces happen, or sometimes even adultery. It's because the pain is overwhelming, David. The natural reaction to pain caused by severe trauma is avoidance—to get away from it. It forces people to seek some sort of elixir."

David had been forewarned about Dr. Buckley's confrontational therapy style. He'd been prepared for it, but he was never one to back down. And he planned to put Sylvester Buckley on notice. "I'm not going to do *anything* to hurt my wife any further, Dr. Buckley." *Not even tell her that I have a son by another woman,* David thought to himself. "If some sort of temptation did occur, I know how to shut it down immediately. And I would. I'm just trying to get through this rough patch in our marriage. That's all."

Dr. Buckley smiled. David was sound. "Very well. Have you convinced her to see someone yet?"

"No. She hasn't even left the house; I think she's afraid."

"Being abducted in broad daylight will do that to a person."

"I'm paying for private security for my family right now—some very well-trained men who were recommended by my best friend. That makes me feel more at ease when I'm away from home."

"David, what is it that you're not saying?"

"I don't know what you mean."

"Of course you do. There's something underneath the person that's sitting before me, David. And I can't help you if you don't tell me what it is."

"I've told you what's going on with me right now. I need to know what to do to get my wife back."

"Really? I think you need to know what to do to get yourself back."

"What?"

"You. You're not together. You're not *back* from the whole

ordeal. You couldn't protect Cherelle. You've been feeling guilty about that, right?"

David couldn't find his voice to respond verbally, but Dr. Buckley was right. There was no sense in arguing with the man. David bit into his bottom lip. He wasn't about to unravel in front of another man. He had no problem crying out to God. But he wasn't about to let another man see him at his weakest point.

"How have you been working on yourself—keeping it together?" Dr. Buckley continued.

David sighed. "Man, I'm just treading water. And I've been treading water for a while—trying not to go under."

"I know you've been praying. That's good. That's the best thing you can do. In addition to that, get out to the gym. I know you don't want to leave Cherelle for extended periods. That's understandable. But take some 'me' moments when you can. Are you done reading the book I recommended?"

"Haven't even started."

"Dr. Buckley laughed aloud. "I've finally met someone as honest as me. My book will walk you through day-by-day steps to deal with trauma from a practical perspective. It's a really good resource. And I'm not saying it because I wrote it. It comes highly recommended by other therapists as well."

"I *will* get around to it this week."

"Is there anything else you need to share, David?"

David hid what was underneath. He'd seriously been thinking of murder. The man they called Jag, who orchestrated Cherelle's kidnapping and who was one of the men who'd assaulted her, was still somewhere free. No one had found him yet. David wanted the man dead. In fact, he wanted to murder the no-good thug himself and watch the life flow out of him.

David smirked. "This is the place where I'm supposed to be

able to say what I truly feel, but what I truly feel isn't acceptable to God or me, so I'd rather not."

"It may not be acceptable, but whatever it is, it is what it is, David. Our thoughts are not always what they should be. But acknowledging one's inner 'truths' helps a person to work through conflict. Ignoring something because it's not acceptable is like lying to oneself. And God is already well aware of the things you're keeping hidden."

"Well, in that case, I want to *kill* him—in a literal sense. I want to *murder* another person." David closed his eyes. "Jag Vincent and those other devils in his crew have taken something more precious than my wife's body. They have taken the life right out of her. And for that, I want all of them to pay. I've never felt like this before in my life. Some days, I pray that the clown is bold enough to come anywhere near us. I dream of giving him just what he deserves with my own hands," David admitted. He opened his eyes and held his hands in front of him. "If I weren't the man that I am and didn't belong to the God of the universe, I would hunt him down and kill him."

Dr. Buckley met David's stare. "I like you, David. I like you because you're honest. And I thought I would have to deal with some larger-than-life pastor who prefers to hide behind the righteous symbol of a clergy robe."

"I ain't got nothing to hide, Doc. I'm telling you that I've been fighting with myself for months to let God handle this thing. But I want to hunt that monster down and give him the punishment he deserves."

Dr. Buckley saw something disturbing in David's eyes. It was the coolness with which he confessed. There was only a thin line that kept a man who was a lover from being a murderer. One of the things that could turn a decent, upstanding man like David into the latter was the evil that had been done to his wife. Dr. Buckley understood that.

"David, nothing would be worth losing your wife and your beautiful kids. To be behind bars for the rest of your life and not be able to enjoy your family. Nothing is worth that."

"The truth isn't always pretty, is it, Dr. Buckley?" David said, standing. "I'll see you next week." He picked up his light leather jacket and walked out of Dr. Buckley's office. He'd committed to the process, and he was in it for the long haul. But it was taking everything he had to stay afloat.

Chapter 33

Still

David had been keeping a close watch on Cherelle ever since the "incident." Simply put, he didn't trust her anymore. He didn't trust her to be alone with herself or the twins. They were four months into this dreadful journey and were back living in Michigan full-time. David had hired Marie to temporarily relocate and move in with them. He was pleased that Marie had been willing to relocate for a short time, although he didn't know how short a period it would be with Cherelle in her present condition. The twins were already used to Marie, and so was Cherelle. He felt more at ease knowing someone was at home *watching* Cherelle when he was gone. Marie was still under strict instructions not to leave her alone for any reason.

Cherelle crept into bed. The sweet smell of lavender and primrose emanated from her skin. David stared up at the ceiling, praying that God would heal her from every emotional wound she suffered. It pained him to see her so lifeless. Cherelle turned on her side, then her stomach. Then, on her back.

The sound of her voice broke the silence. "Honey . . ." she whispered.

"Yes, babe?" David said, turning toward her. "What's the matter?"

"I just wanted to tell you that . . . if you want to make love, we can."

David waved his hand over the lamp on his nightstand, and light shone on his face, illuminating Cherelle as well. He turned to her and rested on his elbow. Her eyes were closed, and David noticed the wetness escaping them. He touched her face gently, and she didn't flinch. "Kit, look at me." Cherelle opened her tear-filled eyes and stared at her husband. "I want you to listen to me, babe. I love you. You are everything to me—everything. You are *still* my Kitten. My desire for you is just as strong as it has always been. And I do still want you and need you, but never at the *expense* of you, babe," David said. He took her hand and brought it to his lips, and kissed it tenderly before intertwining their fingers, and she allowed him. "When it's time, it will be time. There's no rush. Nothing has changed with our love. We *will* have our time again. And it will be right. Don't rush for me. We'll make love when it's right for *you*. You will know, and so will I. But not tonight, okay?" David said. He kissed her forehead. Relieved, Cherelle scooted under his arm and released the cry she'd been holding.

* * *

DAVID WOKE up early and dressed. It was five a.m. when he kissed Cherelle on her forehead. "Hey . . . I'm gonna be gone most of the day. I'll be back later this evening," he said to her.

"Okay," Cherelle said, turning over.

"Julius and Kedar are inside. Nelson and Keenen will be with me. Marie's here too."

This time, Cherelle only nodded. He didn't tell her he was going to Chicago.

* * *

DAVID STOOD at the door of Dominique's loft. Keenan stood to the left of him while Nelson stood just outside the car, keeping his eyes on everything else. David rang the doorbell again and waited. "Back in the car," Keenen ordered as he stepped in front of David. He didn't have a good feeling about Dominique taking so much time to answer the door. He used his hand to nudge David backward. David turned reluctantly and headed toward the car. "He's coming back," Keenen said to Nelson through the wireless microphone attached to his shirt.

"Roger that," Nelson said.

Dominique's groggy voice came over the intercom. "Dave, I'm sorry. We're still sleeping around here," Dominque yawned. "We had a late night. I'll buzz you in."

Hearing Dominique's voice reassured David that all was well. He pivoted and walked back to the loft door.

"No. I need to clear it first, "Keenen said and motioned for David to get back in the car with Nelson, as he had instructed him the first time. Keenen wasn't satisfied until he had checked the place thoroughly. Dominique held her peace as usual. She met David at the elevator entrance into the loft when Keenen finished his duties, and Keenen got into the car with Nelson. After four months, the team had relaxed a little. They used their judgment as to when David could be left alone while he was in a non-public space.

"She's quite a looker, isn't she?" Nelson asked Keenen.

Keenen nodded. "Yes, she is, but there's something about her I don't trust," he admitted.

226

"I think everyone on this team feels that. I'm praying he doesn't slip up with her," Nelson said.

"I think he's good . . . just trying to do the right thing, that's all. You have to admire that."

"He's a better man than most. That little outfit she's wearing had me licking my lips," Nelson kidded, swiping his tongue across his lips.

"Not me. I got a feeling she's nothing but trouble," Keenen said, fiddling with the small, inconspicuous body cam on his tie that had allowed Nelson to track his every move in Dominique's home and see everything from his vantage point. "This works pretty well, then?"

"Oh, yes, it does!" Nelson joked.

* * *

DOMINIQUE STOOD in front of David with her toothbrush in her mouth. Her naturally curly hair was massive and untamed, swaying as she moved. She mumbled and motioned for David to follow her upstairs to the third level of the penthouse loft. Her stretch-jersey and lace, two-piece, blue camisole was halfway innocent and halfway seductive. The material clung to Dominique's petite curves and showed off her beautiful cocoa skin. Her pretty painted toes and nails were light blue with psychedelic colors on the tips.

When she climbed the stairs ahead of David, he averted his eyes and steered his mind to other things. Dominique and David Anthony shared the huge loft bedroom. Her wrought iron bed lay in the center of the room, and David Anthony's fire-engine-style bed was next to it.

Dominique walked into the bathroom and continued to brush her teeth while David stood near her bed. He stuffed his hands in his pockets and walked over to where David Anthony lay sleeping in his fireman pajamas. His limbs were turned every which way, and he looked as if he was enjoying the sleep that came as a result of hard labor. David smiled, looking down on his son with fatherly love and admiration.

"Good Morning, Dave. I didn't want to blow dragon breath on you," Dominique chuckled, touching David's arm.

David turned slightly. "Hey. . . . Good morning. You guys stayed up late?"

"Yes! I'm so sorry. I had planned to have him ready and dressed when you got here, but he wore me out yesterday. We watched all kinds of animated movies and played with his little fire engine trucks until my eyes were blurry. I haven't had a moment to collect my thoughts all week."

Guilt strained David's face. Dominique was managing David Anthony alone, while he and Cherelle had plenty of help. "How's it coming finding someone to help you out?" David asked.

"I interviewed two people this week, but I didn't think you would like either. So, I don't have anyone yet, Dave." Dominique bent over and picked one of David Anthony's toys off the floor, and then another. And David realized he was tracking her movements with his eyes. He stopped and looked at his watch.

"Okay. I think it would be good for you to get some help soon. I don't want you to feel worn out. You have a lot on you. I realize that, and I want to help you in any way I can," David said sincerely.

"Thanks, Dave," Dominique said. She looked up at him with a questioning glance, taking his hands in hers, rubbing her thumbs over them softly. It was a gesture David often made to show affection when they'd dated. "That really means a lot to me," she continued. "You are an excellent father to DA. I couldn't ask for any better." Dominique held David in her stare, and David felt just a tinge of discomfort. She released his hands and smiled. "You might as well go ahead and wake up the fireman. And if you give him a bath, I'll fix breakfast for you guys."

"Oh, sure. I'll give him a bath, but you don't have to cook breakfast. I can take him out to eat."

"No . . . he likes his mommy's special banana pancakes. It's his Saturday morning ritual. He'll be expecting his pancakes, Dave."

"Well, okay, then. I'll get him ready."

"Go ahead and wake him up. I want to see if he gives you the same hard time he gives me," Dominique laughed.

"Oh, so you're trying to keep score?"

"Yep."

David was glad that he and Dominque had been getting along so well. They truly were co-parenting. He took off his jacket and laid it on a chair near David Anthony's bed. Dominique eyed the way David's t-shirt stretched across his solid, muscular chest and how the muscles in his arms flexed when he lifted David Anthony from his bed. The way his well-worn Levi's rode his thighs.

David held David Anthony and rubbed circles on his back. It was his signature move.

"Is that your wake-up method?"

"Yes, it is. There's a science to this, woman," David chuckled.

David Anthony's head rested on David's shoulder. And David continued to rub circles on his back. "Hey man, Daddy's here . . . wake up. Time to go to the zoo . . . . Time to go to the zoo."

After a few moments, David Anthony squirmed. Sleepily, he lifted his head off David's shoulders and looked at him oddly.

"Daddy came to take you to the zoo, man. You ready? You still want to go to the zoo, right?" David asked.

David Anthony nodded. "Daddy," he said, circling his tiny arms around David's neck. "Morning, Daddy."

"Good Morning, fella," David returned, kissing David Anthony on the cheek. "You have to get a bath and then we can go to the zoo, okay?"

David Anthony nodded his head excitedly with a knowing smile on his face.

Dominique rolled her eyes playfully and steadied her hands on her hips. "I don't believe this. So, he *can* wake up without a bunch of fussing."

"Gotta have that Cole touch, woman."

Dominique rolled her eyes again. "Whatever," she said, smiling.

* * *

AFTER BREAKFAST, Dominique cleaned the kitchen while David Anthony and David readied themselves for their zoo journey. David had purchased a red wagon to cart David Anthony around when he got tired of walking. He'd had it delivered to Dominique's place earlier in the week. Nelson came to the door, picked up the wagon, and put it into the truck. David put on David Anthony's jacket and his baseball cap.

"Okay . . . we'll see you a little later," David said to Dominique as he held David Anthony's hand in his. "Tell mommy bye-bye," David said to David Anthony.

"Bye, mommy, see you later! Horsey ride, Daddy!"

"Okay," David said, lifting David Anthony onto his shoulders.

"Oh! Wait, guys!" Dominique trotted to the kitchen and

returned with David Anthony's backpack and a small cooler. She handed both to David. "I made lunch for you guys—corned beef—both of you guys' favorites."

"Kiss, Mommy!" David Anthony said from David's shoulders. David bent a little so that Dominique could reach David Anthony. She stretched on her tiptoes and pressed her breasts and the rest of her soft curves against David's body as she kissed David Anthony.

"Muah . . . muah. . . muah," Dominique said as she planted three sloppy kisses on David Anthony's face. She stepped back unhurriedly, capturing David's eyes.

Chapter 34

I Know You Want Me

David rested on the sofa in the living room area of Dominique's place, reading financial articles on his laptop. He and David Anthony had enjoyed a long day, and the rambunctious ball of energy was napping upstairs. David had worn him out at the zoo and a nearby park. When the toddler awoke, David planned to spend some time playing with him and then eat dinner with him. Afterward, he planned to give his son a fun, toy-filled bath and put him to bed.

Dominique entered the large living room space and flicked on the 72-inch television. She had showered and changed into a pair of cut-off, Daisy Duke shorts and a spaghetti-strap tank top. No bra. She plopped onto the red, high-heeled accent chair across from David. He glanced her way and turned back to his laptop screen. He wondered why she was half-dressed, but it was her house, not his. So far, they'd been able to co-parent without any drama, and David wanted to keep it that way.

Dominique had been exceptionally pleasant all day. She'd prepared lunch for his and David Anthony's father and son Saturday adventure, and she'd already made lasagna for dinner, one of David's favorite meals. Although their dealings with one another centered solely around conducting co-parenting business, she had been nothing but accommodating and agreeable. Perhaps she was just trying to make the best of an unanticipated situation, just as David was, or maybe, becoming a mother and caring for David Anthony made her want to elevate herself and become a better human being. She seemed to have grown more than David figured was possible for her.

"Dave, do you mind if we talk while DA is napping?"

David looked up from his laptop. "No, I don't mind. What's on your mind?" He'd been kind to Dominique ever since he discovered that David Anthony was his son, and he'd pushed aside all the ill feelings he held toward her for David Anthony's sake. As a pastor, he'd seen too often how men and women disrespected their co-parents and caused all sorts of family problems that negatively affected their children.

He vowed to keep communication peaceful and civil with Dominique so that David Anthony would grow up knowing that his father respected his mother, no matter what their family circumstances were. It would reduce everyone's stress, and his son would never feel that he had to take sides.

"I was thinking about what you said about finding somewhere safe for DA, so I looked at a couple of places, and I want to show them to you."

"Okay, let me see what you've got in mind."

Dominique hesitated. "Dave, you didn't give me a budget amount, so I wasn't sure what price range to look at."

"Just let me see what you like, Nik. I didn't give you a range because I didn't have a specific range in mind at the time."

When they'd dated, Dominique never discovered David's secret that he was a low-key millionaire. She knew he was well-connected socially and politically, but they had never progressed to a stage in their relationship where David gave her access and insight to every part of his life like he'd given Cherelle.

Dominique picked up her tablet and sauntered over to the spot next to David. When she sat in his personal space, he could more keenly smell the scent of the perfume or body lotion she wore, and the scent of her hair. It was freshly washed and coated with the same alluring potion he once loved. A smell that used to cast a sensual spell on him. Maybe he was overreacting, but he had the feeling that Dominique was trying to push his buttons.

She scooted closer with practiced innocence and proceeded to scroll through the homes she had saved on a popular real estate app. "I'm sorry," she said, moving her hair from David's face. It always swelled after she washed it and allowed it to air dry. It was becoming massive. She took an elastic band off her wrist and put her hair into a fat, bushy ponytail.

David's body gravitated on a spectrum from relaxed to rigid. He mulled over the events of the day. When he'd arrived that morning, Dominique had been wearing that short, body-hugging, cotton-stretch, get-up that barely covered her. She had walked up the stairs ahead of him, giving him a clear view of her rear end. He had shrugged that off; he wasn't her pajama police.

Then David recalled the *innocent* way she had pressed her body against his as they'd navigated around David Anthony, getting him ready for his father-son day. He'd counted that as unintentional. But considering what he felt in his spirit at that very moment, all the events of the day fit perfectly together, like pieces of a puzzle.

Yes, there had undoubtedly been a subtle teasing going on all day. He'd missed it earlier because his mind had been on David Anthony. Now, he couldn't miss it. It was almost as if

Dominique somehow sensed that he had been longing for phys-ical and emotional intimacy. He'd been deprived of it for months now. He hadn't spoken a word to Dominique about Cherelle or anything that had transpired in their home. And yet, somehow, Dominique was speaking to the parts of David that begged to be nourished.

David calculated his moves like a master chess player and reviewed his strategies like a savvy attorney. Dominique was a smart woman. She knew him. She remembered his fleshly secrets well. He heard her speaking as she showed him the suburban Chicago Craftsman she said she liked. He saw all the pictures of the staged bedrooms and the roomy backyard with the durable plastic, log-style, jungle gym.

His brain took in all the information Dominique shared about the home being in an area where the high school, middle, and elementary schools were all blue-ribbon schools. But David's preeminent thought process caused him to focus on his next move—the next words that would come out of his mouth and what would unfailingly transpire afterward.

Dominique had breached his personal space, an area that was specifically reserved for Cherelle. And she had seized the opportunity to pry open a door David had closed two years ago. He could feel the very essence of her aura pressing beyond his barriers like a mist absorbing into his skin.

David shifted slightly. Dominique would not have even noticed if she hadn't been sitting so close to him. She paused and looked up at him with eyes that used to seem as if they sparkled. Her gaze transformed from friendly and innocent to a sensual, questioning pull, like a charmer hypnotizing her victim.

David wondered if Dominique could see past his signature straight face. He wondered if she had any idea what he was thinking and feeling. His eyes blinked slowly and lowered. He gently tugged the tablet from Dominique's hands and set it on the glass and chrome sofa table. He seemed to move in slow motion. Dominique's breath hitched before she breathed a sigh of victory.

She toyed with her hair. She needed to do something with her hands while she waited for David to make his move. She'd been playing this game for over four months now. Playing the role of a civil co-parent. Suppressing the thoughts of the intimate past she once shared with him. She'd been smothering thoughts of his kisses. His strength. The side of him that only lucky women knew. How sensual he could be. How nurturing and attentive he was. How fine he still was. She'd been with him many times and knew that he was rarely hasty about anything. She had enough patience to wait for him tonight.

David repositioned himself, turning slightly. There was no turning back from here.

"Nik . . . let's stop pretending that *something* isn't happening right now . . . " David said. Dominique had labeled him the Quiet Storm, and she believed she had set that storm in motion. Her eyes batted sensually as David continued. "You know me in ways most people don't, Nik. You know some of my strengths and you're familiar with some of my weaknesses—some of the things that speak to my manhood—because of what we once shared. And now here you are. You're in my space right now . . . and I see you. I smell you. I *feel* you next to me. It's alarming and reassuring at the same time, Nik."

"Dave, I—" Dominique started.

"Let me finish, Nik," David said. "Having you next to me like this is alarming because, for the last few years, no woman besides my wife has been this physically close to me in any setting—let alone a private one," he continued. Dominique's lips turned into a soft smile. "And at the same time, seeing you, smelling you, and having you this close is reassuring because I know without a single doubt that I *don't* have an *appetite* for you anymore, Nik," David said. Dominique's smile inverted. "When I think about smelling a woman, touching a woman, and making love to a woman, I'm thinking about *Cherelle Cole*. Everything I need from a woman is in *her*.

"With that being said, please, don't mistake me for someone I'm not. I want to continue to co-parent with you so that DA's life can be as normal as possible for a kid whose parents are not together. I don't want my coming here to see my son to turn into something awkward between us, Nik. This is your home; I can't tell you how to dress or what to do. But I can tell you with absolute certainty that there is nothing for you and me to ever go back to."

Dominique rose without saying a word and retreated upstairs.

Chapter 35

Normal

Four months had passed since Dominique played the seductress with David. They'd silently agreed to put the incident behind them and had come to terms with their arrangement. David had moved Dominique and David Anthony into a beautiful, four-bedroom, blue-gray craftsman with white trim. It had a huge yard for David Anthony to play in and was in a well-kept suburb with tree-lined streets in the cul-de-sac of a stable, affluent neighborhood.

The home was in an ideal location for David Anthony to grow up and walk to nearby schools when he was older. David rented himself a house two blocks away—within walking distance—so that he could have private visits with David Anthony and wouldn't have to be in Dominique's space when he came to Chicago to visit his son. He washed the remaining dishes in the sink of his rental home and glanced at his watch. He finished cleaning the kitchen and locked up the place. He walked the short distance to Dominique's and rang the doorbell.

Dominique answered, wearing a yellow eyelet dress with

taupe heels. Her face was beautiful, and her hair was pulled up into a bun. "Hey, you look nice. I didn't know you were going out—" David started before he checked himself. "I mean, that's none of my business," he laughed.

"No, it's fine. I need to do some adulting. Thanks for watching DA overnight for me. He's knocked out, though. And my date will be here in thirty minutes. He's very timely, so let me finish getting dressed. I need to choose my jewelry and a shawl."

David didn't know why, but a comparison popped into his head. Cherelle was so fashion-conscious and prissy that she always laid out all her jewelry, clothes, shoes, and makeup, right down to the shade of lipstick she would wear before they went to an event. Fashion was a job. He missed that part of her.

"Is this someone you're serious with? Will he be around DA a lot?" David asked out of pure concern for his son's safety. Dominique didn't have the greatest track record when it came to men. Her last dude had tried to off her and had almost killed him in the process.

"He's a good friend. But he and I can't really be serious, Dave."

"And why is that?" David pried.

"There are a lot of reasons . . ."

"I'm listening."

"Dave, I don't want to discuss my personal life with you—because it's uncomfortable—not because I'm trying to hide anything from you. I know that you have every right to be concerned about DA, and I respect that. There's no problem with my friend, and he won't be around DA at all. I just—" Dominique started. "I just need to feel like a *woman* tonight. I hope I'm being clear enough for you."

It was none of his business. David truly didn't care who Dominique dated. He heard the undertones of her statement loud and clear. '*I just need to feel like a woman tonight.*' That definitely wasn't his business. "As long as this guy is safe and won't compromise the safety of my son, I'm good. That's all I'm concerned about. I'm not your father," David said as his cell phone rang. It was Nelson.

"Hey, is she expecting someone?" A car just pulled up. Late model Bentley. Caucasian man exiting," Nelson said.

"Is your date Caucasian? Drives a late-model Bentley?" David asked Dominique.

"Yes, he's early. Why don't you get DA so you can go ahead and take him with you? I didn't know he would be early."

"That's a copy," Nelson said, after overhearing Dominique's explanation to David.

"No problem," David said, but he didn't move.

Dominique's doorbell rang. She turned into a frazzled mess in two seconds. Hurrying to the door, she felt both dread and anticipation. She had looked forward to adulting. But she hadn't ever planned for David to meet *him*. She wanted to shoo David away, but that would make him more suspicious.

Dominique opened the door. "Hey . . ." she said, a bit flustered. "You're early. I'm not quite done getting dressed."

"I couldn't wait anymore," the man said before he pulled Dominique into his arms and kissed her reverently. He was oblivious to David's presence just a few feet away, as they moaned into each other's mouths.

As if Dominque had remembered David was there, she pulled away from her date and whispered. "DA's father is here to pick him up."

"I'm sorry. I didn't know I had an audience," Dominique's date said with a chuckle.

David sensed Dominique's nervousness and wondered what it was about. He'd been honest when he said he didn't care who she dated. But now she had him curious. He introduced himself first. "I'm David Kent Cole—DA's father," he said.

"Peter Stone," the guy returned, with a firm handshake. "You're a very well-known man," Peter said.

Dominique held her breath and looked as if she swallowed a frog.

"Am I?" David asked, sizing up Peter Stone; he'd made an odd statement that had put David on alert. David's brows furrowed as he considered how he would respond to Peter.

Peter sensed David's level of intensity and attempted to smooth him over. "I've read a few articles about you—especially the one in the GQ—very, very impressive work you do in the city of Detroit."

Dominique didn't want to leave the two alone, but the longer she tarried, the longer they would talk. "I just need to get my earrings and shawl, Peter."

"Take your time, lovely," Peter Stone said. He ogled her until she was out of sight.

"So . . . you know what kind of ministry I do. What kind of work do you do?' David asked.

"Oh, I'm into a little bit of everything. I consider myself a serial entrepreneur. I'm primarily focused on pharmaceuticals, though . . ." Peter said with a voice that trailed off like he regretted the disclosure.

"Passion is everything," David responded, wondering why it felt like Peter Stone regretted telling him about his main business. Dominique walked back into the room and usurped Peter's attention.

"Indeed." Peter Stone said absently, dismissing David. His eyes were fixed on Dominique.

"Dave, can you lock up for me? I'll pick him up from you around two p.m. tomorrow. Thanks again," Dominique said.

When David returned to his rental home, he Googled

"Peter Stone Entrepreneur." *Billionaire. Interesting.* And as Peter Stone had said, he was into a little bit of everything. Stone had made most of his money in the pharmaceutical industry, and he owned several businesses in the medical sector, including medical laboratories.

* * *

SINCE DAVID ANTHONY was taking a nap when Dominique arrived to pick him up the next day at two p.m., as she'd promised, David took the opportunity to find out how Peter Stone would fit into David Anthony's life. "So, how did you meet Peter Stone? I've always been curious as to how women met *billionaires,*" David queried.

"I thought we weren't gonna talk about my personal business, Dave," Dominique said.

"I'm just asking a question."

"What did you do, Google him?"

"Yes. He's going to be around my son, so yes."

"But I told you he *wasn't* going to be around him."

"You've told me a lot of things in the past . . ."

Dominique nodded. The implication stung, but she wasn't going to get into an argument with David. Truthfully, he'd been way too good to her and David Anthony for her to do that, so she acquiesced. "What is it that you want to know, Dave?"

"I want to know if you think having a relationship with a married man is setting a good example for our son."

"Here we go with this holy roller stuff."

"Answer the question."

"DA doesn't have to know my business, and he won't."

"What if he was old enough to find out? Then what? It's ungodly and it's tacky. I'm sure there are plenty of single men to date."

"Is there anything else you want to ask me?" Dominique said.

"Considering you haven't answered the first question, no."

Dominique detected David's distance, and she did not want to run him away. But she also knew that she had to be careful about the information she shared about Peter Stone.

"I met Peter through a work colleague who provided private security for him. Then, later on, I provided private security for Peter as well. As far as his marriage, he has an open marriage—they have an understanding. It's not my business."

"Is that what he told *you?* I bet if you asked his *wife,* she may have a whole different take on the situation."

"Everyone is not as perfect as you, Dave."

"Forget it. My wife's name is Cherelle *Cole,* so do what you want. Keep that stuff away from DA. But you should want him to be proud of his mother. You should represent the kind of wife he will choose to marry one day. Do you want him to be with a woman who dates married men? That's the example you're setting. But I'm done with it. I can only control what goes on in my home."

"Right. You can only control the *queen,*" Dominique said spitefully.

"Well, one thing about a *queen,* she knows who her king is. He doesn't have to worry about her going anywhere else, because she has morals and standards. And she knows she has the king's heart and everything that's his. That's pure contentment for a real queen."

"Cherelle is no better than any other woman!"

"Oh yes, in my eyes, she is," David said before walking away.

Chapter 36

Fearfully and Wonderfully Made

Cherelle put the twins down for their naps. Marie had the house smelling like the finest restaurant in town. Cherelle couldn't quite put her finger on what was cooking, but it smelled delicious. A part of her missed being in the kitchen cooking. It was something she once loved. It was a relaxing pastime, and she used to get excited just thinking about mastering new recipes. She had no energy for any of the things she loved—not even David and her babies. It was still a struggle to feel anything but pain.

She needed to interact with the twins more, and they needed to hear her voice. They needed more nurturing. Marie was great, but she wasn't their mother. David had said it compassionately. Nevertheless, he'd said it.

Marie chopped veggies on the cutting board with the precision of a chef. "Are you hungry? Everything is done. I'm just chopping vegetables for a tossed salad. Pastor Cole said he'd be home in an hour. But you can eat now if you're hungry," Marie said when Cherelle walked into the kitchen.

"What's for dinner?"

"Lamb Chops, curry rice, and garlic bread. I made regular brown rice for you because I know you don't like as much spice as Pastor. Let me make you a plate," Marie said. She stopped cutting the vegetables and washed her hands. For Cherelle, the offer was too good to pass up. Her appetite was in high gear today, and she didn't think she could wait another hour for David. She washed her hands and plucked an apron from a drawer. She took over the vegetable cutting while Marie prepared a dinner plate for her. Marie didn't discourage her. "You see, I got plenty of red onions just for you. They'll give the salad a kick," she said over her shoulder.

Cherelle felt something inside. She wanted her life back. She wanted to be the woman she was before the assault, but she had to find that woman again. She finished cutting the vegetables and tossed them into a large wooden bowl with mixed field greens. She added cranberries and walnuts. Marie set her plate on the island, and Cherelle dug in.

"You have a stack of magazines here you might want to read," Marie said, placing a few fashion magazines next to Cherelle. "I'll leave you to your quiet time. Enjoy your meal."

"Thank you." Cherelle hadn't read her fashion magazines in months. But looking through the magazines did the opposite of what Marie intended. Instead of cheering Cherelle up, they made her feel inferior, like she didn't measure up to the women on the pages. They had life and vigor. They looked desirable. She felt worthless. The dark cloud was relentless. Overwhelmed with emotions she couldn't harness, Cherelle dashed up the stairs to her bedroom. She went into her closet and closed the door. Leaning against one of the center islands, she cried.

"Lord, I can't . . . I can't break through this stronghold. I feel useless and dirty. I *am* dirty and worthless! It won't go away, Lord."

Cast your cares on the LORD and he will sustain you; he will never let the righteous be shaken.

"I'm never going to be the same again, Lord. How can I? I'm not the same woman anymore. What did I save myself for, Lord? I saved myself for David, but they took everything away. I'm used up!"

I have loved you with an everlasting love; I have drawn you with loving-kindness.

"Where is my testimony, Oh, God? I am destroyed. What am I to You now? What am I to my husband? To anyone!" Cherelle cried.

The Lord reminded Cherelle of Psalm 139, one of her favorite scriptures.

I will praise you because I am fearfully and wonderfully made; your works are wonderful, I know that full well. My frame was not hidden from you when I was made in the secret place, when I was woven together in the depths of the earth. Your eyes saw my unformed body; all the days ordained for me were written in your book before one of them came to be. How precious to me are your thoughts, God! How vast is the sum of them! Were I to count them, they would outnumber the grains of sand—when I awake, I am still with you.

He loved her. The Word was true and indisputable. He was with her.

* * *

DAVID KISSED Marie on the cheek and washed his hands in the sink. "I'm so glad to see you!"

"No, you're just glad that dinner is waiting on you because you're hungry."

David laughed. "I missed you, too, Marie."

"Tell it to someone who believes you. I ain't thinkin' 'bout you, Pastor Cole," Marie said, chuckling. She was old enough to be David's mother.

"Where's Kit? Is she sleeping? Did she eat today?" David asked as Marie prepared his plate.

"One question at a time, Pastor Cole. She went to her room. I didn't want to disturb her. I think the Lord is dealing with her. She came down to eat, and she helped me cut up some vegetables for the salad. She's trying to get back to normal. I can tell. It just takes a whole lotta prayin'."

"I know. I pray for her every day. I'm just glad she's back."

David heard the twins before he saw Cherelle coming toward him carrying them.

"Hi . . . You made it," Cherelle said.

"Hey, babe. How are you feeling today? Did you get enough rest?" David asked before he started gushing over his babies, entertaining them with crazy, animated faces.

"I feel okay. I got enough sleep."

"Let me take a quick shower so I can help you out with the kids and eat dinner."

Marie noticed Cherelle had been crying again, but she knew that tears didn't always mean sadness. Some tears were healing tears.

Chapter 37

Signs of Life

Cherelle stood in front of the patio door, looking outside. She tightened the belt on her robe and unlocked the sliding door. She slid it open just enough to be greeted by the chilled air. She took a deep whiff and opened the door a little wider. David walked into the kitchen and watched her without making his presence known. Cherelle reminded him of a child who longed to venture outside but couldn't. After a few moments, she surprised David when she said, "I'm okay, honey. I just wanted a little fresh air."

David smiled. It was refreshing for her to notice his presence. She'd been in her own world for so long that he had gotten used to coming in and out of her presence without her acknowledging him. This was a good sign. "I'm sorry. I wasn't spying on you, babe. I didn't want to startle you," he said.

Cherelle closed the patio door and locked it back. "I'm trying, honey . . ." she said, turning to face David.

"I know, babe. We're fine. No one is rushing you."

"I want to be normal again, honey."

David took a few steps toward her, and Cherelle didn't

back away. "In due time. Everything has its season. Can I get you some tea and honey?" he asked. He wanted her to sit down and converse with him. He would even settle for her just sitting at the table with him. He missed her.

"Yes, thank you," Cherelle said. She took a seat at the kitchen table, and David felt like he'd struck gold.

"What's your pleasure? We've got green, black, chamomile, and rosemary," David said, moving the tea boxes around in the cabinet.

Cherelle smiled. "Rosemary."

David wanted to keep her talking. "I let a few of the talented artists at church paint a mural in the church's fellowship hall. I was a little nervous, but I'm glad I gave them the opportunity."

"Is it done?"

"Yes. It's all done. I think you'll love it." David placed the whistler on the stove and jogged to his office to retrieve his cell phone. "Here, look at these," he said, handing Cherelle his cell when he returned to the kitchen. His heart had been prepared for her to pull her hand back if their fingers touched, but she didn't. She took the phone from him and scrolled through the pictures. Her eyes brightened.

"Who did this, honey?"

"Let's see . . . Sarah Stokes, Armani Nicholson, and Omar Jones—he's fairly new. He joined last month. I think he and Sarah like each other because, from what I hear, they argued the whole time they were painting. I have a picture of all three of them at the end, babe."

The whistler screeched, and David poured hot water over a tea bag in Cherelle's favorite cup. He added an extra teaspoon of honey. He handed the cup to her and waited to see if it was to her liking.

"It's good, honey," Cherelle said.

David sat down and watched Cherelle scroll through the pictures of the mural and the kids. He'd taken a million shots of them.

"The kids wanted me to tell you they miss you, babe."

Cherelle looked up from the phone. "I miss them, too, honey. You're not drinking with me?"

"Sure, I am." He got up and poured a cup of tea for himself. He usually drank straight black coffee religiously, but for this occasion, he would drink whatever Cherelle was drinking. They sat together for over an hour, and David thought of everything he could to keep her talking. Cherelle reached her hand across the table, and David took it in his and kissed it. He knew God was working.

* * *

"Mrs. Cole?" Marie said, knocking on the bedroom door.

"Marie, I'm fine. I'm in my closet praying."

"May I come in for a moment, please?"

Cherelle sighed. She knew Marie didn't trust her. "Yes, you may," Cherelle said. In moments, Marie stood at the entryway of Cherelle's boutique-style closet.

"I'm sorry to disturb you, but I—I just wanted to make sure you were okay. You've been quiet," Marie said, looking around the mini boutique to see if anything was amiss. Cherelle sat on her heels in the middle of the floor. Two Bibles were on the carpet next to Cherelle's prayer journal.

"Marie, I know that Pastor Cole wants you to check on me. Let him know that I'm praying, okay? I want to get back to my time with God. Everything is fine. I promise."

"Yes, ma'am. I'll let you pray," Marie said.

"Thank you," Cherelle returned.

Marie backed away with a grin on her face because there

was a bit of sassiness in Cherelle's polite tone, and her hair was combed. She was dressed in a casual, fitted yoga outfit, and she was wearing eyeliner and lip gloss.

"Yes, Lord, just like that song says, You are a way maker and miracle worker," Marie said on her way out of the bedroom.

Chapter 38

Covert Operations

It was Gus's birthday, and he planned to spend it hanging out with his brother and the rest of the family. In the years since Gus had been in the CIA, he could count the number of times on one hand that he hadn't been working or out of the country on his birthday. It felt good to be with his family as he celebrated another year. In true Gus fashion, he insisted on doing the cooking. He'd purchased several live lobsters, along with crab legs, shrimp, and scallops. It was enough food to feed twenty people. He prepped the food in David's chef-style kitchen.

David entered the kitchen after having showered. "Hey, what time did you tell Mom and Pops to get here?"

Gus jumped. "Bro! You just scared the living—you just scared me!" he said. "Six o'clock."

"Right. Watch your language. And you're supposed to be CIA. How is it that you let your guard down and let me sneak up on you—even though I wasn't trying to, considering this is my house?"

"Man, I'm at home. My guard is down. I'm relaxed, fool."

David chuckled. "You better make sure you have this kitchen back as spotless as it was."

"Nope. That's your job. I'm cooking—and it's my birthday. You on somethin' if you think I'm cleaning."

"Well, you better hope Mom and Pops help you because I plan to relax."

"You bum."

"Whatever, hater," David said. He opened the refrigerator. "What are these?"

"Two strawberry cheesecakes for Cherelle. She said she's been craving them. Anything you want to tell me? Am I about to be a godfather again?"

"Man, I wish I could do what it *takes* for you to be a godfather again," David said. He realized he'd said too much and regretted it. He didn't make a practice of discussing his and Cherelle's business with anyone—not even his brother and best friend. Aside from God, Dr. Sylvester Buckley was the only one who knew the intricacies of his situation.

"Give it time," Gus said compassionately. He'd known David since they were kids. He discerned everything David didn't say. "I can tell she's getting better."

"Yes, I know. She's been talking more, and she's eating more. Putting her weight back on. And she's been working out with her trainer for the last two months here at the house."

"I'm so proud of you guys, bro. The two of you have been through so much, but I can't feel anything but love when I walk into this house. It's so refreshing."

"Yeah, thanks, bro. We're not back to normal, but God has been keeping us. For that, I'm grateful," David admitted.

"I can only imagine how rough it's been, but like you always say, 'God is not wasting your experiences.' He'll use them for your good," Gus said.

"You're right. Hey, listen . . . I want to ask you something, but I can't answer a bunch of questions about it right now. But I promise, I will let you know as soon as I can. I just need you to trust me."

"What's up?"

"Can you find out any information about a dude named Peter Stone—the billionaire?"

Gus went still. He didn't want to get himself put in a trick bag. And he didn't want to flat-out lie to his brother. He tried not to look surprised or concerned. He had to talk to Cherelle first. "What do you want to know?"

"Like, is this guy a clean businessman? I may have some minor business dealings with him, and I want to know what kind of person he is." David didn't tell Gus that there was something about Peter Stone that set him on edge.

"How did you come to have any dealings with him?"

"I just said I'm not at liberty to share all that right now."

"Right. Okay. I'll check into it. No problem. I'll get back to you and let you know."

"Thanks," David said.

"Hey, Gus!" Cherelle said excitedly. Her eyes were bright, and she gave him a welcoming smile. "Happy Birthday!" When she hugged Gus, the move surprised David. She hadn't hugged David in so long that it was hard for him to remember her touch. He felt a twinge of jealousy.

"Hey, sis. How've you been doing?" Gus asked.

"I've been doing well. Mama Leah and Papa Joe have had the twins for the last three days. Every time they say they'll bring them back the next day, they end up calling and saying they are going to keep them longer," Cherelle said. "So . . . I have been sleeping and binge-watching Netflix. And the king and I had a couple's spa day at home yesterday."

"I'm glad you've been enjoying yourself," Gus said.

"I have," Cherelle said, her beautiful brown eyes pinned on

her husband. David took pleasure in the way she looked at him, like he was the king of her heart, and there was no room for any other man. He missed her so much. She bent down and looked inside the built-in wine cooler. "Aw, man. King David, can you check the wine room and see if there is any more Risata?"

"Yes, ma'am," David said. He jogged down the steps to the basement, where they had a small temperature-controlled wine room. Gus walked close to Cherelle and whispered. "Have you told him anything about the conversation we had before you guys got married, or what I did for you? I don't ever want him to not trust me, Cherelle."

"No. I haven't. Why do you ask?"

"He told me he may have an opportunity to do business with Peter Stone, and he wanted to know about his character."

"A lot of representatives for business people and celebrities contact the church for various reasons to participate in programs or to donate money so they can have tax write-offs. Maybe it's not Peter Stone directly, or maybe it's just a coincidence."

"In my line of business, nothing is ever a coincidence, Cherelle. I don't want DC to know what I did. That has to stay between you and me—forever. He's the only brother I have; I don't want him to feel like I go behind his back. It could ruin our relationship. I can't let that happen, Cherelle."

"I understand, Gus. I won't ever say anything about it."

"Okay. I'll just give him what he asked for," Gus said. His gut was telling him that he and David needed to talk, but then he'd be betraying Cherelle. He couldn't do that either. He knew their situation was fragile right now. Gus heard David coming back up the stairs, and he put distance between himself and Cherelle. "Your hair looks beautiful, by the way, Cherelle. Nice."

Two days ago, a loctician had come to the house and interlocked Cherelle's hair. She'd given Cherelle a color treatment that left her hair a sassy light brown and honey-blonde color. Then she'd styled Cherelle's shoulder-length locs in a curly mohawk that looked regal and sophisticated.

"Thank you, Gus. It was such a big step for me, but I felt like it was time. I had been thinking about joining the Loc Nation since forever. It just fits who I am as a natural black woman."

"Man, you better stop flirting with my wife," David kidded as he put one bottle of wine in the cooler and the other on the counter for Cherelle. "She knows she looks good," he said. He opened the bottle and poured Cherelle a glass. "Here you go, babe."

"Thanks, honey," Cherelle said. She placed a quick peck on David's cheek. He felt like he was in second grade getting his first kiss. It had been months since they'd had any real physical contact. He wanted to hug her and kiss her in response, but if she stiffened or rejected him, his heart wouldn't be able to handle it, so he let the desire of being close to his wife pass.

"I'm gonna go put the finishing touches on the scrapbook project I'm working on for Mama Leah from the twins. It's a surprise for her; I want to give it to her tonight."

"I'm sure she'll love it," Gus said.

David watched Cherelle as she walked out of the kitchen and up the stairs to the second level. She was wearing fitted navy blue ankle pants and a fitted baby blue button-up. Her curves were back with a vengeance. "Ooh . . . she so doggone fine."

"Yes, she is," Gus joked.

"Don't get a beat down on your birthday," David said.

Gus chuckled. "I was just agreeing with you, bro," he said. He loved to irritate David.

"You better find something else to agree about."

Chapter 39

Ready

Cherelle chased after Caleb as he speed-waddled from the family room into the kitchen area, giggling and babbling. She was afraid he would injure himself. Caleb thought it was a game; he seemed to be having the time of his life. It was hard to believe the twins were ten months old now. Time had flown by. Caleb was as quick as a flash of light, enjoying the newfound freedom of legs that could stand and walk—sometimes run—like now. Chloe sat up in the playpen watching, babbling words only she and her brother understood.

"Boy! Come here!" Cherelle laughed, running after Caleb. "I know I need some exercise, but you're getting ridiculous!" she said, reaching down and scooping Caleb into her arms. "You running from Mommy? Huh?" She tickled him. He giggled gregariously, which made Cherelle laugh. She walked him back to the playpen and lowered him in. Chloe babbled loudly, and Caleb babbled something back. "That's right, you two keep each other company while Mommy gets dinner ready. We don't want Daddy cooking, do we?" Cherelle laughed.

They giggled as if they knew what she was saying. "You two are too cute."

The patio door slid open, and David stepped in with the ingredients Cherelle had sent him to fetch for dinner. Marie had been on vacation for two weeks. "The three of y'all in here ganging up on my cooking?" he asked, crossing the threshold.

"No way, King David, we love all your little burnt delicacies," Cherelle said, batting her eyes and blessing him with a wide, silly smile.

It was a beautiful thing to see her smile like this again. She'd been showing signs of the old Cherelle for the last few weeks, and David couldn't have been happier about it. "Is that right?" David teased. He knew his cooking was bad.

"Certainly," Cherelle replied. She walked over and stood close to David. "Thank you, honey," she said as David placed the eco-friendly grocery bag on the counter. She stood on her tiptoes and kissed her husband softly on the lips—timidly at first, then with urgency. For a tender moment, David lost himself in the completeness of their intimacy. And like a sudden change of heart, he suppressed his desire. He took a small step back and eyed Cherelle curiously. She hadn't done that since before her abduction. They'd held hands and shared kisses on the cheeks recently, but that had been the extent of their interaction.

He'd known since this journey began that it had to be Cherelle's decision when they made love again. He knew they would eventually, but for the sake of her need to heal in a way that was most beneficial to her mental health, he'd left the decision solely up to her. David planned to wait, no matter how long it took.

Cherelle eyed her husband lovingly and kissed him again.

"Kit, are you *okay*?" David asked.

"Very much so," she said. She verified her answer with

another delicious kiss. This time, David indulged without restraint.

How she loved him. He truly was her king. He'd been so patient with her over the last nine months, never ceasing to demonstrate his love for her, even when she couldn't reciprocate. Even when she was unable to simply sit and have a normal conversation with him, and show interest in his life.

Despite it all, David had continued to bring her roses regularly and spoil her with jewelry. He continued to profess his love for her in the letters and notes he wrote to her when he had to be away for more than a few days. He'd treated her like his queen and had been the greatest dad on the planet in the process, all while pastoring his church and attending to the needs of others. Yes, he was her king.

David allowed himself to fully experience their closeness as he held Cherelle in his arms. Cherelle paused briefly and said, "I love you . . . I miss you . . . I love you."

And David knew it was their time.

DAVID STRODE into the master bathroom and circled his arms around Cherelle's waist as she brushed her teeth. He buried his nose in the crook of her neck and spoke into her delicious-smelling skin. "Good morning, babe. I love you."

Cherelle rinsed and swallowed before turning in his arms. "Good morning, my king! Happy Birthday! I ordered something," Cherelle said, looking up at her husband. She motioned to unravel herself from him so that she could retrieve his gift from her closet, but David held her steadily, unwilling to let her go.

"It can wait, babe. I just want to hold you," David said, squeezing her to his body. He was a man in the desert who'd found the purest stream of water. His thirst had been quenched in the most wonderful way.

Cherelle rested in her husband's arms and held onto him. Their relationship had been restored and rejuvenated. She buried her head in his chest and sobbed. "Honey, I'm so sorry, please forgive me. I didn't mean to keep us apart for so long."

David tilted his wife's chin and wiped her tears with the pads of his thumbs. "No . . . babe . . . don't cry. It doesn't matter. We're together. We are *one*. I told you that we would get through whatever we had to get through *together*. And we've done that. Just let me love you . . . that's all I want . . . that's all I need . . . " David said, kissing his wife. And just like that, Cherelle was under her king's spell again.

* * *

DAVID AND CHERELLE sat on their expansive, three-tiered backyard deck, enjoying a candlelight dinner. He'd ordered food from her favorite Italian restaurant. Earlier, he'd had her manicurist come to their home and give Cherelle a manicure and a pedicure, followed by her massage therapist. Then a personal shopper came with racks of clothing. Cherelle selected several dresses, pairs of shoes, and lingerie. She'd been pampered the entire day.

"Honey . . . do you like your birthday gift? I feel like it's my birthday instead of yours. I wanted to celebrate *you*. But you've done everything for *me* today."

David refilled Cherelle's wine glass. "Babe, yes. I love my gift," he said, lifting the unique white gold dog tag pendant from underneath his t-shirt. It had Cherelle and the twins' pictures laser-etched on both sides with an inscription that read: My heart and soul. It was bordered by modest diamonds on both sides. Cherelle had it specially made by her friend,

Donovan Stamps, a celebrity jeweler. "This is the best gift I've ever received, besides my real-life wife and kids," David chuckled.

"I just feel like it's my birthday instead of yours. I want you to feel special," Cherelle said.

"Babe, trust me, I'm feeling really special right about now," David grinned mischievously. "You gave me my birthday gift all last night and early this morning and this afternoon."

Cherelle blushed. "You are so silly!"

"Babe, I'm so serious. Having you back that way—being able to make love to you again—being one with you again is everything. I did all this for you today, babe, to reiterate to you that you are my queen and I love you."

"I love you too, honey."

"I do. I will. I am," David said, holding out his wine glass for a toast.

"I do. I will. I am," Cherelle said, clinking her glass to his.

Chapter 40

Super Bad

David strutted into Dr. Buckley's office, feeling like he had conquered every feat there was. His swag was infused with something that had Dr. Buckley curious. "How are you today, David?"

David grinned like a Cheshire cat. "Man, I'm great! I feel like James Brown. "I got soul, and I'm super bad . . ." he sang, mimicking James Brown's raspy voice.

"I take it your week went well. You celebrated another birthday the other day, right? Happy Belated."

"Yep. Thank you. And it was the best birthday ever!" David chuckled. He lifted the top off Dr. Buckley's candy jar and took a few Starburst candies out. Dr. Buckley smiled curiously and waited for David to share. "Cherelle and I . . . we're *back*," David said.

"I see," Dr. Buckley said. "No wonder you look like you just hit the lottery."

"Yeah . . . it was the night before my birthday, and it was right on time!" David laughed.

"I bet," Dr. Buckley said, laughing along with David. "God is good!"

"Man, He sho is! Mmm hmm!"

"So, I need to ask—and I hope I'm not being too personal—was Cherelle okay afterward?"

"Yes. . . yes, she was. Everything's been great! She's almost back to her old self, except she hasn't been off our property or to church yet. Anytime she's wanted to receive any pampering services, like getting her hair styled or getting a manicure, I've had people come to the house. Her fitness trainer even comes to the house three times a week."

"She'll get around to venturing outside the house when she's comfortable. Remember to ask her about going out, but don't push her. And I don't want to burst your bubble, but I do want you to understand that intimacy can be a touch-and-go type of thing. I don't want you to feel deflated if Cherelle goes back to square zero as far as intimacy is concerned. Rape trauma is complex, David. She's going to continue to need your patience."

"I know. I've been doing a lot of reading on the subject, and I joined a support group. I'm prepared to take it one day at a time, Doc—whatever she needs. Right now, though, I'm enjoying living in the moment. I think she brought me back to *life!*" David joked.

"I get that. You're right. I just don't want you to be frustrated if you hit a roadblock."

David's expression turned serious, and Dr. Buckley sensed the change in his energy. They'd been meeting for months now, and Dr. Buckley had a clear handle on David's personality and his emotional temperament.

"Spit it out, David. What's on your mind? Are you worried that intimacy will be short-lived?"

"No . . . no. It's not that. There's something that I've been keeping to myself. And I need to talk to you about it."

Dr. Buckley sat back in his chair and steepled his fingers. David was used to his no-nonsense mode. "I'm listening . . ."

David blew out a long breath, and the light that was in his eyes just a few minutes ago had dimmed. He adjusted himself in his seat and scooted to the edge. "Before Cherelle and I got married, I had a short relationship with a woman, and unfortunately, we were intimate. I broke things off with her after a while because God had made it clear to me that she wasn't the one for me. And I knew as a man of God, I was living a double life when I was with her.

"On the night I was shot, she'd told me she was pregnant with my child. While I was in rehab, she came to me and led me to believe she'd had an abortion. And I was so angry with her—I hated her for doing that. The sin of our relationship led to another more devastating sin, with my child's life being taken without any consideration for how that might hurt me for the rest of my life."

Dr. Buckley sat up straight in his chair and hung onto David's every word. "Hmm . . ." he said quietly, knowing that David was about to drop something heavy.

"Well, I found out nine months ago that she *didn't* have an abortion. I have a son. And I haven't told Cherelle yet. I wanted to wait until she was better emotionally. But I've waited long enough. And I'm afraid of what it will do to her—to our marriage. But I love my son, and I want him to be a part of our family." David filled Dr. Buckley in on the last nine months of his life with David Anthony and Dominique.

Now it was Dr. Buckley who sighed long and hard. He looked at David pitifully, feeling sorry for him. "How are you going to handle this?"

"I plan to tell Cherelle this weekend. A part of me doesn't

want to because I never want to hurt her, and this is going to hurt. She knows about the situation with the other woman. But, like me, she thought it was something in the past that was over. But it's hardly over with—and won't ever be over with because I have a son."

"I understand that you wanted to protect Cherelle. But I think nine months of secrecy is way too long for a good marriage. You've got to put it on the table and get it out there in the open. I'm not ignorant about your past, David—at least what was printed in the papers. I'm assuming the woman you are talking about is the woman whose boyfriend ordered a hit on her and almost killed you, right?"

"Yep."

"Did you do a paternity test?"

"Yes. He's mine."

Dr. Buckley nodded. "So, what do you plan to tell Cherelle exactly? Have you been seeing your son?"

"Yes. I've been seeing him at least once a week since I found out that he was mine. Some weeks, I've been able to see him more than once. We've bonded well. He knows I'm his daddy, and he's a wonderful kid. At two and a half, he is smart as a whip," David smiled. "I plan to tell Cherelle just how I found out. I just wish I didn't have to hurt her . . ."

"What's happening between you and your son's mother, David? How's the relationship going?"

"It's cordial. We co-parent. That's it."

Dr. Buckley studied David's facial expression and his body language, and he decided he wasn't buying everything David was selling. "These kinds of relationships can get tricky, especially with what you've been dealing with at home. Be careful." Questions swirled around in Dr. Buckley's head, but he would save them for the next session after David had come clean with his wife.

"I'm good."

"Be careful," Dr. Buckley repeated.

They prayed, and David walked out to his truck dispossessed of the exuberance that he'd arrived with. A post-traumatic headache taunted him. He squinted and rubbed his temples, considering all the possible outcomes of the discussion he had to have with Cherelle. They were healing and headed in the right direction, but his disclosure could destroy their progress with the ease of knocking down a house of cards.

Chapter 41

The One

"So . . . is she the *one*?" Cherelle asked Gus before scooping another spoonful of his famous seafood gumbo.

Gus laughed. "You know you're worse than DC, right?"

"I want to meet her."

"Meet who?"

"Oh, don't even try it, Gus. I heard you and David talking about *Zuri*."

Gus's smile was as bright as a megawatt LED light bulb. "I like her—a lot."

Cherelle batted her eyes. "Like or *love*?"

"Aww, Cherelle, don't do this to me. I uh . . . I don't think I've ever told a woman that I loved her."

"Are you waiting on some other man to tell her?"

Gus's pale skin turned red. "Oh, no."

"Well, you better step up to the plate, Gus! Seriously."

"I've been *showing* her how I feel about her. Speaking of that, I want you to help me make something unique for her—a scrapbook celebrating our relationship."

"Oh, Gus, I'd love to! But you didn't answer the question. Do you love her?

"I think I do."

"You *think?*"

"Oh, my God! You've been hanging around DC too long. You should see your eyes right now. I'm just saying that I've never been in love before, so I can't say what I'm feeling is love. But it feels good and feels right."

"Do you miss her when you're away from her?"

There was that moonbeam smile again. "As DC would say, fa sho."

"Do you find yourself thinking about her when you're away from her, and you can't wait to hear her voice or see her or . . . kiss her?"

"OMG! Cherelle, you should work for the CIA. So many questions!"

"Do you? I'm trying to help here."

"Honestly, I think about her all the time. I'm thinking about her right now. It feels good, Cherelle. And I mean deep inside —not some surface physical or sexual attraction. I mean, she's beautiful and everything, but there's something else. When I'm with her, it's like everything is all good. We could be doing something together or nothing at all. It doesn't matter. As long as I'm with her, it's all good. Is that how it was with you and DC?" Gus asked.

"Yeah, pretty much. Before we even got together—when we were just friends—I couldn't wait to have a meeting with him, just so I could smell him. I looked forward to being with him and hearing his voice. It's corny, but that's how I felt," Cherelle smiled. "Then, after we got engaged and he started courting me properly, it was wonderful. I got to see this whole other side of him, and I was shocked in a good way. He's so passionate about God, and it funnels into everything he does. He could pray rain down from heaven, but I've always felt like he makes the world stop when he's with me. He's so attentive and loving—even through all of this," Cherelle said. "He's been patient and supportive. It makes me want to love him even more. Like, I could just pour myself out for him. And I swear, when he kisses or touches me, I'm fifteen all over again. I pray that never changes."

"That's how I feel about Zuri. I just want to give her all of me—even though it feels a bit scary at times."

Cherelle hopped off the barstool. "Yes! I knew it! You're gonna be getting married soon! I knew it!" Cherelle jumped up and down like a kid.

"Who's getting married?" David asked.

Cherelle turned from Gus and ran into David's arms. "My king is home!" she said before squeezing David. She teased his lips with a kiss, and he kissed her back reverently.

"Did you miss me?" David whisper-kissed into Cherelle's ear.

"Yes . . . all day long."

"How was your day today, sweetheart?"

"It was good. Gus made me some seafood gumbo," Cherelle said as she and David walked hand in hand.

"Bro, what I tell you about coming to town and romancing my wife with food and stuff? Stay in yo' lane," David teased.

"You better learn how to cook, bro," Gus said, pointing his spoon at David.

"I know how to cook where it counts," David said. He turned to Cherelle. "Ain't that right, babe?"

"Yes, indeed," Cherelle agreed.

David swatted her behind, then turned to Gus. "Hey, I'm gonna run up and take a shower and change. I'll be right back, and then we can roll." He'd had counseling appointments at church all morning, but his afternoon schedule had been cleared so that he and Gus could hang out with the fellas.

"Where are you guys going?" Cherelle asked, cozying up to David.

"We're gonna go check out some junior boxers and watch an amateur fight right after. Then we plan to catch up with the crew for a while," David said, referring to the rest of the brat pack, which included Mayor Walter Kincaid, his chief of staff, Reginald Williams, Chase Martin, owner of Chase on the River, and Cherelle's brother, Corey. "After that, I have to drop Gus off at the airport so he can get back to Tennessee; he and Zuri have plans early tomorrow. It'll be after midnight when I get back, babe." Cherelle made a sour face. "Come here . . . don't do that," David said. He pulled Cherelle by her waist and whispered into her ear, and she squealed. She whispered back into David's ear. Like two romantically eager teenagers, they teased one another.

David held a mischievous grin. "Mmm . . . mmm! Woman, I'ma hold you to *all* of that when I get back here!"

"Cherelle, please leave this dude alone so we can go. We'll never get out of here if you two keep that up," Gus said.

Cherelle's girlish giggles filled the room. "Okay, let me get started on your scrapbook for *Zuri*."

"Scrapbook?" David questioned. "Oh, you might as well go on and get that ring, bro. Just sickening!" David joked.

"Leave him alone, honey. Gus is getting right to her heart."

David winked. "If he goes ahead and gets that *ring* and makes it *legal*, he can get down to her *soul* like he really wants to do!"

Gus roared with laughter.

"And that is a perfect example of your incorrigibility," Cherelle said to David. She walked around to Gus's laptop that was sitting on the island and scrolled through some of the pictures Gus had taken with Zuri. "Ooh . . . these are so beautiful, Gus," Cherelle said. Why don't you tell me what you guys were doing on these, and I'll take notes so that I can make the scrapbook look good and have some meaningful quotes."

David rolled his eyes. "Man, you are a goner," he said, heading toward the stairs.

By the time David had showered and dressed, Cherelle had all the information she needed from Gus. She walked the two to the door. "Should I wait up for you, honey? I'm gonna be working on Gus's scrapbook for a while," Cherelle said to David.

David cupped Cherelle's face in his hands. "No, don't wait up for me. If you get tired, babe, get your rest. You're gonna need it," David said, planting a kiss on his wife's lips.

"Y'all 'bout to make me throw up, bro," Gus said, pulling David out the door.

Cherelle returned to the counter and scrolled through Gus's pictures, moved by the emotion in Gus's face. He was happy. In each photo with Zuri, the dark chocolate beauty, Gus wore a gleaming smile. They looked to be a perfect pair. Cheesing and overly excited for Gus, Cherelle picked twenty of the best photos for the scrapbook. She opened a kitchen drawer and looked for an extra flash drive to save the photos so she could work in her arts and crafts room. She rummaged through the drawer before giving up.

She strolled into David's office and pulled out his middle desk drawer; he had several flash drives there. She tried one that turned out to contain backup files for their real estate business accounts, and she placed it back. She pulled another one that contained a bunch of JPEG files. She clicked on one of the files.

Bent over David's desk, Cherelle felt her knees wobble. She forced her weight to the palms of her hands and pushed her butt into David's plush, brown, executive-style office chair. Cherelle's right hand trembled as she reached out to touch the screen—to touch David's face in the photos where he smiled next to Dominique with a little boy in the middle of the two. She covered her mouth to muffle the cry that rose from the bottom of her stomach to her throat. Photos went by in blurry fragments like cars on a highway, as Cherelle swiped her fingers across the touchscreen monitor feverishly. "No . . . no . . . God!" she cried.

She felt a sharp pain in her stomach, and her insides lurched out. She grabbed David's small wooden wastebasket and vomited out her emotions, as her heart imploded. She stammered into David's office restroom and rinsed her mouth. Then she splashed her face with water. David's words came back to her—the ones he told her when they said their vows on their wedding day—the ones he still reminded her of from time to time: 'I'm yours and you're mine.' Surely her husband wouldn't do something like this.

The David she knew so well wouldn't. But up until a few nights ago, Cherelle had to admit that she'd been unavailable to him emotionally and physically for the past nine months since her abduction. As close as David was to God, and as much as he loved his family, he was human. Her head throbbed. What if everything that had transpired had inadvertently pushed him into Dominique's arms?

She sat and sobbed at David's desk for more than an hour before a scripture burned in her heart. It was Deuteronomy 1:21.

See, the LORD your God has given you the land. Go up and take possession of it as the LORD, the God of your ancestors, told you. Do not be afraid; do not be discouraged.

One Sunday, while she was pregnant with the twins, David

had preached a sermon titled, "When God Gives You Something." Cherelle could still hear David preaching to his congregation, encouraging them. *'If the Lord has given you something, He hasn't changed. He isn't wavering. You gotta possess it! You can't turn and wimp out when things get rough. You can't be scared! You can't be discouraged. It could be your marriage, your job, your family. It's yours! The Lord has given it to you; what are you afraid of? Possess it! God said it belongs to you! I don't care if you gotta fight for it—then fight! Whatever you need to do to keep and honor what God has given you, you better do it! Possess the land!'*

Chapter 42

Woman to Woman

D ominique received a text from a number she'd never seen before.

Hey . . . it's David. I'll be using this number from now on. I'll explain in person. How's my guy doing?

Dominique: He's good. I'm working today, so he's with my Dad.

David: I'll be in town for a few hours. I need to talk to you about something. What time will you be home?

Dominique: 6:30.

David: Can you get home any earlier?

Dominique: Maybe an hour.

David: Ok. Do me a favor, don't call or text
the old number—even if you receive a call or
text from me—ignore it. Please.

Dominique: Ok. Do you still have access to
the door code?

David: Nope. In the other phone. I'll explain
when I see you.

Dominique: 784987

David: Thanks. See you in a few.

* * *

DOMINIQUE USED the keypad to enter. "Dave, are you here?"
she called out. But the first person she saw was Nelson. She
gasped and instinctively went for her weapon. Keenen was on
the other side of her with his gun already drawn. "Move your
hand away from the weapon. It isn't necessary," he said.

Cherelle came strolling out of the kitchen with a glass of
wine in her hand. She was impeccably dressed in a white,
embroidered, pencil dress with a wide red belt and elegant red
patent leather heels. White always looked beautiful against her
chocolate skin. Her hair. Her nails. Her make-up. Everything
about her was polished.

"Have a seat, dear," Cherelle said, motioning to
Dominique.

Dominique rolled her eyes. "What are you doing in my
house?"

Without answering Dominique's question, Cherelle took a
seat across from where she'd motioned Dominique to sit in the
living room. On the table in front of Cherelle was an expensive

luxury tote. Cherelle moved it next to her feet so that she and Dominique's view of one another wouldn't be obstructed.

"Have. A. Seat," Cherelle said more assertively.

"I'm going to call the police. You have no business here," Dominique said, taking out her cell phone.

Cherelle's voice remained calm. "I promise you, if you do that, you and your child will be looking for someplace to stay tonight. Sit down. I'm not going to say it again."

Dominique complied. Cherelle studied her, wondering what, if anything, David saw in her now. She was pretty, but she was a wicked little witch with no soul.

"Why are you here, Cherelle?"

"I'm here to extend *mercy* to you, Dominique. You see, you are this close," Cherelle said, pinching her fingers together, leaving hardly any space in between, "to experiencing my wrath in biblical proportions."

Dominique smiled a sly smile. "Ms. Insecure," she goaded.

Cherelle chuckled. Dominique was nothing more than an insufferable nuisance. "I have nothing to be insecure about, Dominique, "I'm *Mrs*. David. Kent. Cole. And *you* are a wanna-be," Cherelle retaliated coolly before she glanced at her watch. Dominique couldn't miss the luxury brand that sparkled on Cherelle's wrist. "I'm going to be quick because I have to get back to *my husband*." Cherelle took another sip of wine and set the glass on the table in front of her.

Classy and sophisticated, Cherelle didn't show an ounce of anger, though it ran through her veins just as swiftly as her blood. "This will be the last time you will have any contact with me, my husband, or anyone else I know. This is not a warning. This is my last straw. Your little charade is over. My husband is a good man. He always tries to do the right thing by God and others. And you are trying to take advantage of the goodness in him. You were a mistake from the beginning. A *blemish* on his past."

"We had something, and we have a *son* together."

Cherelle shook her head. "Dominique, you had nothing then, and you have nothing now. You don't have *a single thing* with my husband," Cherelle said, deadpanning Dominique. "You are a wicked little liar."

"Dave took a blood test; DA is his! So maybe you need to get used to that!"

"I call your bluff," Cherelle said, scooting to the edge of her seat. She was poised like a tamed lioness who charmed one with beauty and then struck for the kill without warning. "I'll bet you a million dollars that David Anthony is the son of Brent King. Cherelle rattled off Brent's inmate number like it was her own birthdate and flashed a knowing smile.

Dominique's whole body shook. "No, he's David's son."

"David Anthony Street is Brent King's son. You know that. You've known that for a while now. So, if I ever hear your name again, see your face, think about you, or even dream about you while I sleep, Brent King will find out that he has a son. And then you will have to deal with whatever happens afterward.

"You know, as a mother, I can empathize with your need to protect your child. I get it. I do," Cherelle said sincerely. "You ran to the one person you knew you could count on if he believed he had a child with you. You knew he'd do the right thing. But as the *wife* of David Kent Cole, I couldn't care less about you or your baby daddy *drama*," Cherelle said. She picked her bag off the floor with innate gracefulness and stood. "I hope I've made myself clear—you don't want to test me. Please believe me. Peter Stone won't be able to save you. And you've got thirty days to get out of here!"

Dominique stood. "What are you talking about? This is my

home!" She was weary from the emotional punches Cherelle had thrown.

"What do you pay for rent, Dominique?"

"Dave takes care of that. It's not your business."

"There you go. Just when I was trying to be nice. I thought I told you once before that anything that concerns David Kent Cole *is* my business." Cherelle said in a voice that was too calm to be harmless. "So, basically, you pay nothing."

"Like I said, it's not your business," Dominique countered.

"You know what? I see that you *don't* know my husband, Dominique. The reason why you are living scot-free is that my husband was making sure that the son he *thought* he had was being taken care of. Now, that's the sign of a good man. But if you did a little research, you would find out that the owner of this property is Kitmark, LLC. Allow me to let you in on a little secret. If you didn't know, my honey calls me Kit—short for Kitten. This is just one of the properties in *my* portfolio that my husband purchased for me.

"We lease them out to corporations for their business executives when they relocate or for the short-term stays of their employees. Very profitable. So, you see, when you fix your mouth to say, "Dave takes care of that," Cherelle said, mimicking Dominique. "What you're really saying is that *Cherelle and David* take care of that." Cherelle leaned against a column. "Me. This home belongs to me and my husband. Thirty days, miss," Cherelle said before walking out the door behind Nelson, with Keenan following.

Outside, as Keenan helped Cherelle down the porch stairs, Nelson turned around and said, "You are a beautiful savage."

The three laughed.

Chapter 43

Trust

David entered the house through the front door and saw a flicker of candlelight as he neared the kitchen. Cherelle was perched at the kitchen table, and she stood when he came into view. She was wearing his favorite blue wrap dress—the one she had laid out to wear on the day she was abducted nine months ago. Her locs flowed on her shoulders, and David noticed the soft, neutral color of polish on her hands and feet. Why was she dressed to go out at this time of night? And as stunning as Cherelle looked, she was surrounded by a dark, somber cloud.

Cherelle spoke first. "Hi, honey . . ."

David stepped closer to take a good look at her. "Hey, babe. What's going on? Why are you still up? I told you that you didn't have to wait up for me. Where've you been? You look and smell beautiful," David said, kissing Cherelle on the lips. It was a relief to be able to do that without her flinching.

Cherelle tried to fight the tears that brimmed in her eyes. And David knew something was askew. He scratched the top of his head. "Are the kids okay?"

"Yes, honey. The kids are still with Mama Leah and Papa Joe. They're fine. Please sit down . . . I need to talk to you."

"Kit, what's wrong?"

"I have a lot of things on my mind. And I need to talk."

David remembered what Dr. Buckley had advised him about being receptive to listening when Cherelle was ready to talk about her ordeal. "Okay. I'm right here for you, you know that," David said lovingly. He stroked Cherelle's face with his finger and kissed her forehead. He hugged her.

Cherelle pulled apart. "Let's sit down," she said. It was all so overwhelming. She didn't have the energy to stand any longer. She took David's hand and they sat next to each other at the table. Maybe she was ready to discuss the assault. Whatever it was, David wanted to give her his full attention.

"Honey, I need you to tell me the truth . . ." Cherelle began.

David's eyes were full of patience. "Whatever you need, babe, okay?" he said. He scooted closer. "What is it?"

"Do you still love her?"

David shook his head from side to side. What on earth was Cherelle talking about? He was trying to figure it out as trickles of heartache rolled down his wife's beautiful face. Cherelle swallowed hard and let go of the breath she was holding. It came out with force like someone struggling to breathe. "Or was it because I—I couldn't make myself *available* to you for such a long time? Just please tell me the truth. I want to stay with you. I love you. I'm so sorry . . . I'm so sorry, honey," Cherelle sobbed hard.

She was not the confident lioness she'd been earlier when she'd flown to Chicago on their charter jet and confronted Dominique. It dawned on her that there was an unwanted possibility that David had shared more with Dominique than his responsibility of being David Anthony's father. Perhaps in his heart, he still had feelings for her.

280

One half of Cherelle wished it all away, but the other half needed to know the truth so that she and her husband could tend to their marriage. She wasn't giving up without a fight. But it still hurt to think David would betray her in that way after all they'd been through together.

David stood and pulled Cherelle into his arms. "Babe, please help me understand what's going on. I love you. What are you talking about? Still love *who*?" David asked. Was Cherelle having another breakdown of some sort? Not sure what to do, he held on to his wife until she pulled away from him.

Cherelle walked over to the kitchen drawer and pulled out a manila envelope. She handed it to David. She watched as he bent the metal clasp, opened the envelope, and pulled out the pictures she had printed of him, Dominique, and David Anthony. They looked like they were a family. David closed his eyes and raked his hand down his face. He'd screwed up big time and done the very thing he'd been trying to avoid doing— break his wife's heart, crushing the one person he loved beyond reason.

Lying by omission was just as treacherous as telling an outright lie. He had planned to tell Cherelle about David Anthony the coming weekend. For her to find out this way broke David's heart all over again, knowing he had contributed to hurting her after all she'd gone through over the past nine months.

"I'm sorry, babe. I haven't been honest. That's my son, but I don't love her, nor do I want her. I love *you*. Please believe me. I didn't want to hurt you—that's the only reason I didn't tell you. When I found out about him, you had just come back home, and you were here physically, but you weren't all here. I thought finding out about him would be too much for you. That's the *only* reason why I didn't tell you. God as my witness!

"Have you been with her? Are you sleeping with her?" Cherelle asked, fearful of what David might say. She breathed in deeply and let her breath flow as if she were preparing for some horrific verbal assault. "And please don't lie. I need you to tell me the truth from now on. I want to trust you . . . I want to love you," Cherelle sobbed.

David pulled Cherelle close to him. "No, Kit. I have not touched her or *any* other woman. Please, don't cry, babe. If you hate me for lying to you about DA—I understand that—I deserve that. I thought I was doing the right thing under our circumstances. Kit, please . . ." David said, wiping her tears with the pads of his thumbs.

The tightening of his chest made it hard for him to breathe. His head and heart ached. "I need you to know that I would never disrespect you and what you are to me. I have not *touched* her. You are still the only woman I want, babe. I need you to believe me. It was always about my son. I was trying to do right by my son. That's all. You are everything to me. I swear to you that I haven't done anything that would violate you or the covenant I made with you and my God. You saved yourself for me before we were married, and I waited for you through our struggle. There's been no one but you, Kit. I swear. You have to believe me!" Beaten by his failure to protect Cherelle for the second time, David was moved to tears.

Cherelle rested in David's arms and sobbed heavily. "Oh, God. What have I done? I'm so sorry, honey. Please forgive me," she said.

"No . . . this is my fault. I made a mistake. But I haven't been unfaithful to you. Put all the blame for everything else on me, Kit. But please don't think that I would ever disrespect you by sleeping with her. I didn't. I wouldn't do that to you. I've been waiting on you—waiting for you. The other night was so beautiful, like I always knew it would be. I only have an appetite for you, babe. You've got my whole heart, Kit," David confessed.

Cherelle looked up at her husband. Defeat tugged at the corners of her mouth. "We don't trust each other. Greg was right. We don't *trust* each other. And I don't want to come back to this space again, David. I should have told you."

"Told me what, Kit?"

Cherelle sniffed in deeply and squeezed out the rest of her tears. "David Anthony is not your son, honey. He's not."

"Kit, I did a paternity test. He *is* mine."

"No, he isn't. Listen to me. After Dominique showed up at your office that day before we were married, I needed to find out more about her. I wanted to know where she lived . . . what she was doing . . . because I wanted to make sure I knew everything about her so that if she ever became a threat to what I was building with you, I would know how to deal with her. I asked Gus if he could find out about her, but he already knew everything because when you were still recovering from being shot, Gus was working on some cyber-terrorism case that had something to do with The Sect. Dominique's long-time lover, Brent King, was connected to The Sect, and so she had been under FBI surveillance.

"She gave birth to David Anthony in Chicago a month before you and I were engaged. The child was tested. Brent King was also tested while in jail, unbeknownst to him. He is David Anthony's biological father. And Dominique wanted to hide it from him. It was her original plan to trick you into thinking the baby was yours, no matter what. When you were fighting for your life in the hospital, Gus gave me a recording of Dominique talking with a billionaire named Peter Stone. Gus told me that if anything happened to you or him, I should give the tape to Mama Leah. On the tape, Dominique tells Peter Stone that she's pregnant by Brent, but if she decides to keep the baby, it's going to be *your* baby. And maybe, like Gus believes, she didn't know which of you was the father before David Anthony was born. But she knew for certain *after* he was born, honey.

"Brent King—the same man who tried to kill Dominique and almost killed you in the process—is David Anthony's father. He doesn't know, and I think for the child's sake, it's best that he never finds out. Peter Stone owns a slew of DNA testing labs, honey. It is very possible that he pulled some strings. This man is a billionaire, David. He's smart and resourceful. He could have easily had those results altered. Even if you were tested at a lab that didn't belong to him, he has the kind of resources to make things happen. I believe he did that for Dominique, thinking he was helping to protect her from Brent. But I know for certain you are not that child's father. I'm sure Gus can get you a copy of the original paternity test. And please, don't be mad at Gus for not saying anything; he thought Dominique was out of our lives for good, so it didn't matter if she had a child or not."

It was all too unbelievable. But something clicked in David's brain. He remembered how fidgety Dominique had been on the day he'd met Peter Stone by happenstance, and how Stone had hesitated when he stated he worked in pharmaceuticals. The labs. David bet that if he investigated thoroughly, he would discover that the lab he used to do the paternity test was one of the businesses Peter Stone owned. It all made sense. It had been a diabolical plan by an evil, heartless woman, who didn't even mind using and hurting her own child in the process.

"Babe, this is all so heavy. I don't know exactly what I'm feeling. A great part of me is angry, but the biggest part of me is grieving. I've been a father to David Anthony and have loved him like my own for the past nine months," David said.

"I understand, honey. I'm sorry that you're hurting this way. I met with her today, and she will not be a thorn in my side anymore. So please, tell me that this is over. I want to move on from what happened to me, and from Dominique and David Anthony. This time for good. Can we please just put the past behind us? I just want to love you and be your wife in every sense. This is the recording," Cherelle said, sliding a digital recorder across the table.

Without hesitation, David picked up the digital recorder and stood. He walked over to the trash can and pushed the foot pedal. The mouth opened, and David tossed the digital recorder inside with a thud. Whatever was on the recording didn't matter. Only this moment with his wife. He pulled Cherelle into his arms and said, "I'm yours and you're mine. Nothing else matters."

"I do. I will. I am," Cherelle said, reminding David of his wedding vows.

"I do. I will. I am," David said back, squeezing her body to his.

About the Author

Sherrhonda Denice is an author, speaker, licensed therapist, and educator. She is a graduate of Michigan State University and holds a master's degree in social work from Wayne State University and a master's degree in teaching from Oakland University. Sherrhonda writes realistic Christian fiction that takes her readers to places where faith and love intertwine to create juicy storylines, and non-fiction to help her readers conquer life's challenges and grow in their walk with Christ. She loves to read, write, and do absolutely nothing but look out the window with a steamy cup of French vanilla cappuccino in hand. Visit Sherrhonda on the web at **www.sherrhondadenice.com**

 facebook.com/sherrhondadeniceauthorpage

 instagram.com/sherrhondadenice

www.ingramcontent.com/pod-product-compliance
Lightning Source LLC
Chambersburg PA
CBHW020947260626
47169CB00006B/1854